The End of Time

A Fabulous Narrative

Volume I: From Waterloo to Meridian

by T.S. Creager

To the one who read this story first
and helped it grow
from the very beginning.

CONTENTS

I. A Past and Future Secret   1

II. The Delirium Has Just Began...   12

III. A Pagan Storm   25

IV. Midnight Sun   42

V. Paranormal Mysteria   56

VI. Guardians of Fate   77

VII. Somewhere Far Beyond   90

VIII. Journey Through the Dark   107

IX. Lost Souls in Endless Time   111

X. Wolves of the Sea   124

XI. Under Jolly Roger   137

XII. Burning Bridges   153

XIII. Another Stranger Me   167

XIV. Bash Out!   187

XV. Return Fire   204

XVI. Rise and Fall   224

XVII. A Dangerous Meeting   242

XVIII. Heading for Tomorrow   258

I

A Past and Future Secret

Once upon a time, in the not too distant future, an old man walked into a bar. This was very odd; perhaps even the oddest thing that had ever occurred in the history of the world, and yet it had happened countless times before, in other places and in other times. It was odd for many reasons, but only one of them, the oddest reason of them all, really mattered.

It was not that he was wearing a blazing red nineteenth-century general's uniform. Quite a lot of people wore that sort of thing and it wasn't odd at all, if they were generals from the nineteenth century, of course. Nor was it the fact that he was in uniform in a bar; that was a bit strange, but it's possible for anyone to wear anything they want into a bar, really.

It wasn't even the oddest thing that he had stepped into the bar through a door which had appeared in the middle of a solid wall. A wall that, up until that point, had done a spectacular job of not letting anyone at all walk through it, which is just the sort of thing one builds walls for. But a wooden door had appeared out of nowhere, opened, and out had come an extremely old man.

The oddest thing, in fact, was that he really was a general from the nineteenth century, and this particular bar was not in the nineteenth century at all, or anywhere close. He had stepped into a time and place hundreds of years beyond the day history had recorded as his death. The white hair poking out from under his bicorne hat and his wrinkled face showed the wide span of years he'd lived, but it still did not appear he had lived for hundreds of them.

What was almost just as odd was that nobody had noticed. The bar wasn't empty, yet as it turned out, everyone else was too preoccupied with their own business to see any part of this remarkable event. Or they were not in the habit of eyeing suspiciously any perfectly ordinary walls in case they developed a bad case of emitting people. Which, ironically, is a habit they might've developed, had they seen anything. But they hadn't. Nor did they notice when he closed the door behind him and it disappeared entirely, returning the wall to its previous solid, doorless state. And still nobody noticed him sneering in disgust as he surveyed the people around him.

Somebody was asleep on a table. Somebody was stumbling out of the entrance doors holding a hand over his mouth. Somebody was arguing with two other somebodies about something entirely inane. A pair of somebodies were mashing their faces together in a poorly lit corner of the room. And yet another somebody sat at a table, motioning excitedly with his hand as he talked to a darker skinned woman on the other side.

"Well that's the problem with this country, isn't it?" this somebody half yelled over the music blaring from speakers nearby, his pale face flushed. "People don't think like me! If everybody had it right, things would be great!"

"What you're saying definitely sounds like a problem, Jylling," the woman smirked, her ponytail of long, black hair gently swinging as she turned her head.

The uniformed man's large, aquiline nose turned towards the two of them as he watched them intently.

Jylling absentmindedly ran his hand through his short, black hair. "Right? This is what I try to tell people—" His hand froze. "Oh wait, you're making a joke about me again. Goddangit, Dhlara."

She grinned, her green eyes twinkling. "You say the same thing all the time! What do you expect me to say?"

"It is not all the same," he grumbled to himself. He lifted his drink toward his mouth, but he halted, holding his arm motionless in the air as he caught sight of the old general striding towards them. He opened his mouth to say something, but only managed to raise a befuddled eyebrow.

"The two of you are coming with me!" the old man barked.

"What? No. Go be crazy somewhere else, man. Is there some convention in town I don't know about?" Jylling responded, turning to look at Dhlara.

The antiquated soldier frowned and held his hands out to each of them.

"Now!" he ordered, his jaw clenched.

Jylling laughed. "Still no! Getting angry about it doesn't matter."

The man suddenly lurched forward, roughly grabbing Dhlara's wrist and the front of Jylling's shirt, and all three of them disappeared. Jylling's bottle fell and shattered on the floor, unheard and unnoticed by anybody as the music played on.

*

An intense flash of white light blinded Dhlara for a moment, and then… darkness. She heard a hiss of rushing steam above her.

"What the—" Dhlara heard Jylling's voice from somewhere within the black. Something banged against metal. "OW!" he yelped.

Dhlara realized she was laying on her back. She leaned forward, put a hand on her knee, and stood up. She stared into the dark with wide eyes, trying to see her surroundings. As her vision adjusted from the flash, she discovered a yellow light emanating from a small square window a few feet away. Its dim glow illuminated Jylling's prone form, who grimaced as he sat up and held the back of his head.

"You okay?" she asked.

"Hit my freakin' head. Whatever nonsense that jerk just did knocked my chair out from under me," Jylling answered. He felt the ground around him with his hands. "I think I dropped my drink, too. Crap. Where did it go?"

"I get the feeling we're somewhere else entirely, Jylling."

"That's impossible. Costumed freak probably just knocked out the lights. Where is my chair? Maybe it fell over around here somewhere..." he got onto his hands and knees and started to crawl away. "Whoah, the floor is all weird here. It feels like metal. And goes... up?"

Dhlara took a tentative step away from Jylling. She felt the floor beneath her slope upward. She extended her hand behind her and it was met by a wall. Running her hand down the metal surface, she felt it curve smoothly all the way to under her feet.

"We seem to be in some sort of... sphere," she said.

"Huh. That's weird," Jylling said as he stood up. Noticing the little window, he moved closer to look through it. "Oh man, redcoats!" he said. "What does that mean?" He looked at her in confusion.

She shrugged and lifted her hands, "What are you talking about?!"

"I think we've been kidnapped by nerds. HEY, LET US OUT, NERDS!" he shouted, pounding his fist on the wall.

A series of metallic clanks and clunks came from beneath the window, and then a portion of the wall around it slowly swung open to the left. A pair of soldiers in red uniforms stood on the other side, levelling the sharp, glinting tips of musket bayonets at Dhlara and Jylling. Jylling stepped through the doorway.

"What the hell, you guys? You can't— Ow! Those are sharp!" he exclaimed as he breasted the bayonets.

"They are sharp because they are made to kill men," said a voice to his right. Jylling turned and peered around the bronze wall of the sphere he had exited. A familiar figure in a bicorne hat stood at the side of the sphere pushing and pulling waist-high floor levers. "Do not waste time; there are matters that demand our attention," he said as he pushed one forward and pressurized steam sprayed out of the top of the machine.

"Waste—what! I don't—" Jylling sputtered.

Dhlara put her hand on his shoulder. "Where are we?" she asked the general.

"The Ministry of Order. I am the Minister of Order," he said, looking at her. He signaled to the soldiers to shoulder their weapons. "You have been transported to this place so that you may set events aright."

4

"I'm not doing anything!" said Jylling. "I don't do things for people who go around kidnapping people."

"You are required to do your duty, sir. You are here, and you will do what you must. That is that."

"What is the Ministry of Order?" Dhlara asked.

The Minister spun on his heel and walked out of the small room holding the bronze sphere, motioning for them to follow. They came into what looked like a library, with the ends of rows and rows of towering shelves of books on their right and left. The bookcases were at least twice as tall as Dhlara. Daylight streamed in through a glass ceiling, but oil lamps along the walls also lit the room.

"The Ministry of Order ensures that events happen how they happened," he explained. He turned to his right and walked down a passage between the bookshelves and the wall of the library. It was a long passageway, as there were hundreds of huge aisles of books.

"I'm reasonably certain that was complete nonsense," Jylling muttered as they followed.

"I'm afraid we don't understand," said Dhlara.

The Minister sighed heavily. "You never do." He stopped walking. "This is where every record of every event that has occurred is kept. What happens must match these records."

"Still not caring! We're not playing your game, buddy! I'm still not over the part where you've kidnapped us!" exclaimed Jylling.

Dhlara stepped aside to look at the spines of the closest books. They read: *AD 1694, November 21, 11 AM*; *AD 1694, November 21, 12 PM*; and more of the like. She grabbed Jylling's arm and pointed at the books. He leaned to the side to read one of the titles, then scrunched up his face in confusion. He slowly put his hand out to pull the book from the shelf.

"What exactly are these events you're talking about? And when?" asked Dhlara.

"All of them. At any time."

"Are you telling me that this," Dhlara motioned with both arms to the rows of bookcases, "describes everything that has ever happened in the world?"

"Yes."

"'Elizabeth Bexstwicke, eleven-seventeen A. M. to eleven-twenty-four A.M.: had a spot of tea'," Jylling read. "'Eleven-twenty-five A.M. to twelve-eighteen P.M.: bit of a nap.' So you're some kind of stalker who keeps a diary and meticulously indexes. That's creepy. And every one of the books in here are just like this?"

"Yes, exactly as I said. Anyway—" started the Minister.

"No!" said Jylling. "No 'anyway'! This is all ridiculous!"

The Minister's eyes flashed. "I am providing you with answers. Do not wear thin my forbearance."

"How is this possible?" inquired Dhlara.

Muscles flexed in the Minister's face as he gritted his teeth, "This is the Ministry of Order. I am the Minister of Order. Events are recorded and kept here, and the Ministry makes certain they are accurate."

Jylling moved closer to Dhlara. "I don't think we're getting anywhere with this guy," he said out of the side of his mouth.

"What do you need from us?" she asked.

"This way," the Minister said. He turned around and walked through the aisle of books, into the center of the vast room where there was a seemingly endless table that stretched far off to the right and left, with equally long benches at its sides and oil lamps on top of it. Many rows of bookcases stood perpendicular to the table on either side of it. Following the Minister as he turned to the right and strode alongside the table, Dhlara could see a massive desk atop a five-foot high platform overlooking the rest of the room. Wooden stairs on either side led to the top of the platform and the desk. In the wall behind the desk was a closed door. The Minister stomped up the stairs and snatched a roll of paper from the desk. Gripping one end, he unrolled it in front of them.

It was a poster. Its artwork showed an army of soldiers clad in blue fighting an army in red. Most of those clad in red appeared to be in the process of fleeing or dying. Near the top she could see a pale man in a white and blue uniform holding a billowing French flag in his right hand, while his left was outstretched, pointing out toward nothing. The bottom of the flagpole rested on the gigantic squid he stood on, which was simultaneously throttling and discarding red soldiers with its many tentacles. Above him were splayed the words, *Battle of Waterloo Centennial!*

"This is the problem," said the Minister. "Old Boney's gone and ruined quite a lot of perfectly good history."

"'Old Boney'?" asked Dhlara.

The Minister nodded emphatically. "Yes indeed."

"I believe that's supposed to be Napoleon on that squid there," said Jylling. "But this is all utter nonsense. Crazy old dude probably drew it himself."

"You may be right," she said. "I'm no expert, but I don't recall any prominent invertebrates at the Battle of Waterloo."

"THAT IS PRECISELY THE POINT, YOU CONFOUNDED HALF-WITS!" shouted the Minister. "This very real piece of filth does indeed show the events of that battle as they are now, after that blasted Bonaparte has done his bit!"

"Ah," she said. "So it wasn't that way, and it shouldn't be that way, but it is that way."

"Yes!"

There was a pause. Jylling looked away thoughtfully, then spoke. "Hang on, so I'm supposed to believe that's real propaganda from France one-hundred years after the Battle of Waterloo?"

"Yes!"

"Why's it in English, then?"

"By God, sir, that is not the Queen's English!" the Minister exclaimed.

Jylling laughed. "I can read it, can't I? I don't know any French."

"Jylling, look again. It is in French," said Dhlara.

He squinted at the poster. The words *Bataille de Waterloo Centennial!* were clearly printed on the poster.

"Huh, so it is," he said. "How is it I can read French all of a sudden?"

"I took the liberty of emplacing translation mechanisms within your minds," explained the general.

"Took the liberty?!" said Jylling. "In what other ways have you violated us?!"

"None at all! And that's hardly a violation, sir! You will find it quite useful, I should say!"

"Is it just French we can understand now?" asked Jylling.

"No, it is everything."

"That does sound useful," said Dhlara.

"No, listen," Jylling shook his head as he talked, "this nutter popped your head open and rooted around! I think that's pretty alarming!"

"I'm not saying I'm pleased with it, Jylling."

"I don't suppose you'll undo it?" he asked the Minister.

"No!"

"Of course not!" Jylling looked around the room, disgusted.

"How'd Napoleon manage to alter the course of history?" Dhlara asked.

"He is the Minister of Chaos," the Minister answered.

"What now?" said Jylling.

"He is the Minister of Chaos," the Minister repeated.

"No, what does that *mean?*"

"The Ministry of Chaos aims to destroy the perfectly planned sequence of events! Bonaparte is the head of that Ministry. In order to retain the good, authentic sequence of events, it is my job to counter the damage done by him."

"Seems like it's getting away from you a bit," Jylling shot back.

"So he's just doing his job?" asked Dhlara.

"He is ruining the history of England! He should be run through and his Ministry dissolved for his crimes!"

"Why would he go back in time to change history, though?" she asked.

"He is the Minister of Chaos!"

"You said that already," said Jylling.

The Minister stared at him blankly.

"Why a squid?" Jylling asked.

"What?"

"Why's there a squid there, on that paper? No, I mean, I

know *why* it's there, but how'd it get there? If you gave me a chance to go back to an event in my life, I could take some winning bets and kick a few people in the shins, but I've got no idea how to get to the point where I'm riding about on a stonking great squid."

"I am not aware of how Bonaparte managed to acquire such a beast. His endeavors have been unknown to me for some time. This is one of the facts that you are tasked with discovering."

"And then you want us to stop him?" asked Dhlara.

"Yes."

"What happens if we don't?" inquired Jylling.

The Minister marched past him and back down the stairs, toward the opposite end of the huge room. After following him for a couple minutes alongside the very long table, they came to a set of two elaborate wooden doors. More soldiers in red uniforms stood at attention on either side of the doorway. The Minister gripped the handle of one of the doors and swung it open. The three of them passed through the doorway, entering into an endless hall full of doorways on either side. The doors and ceiling were made of dark stained wood, as was the paneling between them, whereas lighter coloured boards made up the parquet floor.

"There is a door here for every time," said the Minister as he continued marching. "Through them, you can travel to any year." Soon he came to a stop at a specific door on the left. Dhlara saw four gold numbers on it: *3000.* "This is the future of the world should you fail to do your duty," he said, gripping the handle and shoving the door. As it swung open, a wave of heat washed over the group. Gazing into the doorway, Dhlara saw a setting sun amid an orange sky shining through a haze of smoke. For a moment, Dhlara could hear echoes in the distance of what sounded like the roar of some indiscernible beast. Jylling stuck his head out the door and looked around. Far below, huge swaths of flame raged across the ground, emitting thick columns of black smoke.

"Everything's on fire?" he said.

"Yes. It is all burning."

9

"Huh. Seems awfully real."

"It is indeed, sir! It is imperative that you prevent this!"

"How do we know this isn't just something they do in the year three-thousand? Or maybe there's just a great big fire about then? How do we know this other minister has something to do with it?"

"Stuff and stonsense, sir! Of course he has something to do with it!"

Another roar resounded, this time much closer. The light from the sun briefly darkened; glancing at it, Dhlara thought she saw passing near the sun the silhouette of someone riding a giant winged creature and lifting a bicorne hat above their head. She heard something faint… something that almost sounded like a laugh.

"…What was that?" she asked.

The Minister appeared bewildered.

"The great fiery death of the world, I suspect!"

"No, I meant that, out there!" she said.

The Minister peered out of the doorway at the expanse of smoke and fire, then went back to giving her a confused face.

"Nevermind…"

"Well, how do you expect us to fix this?" Jylling sighed.

The Minister shut the door and led them out of the hall, past the entire length of the table again, and back to his desk. Opening a drawer, he picked up a pair of wrist-watches and handed one to each of them. Jylling turned it over in his hands, examining it. Finding a button on the side, he pushed it, and he promptly vanished. The Minister stared at the spot where Jylling had been with a furrowed brow.

"As you can see, their function is to return you to this place," he said, shifting his gaze to Dhlara. She followed as he went to the small room they had left a few minutes earlier. Rounding a bookshelf, she saw the gleaming bronze ovoid that she and Jylling had been inside. Steam hissed from pipes emerging above the squat metal construct. The door swung open again while a soldier on the left busily pushed and pulled a series of levers. Jylling stepped out from within the machine.

"Huh. That's nifty," he said, looking at the watch in his

hand. The oblong face was almost entirely smooth gold plating, and two square holes in the plating above one long rectangular hole gave the watch the appearance of making a grimace at him. Nothing was visible in the top holes, but there was a single symbol in the hole below: ∞. The Minister grabbed him by the arm and guided him back out into the library.

"Bally good. Now, you have seen the hall over there," the Minister said while pointing to the side of the library where the endless hallway of doors was. "Choose the year you are desirous of entering, then go forth." With that, he walked off toward his desk.

"Hey, wait a minute!" Jylling yelled after him. "That's it?! That's all you've got for us?!"

"It is indeed, sir!" the Minister shouted without turning back.

"Well, what year is Waterloo anyway?!"

"The Battle of Waterloo began at ten o'clock in the morning, on the eighteenth of June, eighteen-hundred and fifteen!"

Jylling looked at Dhlara. They stared at each other, both waiting for the other to speak.

"So, we can travel through time now, I guess?" said Dhlara.

"According to that guy, anyway. And he sure seems like a cracked pot. This thing definitely teleported me, though, so I don't know," replied Jylling, tapping his watch.

"And he teleported us before, to this place."

"Yeah, this is really weird."

"Want to see if we can go to the time he said?"

Jylling shrugged. "Might as well. If we can... Wow. That'd... that'd be crazy. It just can't be real. Things don't work that way."

Dhlara headed for the doors while attaching the watch to her wrist. "Then let's find out."

II

The Delirium Has Just Began...

"I think this might be real, Jylling," Dhlara said as she walked down the hall. "If this is a prank or some sort of joke, it's an awfully expensive one. I think that old guy might really be who he says he is."

"I just don't see how any of this is possible."

"Seems pretty impossible how we got here, but here we are."

"Let's just open one of these doors and see what's what. Oh hey, eighteen-fifteen."

They stopped in front of a door to their right. Dhlara saw gold numbers on the door at eye-level: *1815*.

"Well that's convenient," said Jylling. He stepped in front of her, turned the knob, and pushed the door open.

This particular door, it turned out, was in the middle of a cobblestone street, which was in the middle of a village, which was currently in the middle of a fierce battle. The roar of countless shouting voices and deep, distant thuds of artillery fire immediately assaulted them. Brick houses painted white lined the road, but many of them had gaping holes where their roofs or walls had been blown apart. A few houses distant from the two of them was a crossroads, where the street they were on ended and connected to another street that ran in a perpendicular direction. The second story of one large house overlooking this intersection played host to a raging fire. Corpses of soldiers covered in dust, rubble, and blood lay all around, and some of them were still moving. They wore 19th-century military uniforms, and all seemed to be wearing some shade of blue. The air was thick with smoke, and more was added by the flashes of light that snapped out of windows, accompanied by deafening cracks.

For a few moments, they stood in awe of the scene before them. A group of men ran into view at the crossroad, and they were greeted by a volley of musket fire from the windows of one of the houses near the door. Those who were hit fell to the ground, but the rest went on and charged the house that had fired on them. They poured in through the doorway and windows with their muskets' bayonets held out before them, and soon the defenders found themselves engaged in a fearsome melee.

Suddenly, thick tentacles wrapped around the corner of the building and pulled the brick and mortar down with a crash. A huge, glistening mass of red flesh hauled itself into view with astonishing speed. It was a squid; or at least, it *looked* like a squid, but it was not in the water, and it was as tall as the houses around it. A swarm of arms beneath the sea monster propelled it forward, while somehow also managing to keep its long, bulbous body upright. With a few spare tentacles, it picked up chunks of the wall it had just demolished and lobbed them into the house's newly created hole. Anguished voices cried out in response. At the base of the body, just above the tentacles, its flesh parted and revealed a massive eye. The eye swiveled around, its black pupil rapidly surveying the battlefield. It stopped searching, however, when it saw Dhlara and locked eyes with her. The squid darted toward the doorway standing independent of any building in the middle of the street. Tentacles whipped up to grab the roofs of the buildings on either side of the street and the creature lifted itself up in front of Dhlara. Pushing through a ring of flesh nestled at the center of the bottom of its body, a beak emerged and opened to emit a strangled shriek.

Jylling slammed the door shut.

"Well then, let's try a different door," said Dhlara, walking across the hall to the door marked 1814.

Jylling stayed put, holding the door shut. "There is all manner of buck wild insanity happening out there!" he yelled.

"I saw. Which is why I said we should try a different door."

"I don't think we're properly addressing how completely

unreal this entire business is!"

"It *is* incredible. But we really should move away from this door, because if something does come crashing through it looking for us, I don't think it'll make a difference whether you're holding onto the door or not. It'll make a difference in how much you get hurt, I would imagine."

Jylling jumped away from the door and continued to watch it suspiciously. Dhlara cautiously opened one on the other side of the hallway marked *1814*. Birds chirped and glided over a placid, green, mildly hilly European countryside. There were some trees and buildings, but all sat peacefully under a cloudy sky. She closed the door and opened the next one to her left, marked *1816*. Almost identical. This time, it was a beautiful, clear blue sky.

"Let's go have a look around in here," she said.

"Yeah alright."

They stepped through the doorway. As Jylling exited the hallway, the door behind them swung shut and disappeared.

"Crap," said Jylling. "How do we get back now? I wonder if this still works." He lifted his arm and pressed the button on his watch. He vanished, just as before. Checking her own watch, Dhlara noticed there were now numbers in the slots: *18* on the left, *6* on the right, and *1816* in the wide hole beneath. She put her hands into the pockets of her pants and gazed at the panorama before her. There was a village nearby, and it also had brick houses painted white.

After a couple minutes, the door reappeared and flew open. Jylling stood in the doorway.

"Just checking!" he said, grinning.

"Satisfied?"

"I am! That blustery old fellow's pretty sore about it, but sod him. You should check to see if yours works."

"I'll trust that it does. Come on, let's head over to that village," she said, pointing. "Hopefully we'll find some people to talk to."

Jylling nodded and they set off. "So what's the plan, here?" he said. "Surely we're not going to be working for that guy."

"I don't think we know enough yet about him or the

14

situation to say. Maybe he is working towards a good thing and he's just a jerk. Maybe he's a jerk with a bad cause. We'll see."

"He's kidnapped and threatened us! I think we've gotten to the point where society agrees that that's a bad sort of person."

"Society isn't right about everything."

"That's not the point! Why are you defending him?!"

"I'm not. Like I said, I need to gather more information before I know who or what he is, exactly."

"Okay, well, I've come to the decision that he sucks."

"That's fine. More importantly, we should figure out exactly how powerful that... place is. If we really can go anywhere in time..."

"Even if time travel's really a thing, what on earth was with that squid thing back there?"

"That Minister of Order did tell us about it."

"He showed us a drawing on a poster, and people can put whatever crap they want to on a poster, especially when nobody can take any pictures to prove you're a liar. That's not the same thing. That was a real thing! Just walking around! It yelled at us! Well, more like scarily gurgled at us super loud. Even if we suppose that you *can* go to different times in this place, there's *nowhere* you can go with a squid like *that!*"

"I actually think it's easier for a creature like that to exist than it is to time travel."

"That's my point! There's no way any of this can happen, and yet here I am, wiping dang squid spittle off my pants!"

Coming across a dirt road, they decided to follow it to the village.

"What's up with that guy's stupid clothes, do you think?" Jylling wondered as they walked.

"Who?"

"The Minister."

"I think he wears them, mostly."

"No, I mean *why*, though? Looks to be from about the same time period as Napoleon. Is he getting into the spirit of fighting Napoleon and wearing the appropriate clothes? Or is he from the same time?"

"He certainly doesn't speak in a modern way. And he

sounds British. I don't know, though."

Jylling stopped. "Uh... actually, speaking of clothes, we're going to look pretty weird," he said, looking down at his own attire.

"Hmmm... you're right," Dhlara agreed, observing her own jeans and a t-shirt. "Ah well, it's just a little village. We'll just look weird to a couple of farmers. Besides, it's not like we have a spare change of clothes from the eighteen-hundreds on us."

"I guess..."

They kept walking. After a few moments, they spotted in the distance a man riding a cart being pulled by an animal. As the cart trundled along, however, Dhlara noticed that the animal looked oddly short and too... red to be a horse. Soon, she could make out a mess of tentacles beneath the creature wriggling along the ground.

"So, that cart's being pulled by a squid," she said.

"Yeah, that's what it looks like. What the hell is going on? Do you think we're just both going crazy?"

"If we were, I don't know how we'd both manage to have the same hallucination about land-based applications of marine invertebrates."

"It doesn't make a lot more sense for us to be *actually* seeing what we're seeing, though."

"Well, it appears that we are."

As the cart approached, Dhlara waved to the driver. His eyes narrowed as he drew close; he yanked on the reins attached to the squid and the animal slowed to a halt next to them.

"Good day, travelers!" he said, nodding. He flipped his head back to move his shaggy, shoulder-length black hair away from his face. A length of rope had been wrapped around the squid and tied to two wooden handles on either side of it. One of the squid's eyes on the side of its body peered up at Jylling from below the handle. Its pitch-black pupil surrounded by stark white sclera stared at Jylling.

"Sorry to bother you, sir," said Dhlara, "but we are foreign to this country, and we were wondering if you could tell us where we are."

"That's Plancenoit up ahead."

"And, um... where is that, exactly?"

"You're in the district of Belgium. In the Empire of France," he added after Dhlara and Jylling continued to look confused. "Where are you two from, anyway?"

"Somewhere where travel such as this isn't exactly commonplace," said Jylling, staring back at the squid's unblinking eye.

"There is nowhere but the Empire of France that travels in this way!"

"Who is the... leader of your empire?" asked Dhlara.

The man's eyebrows lifted in disbelief. "Emperor Napoleon, of course! You must come from a distant place indeed, to be unaware of his great victory here last year, and the incredible beast he rode in that battle! It has been the sensation of the world! All the powers of Europe are nothing compared with the brilliance of the Emperor!"

"We'd heard about that," said Dhlara. "We just didn't know there were... little ones."

"With Napoleon, there is always a revolution, even when it comes to my humble farm equipment!"

"I see. Well, thank you for your help, sir!" said Dhlara.

The man nodded and snapped the reins. The squid jerked into motion, pulling the cart forward while still trying to stare back at Jylling. Jylling stood to watch it go for a moment.

"That thing is super creepy," he said.

"Yeah. And it doesn't seem very efficient, either. I don't see how that's better than a horse."

"Well, he seemed happy with it."

"Maybe he has to be."

"Maybe."

Dhlara and Jylling headed to the village. After a few minutes, they started to pass by houses that lined the road, and their appearances were strikingly familiar to the two of them. In fact, when the street they were on joined with another, they realized they were standing at the exact same crossroads they had seen through the other door. There were no soldiers, no squid, and the buildings weren't blown apart, but they did show signs of repair. The corner of a house that the enormous squid had demolished was there, but it had a newer coat of paint than the rest of the building.

As they noticed this, they also noticed people passing them on the street and in the windows of the houses looking at them with puzzled expressions. A woman in a dress straightened up and backed into the doorway of her house a few feet away, then shut the door. An old man leaning against a fence and smoking a pipe watched them with a disapproving expression.

"This is somewhat uncomfortable," said Jylling.

"It's the clothes, like you said."

"I still don't like it."

They hurried on, turning right at the intersection. When they passed a church on their left, they saw a fat man in a long black overcoat limping down another street toward them. When he caught sight of them, he stopped and stared at them. He sneered as they passed by. They rounded a bend in the road and another crossroads lay before them. In the center was a huge bronze statue of Napoleon atop a gigantic squid.

"That's a fast commemoration," Jylling remarked.

They approached with upturned faces as they examined it. Jylling put his hand on his chin and cocked his head. A plaque on the square base of the statue celebrated the French Empire's repulse of the Prussian field marshal Blücher at Plancenoit as part of Napoleon's victory over the Duke of Wellington at the Battle of Waterloo. Napoleon, as the plaque explained, had directed most of the battle while riding the squid (specifically named 'Pote Gluant'), but the squid conquered Plancenoit on its own at his direction.

"Well, that Minister of Order is right about this, at least," said Dhlara. "Something really has gone wrong here."

A pause.

"That squid's awfully... beefier than I remember," said Jylling.

"What? Hmmm... Hey, you're right! I think those two tentacles are supposed to be flexing their biceps!"

"I wonder if they added a set of abs, too—WHOAH!"

A deafening crack startled them. Dhlara whirled around.

She saw the man in the overcoat again, this time standing behind a puff of smoke pointing a flintlock pistol at her. Half of his overcoat was thrown over his shoulder, revealing a pistol holster hanging at his side. Jylling's hand jerked over to his watch and he disappeared. The man started drawing another pistol from beneath his coat with his other hand. Dhlara brought her watch up to her face and pressed the button on its side.

*

A white flash, a hiss of steam, and darkness. The great metal door swung open and light poured into the time machine in the Ministry of Order.

"I almost got shot, Dhlara!" Jylling exclaimed as they exited.

"Well, you didn't, right?"

"Yeah, but I could have been!"

"Then we're okay. And for all you know he was aiming at me."

"I don't know how that's better."

"The point is we're fine."

"Why'd he do that?"

"I don't know. There was certainly more going on there than just how we're dressed. We ought to head back, see if we can figure it out."

She headed for the hallway. The Minister looked up from his desk and glared at them from a distance while Jylling caught up to her, protesting.

"What?! No! I'm pretty keen on not getting shot. Wait! Or shot *at*. I don't like that very much either. One tends to lead to the other, you know."

"Really, Jylling?"

"Alright, don't get sarcastic with me. I'm just saying I don't like it."

"I don't either, but that guy has some reason to shoot at us and I'd like to know it."

"Won't do us any good if we're dead!"

Dhlara pushed through the doors, but right as she entered the hallway, she froze. There, on the floor of the hall, was a head. A real, living head. And only a head. It, or he, was upright, the stump of a neck held up by a small metal platform which had two sets of four spindly metal legs connected to either side of it. The tail of a fish sticking up out of the floor was held firmly in its mouth. Dhlara could not see the rest of the fish, just the tail jutting out of the floor, thrashing and wriggling against the mouth that had chomped it. The head growled through clenched teeth as he struggled with the tail. The tail gave a jerk of renewed effort to escape and slammed the head's face into the floor.

"Grrrrr-RRRGH!" went the head as he turned from side to side, still struggling as his sharp nose was mashed into the wood. His metal feet scraped against the wood floor as they braced themselves in his effort to pull the tail back out. Suddenly, the head whipped back, flipping his few inches of messy brown hair into the air, the back of its skull thumped against the floor, accompanied by the metallic clatter of his legs as they fell down. Dhlara walked over to him; he had a round and boyish face with pronounced cheekbones and, at that moment, a dazed expression.

"Pftoo!" The head spat something out. A chunk of the tail that he had bitten off in the struggle shot up into the air and landed next to him. His brown eyes lit up as he spotted Dhlara.

"Hi! I'm Melvin! The previously embodied head!" he announced, grinning up at her.

"Uh... hello, Melvin..." she replied.

Jylling peered over her shoulder, also befuddled by the display. "...What... the hell?"

Melvin's thin legs propped himself back up. "Hi! I'm Melvin! The previously embodied head!" he said again, this time facing Jylling.

"Who are you?" asked Dhlara.

"I'm Melvin! The—"

"We got your name, Melvin. And what you are, for that matter. But who are you? No, sorry. Yes, yes, you're Melvin," she hastily corrected herself as he eagerly opened his mouth to answer. "I mean, what is it you do here?"

"I'm the Minister of Maintenance!" he said, continuing to be absolutely thrilled.

"Maintenance?" said Jylling.

"Yes!"

"So... what, are you a janitor or something?"

Melvin looked up, thinking. "Yes!" he answered, after a moment.

"Brilliant. I mean, what is the Ministry of Maintenance? What do you do?"

"I make sure everything is how it should be!"

"Isn't that what the Minister of Order says *he* does?" asked Dhlara.

"Well... yes! He makes sure everything in *there* is how it should be," he said, swiveling to point his nose at the closest door and nod at it, "and I make sure that everything is how it should be in *here*!" He turned back and nodded at the floor.

"How should it be in here?" she asked.

Melvin seemed confused for a moment. "As it is!" he said.

"That makes it sound like you don't have much of a job to do," said Jylling.

"Or, I'm really good at my job! Hooray!"

"What were you doing, just now?" asked Dhlara.

"Keeping the fish out! They get in here sometimes, you know," he said, his eyes narrowing. He stared up at random areas of the ceiling.

"Uh-huh..." said Jylling.

"Who are you?" asked Melvin.

"Dhlara."

"Jylling."

"Okay!"

"So how many ministries are there, Melvin?" asked Dhlara. "We've met the Minister of Order, and heard about the Minister of Chaos."

"Five! The Ministry of Order, the Ministry of Chaos, the Ministry of Maintenance, the Ministry of Planning, and the Ministry of Action!"

"Good lord, there's more of them," Jylling said to Dhlara,

motioning with his hand to Melvin.

"More of who, Yuhling?" said Melvin.

"No no no, my name is 'you-ling'."

"Okay!"

"Do you know the Minister of Order?" Dhlara asked Melvin.

"Yes!"

"Can you tell us about him?"

"Yes!" Melvin's smiling mouth hung open excitedly, his eyes darting back and forth at each of them.

"We've been specially chosen to do a job for him," said Jylling. "Do you know anything about it?"

"No you haven't."

"What?"

"You haven't been specially chosen. He just yanks on those levers in there and people pop in all the time. There's whole bunches of yous!"

"That actually makes a lot more sense," said Dhlara.

"What's happened to everybody else, then?" said Jylling.

"The people like you? They've all gone through these doors and most of the time I never see 'em again! Sometimes they come back when they're dying and leave a bloody mess for me to clean up in the time machine. Seems inconsiderate of them."

"'Dying', Dhlara," said Jylling. "You hear that? That fat bastard's probably shot somebody just like us already! And who knows who else is waiting for us!"

"What's the deal with the Minister of Order?" asked Dhlara. "Why's he so angry?"

"He wasn't always that way," said Melvin. "He and Napoleon have been at it for a long time. Maybe he's mad about that!"

"Why does he dress funny?" asked Jylling.

"I don't know, but everybody dresses like that where he's from."

"And where's that?" asked Dhlara.

"Somewhere in the nineteenth-century."

"Really? He used to be somebody in the past?" she asked.

"Of course! He's the Duke of Wellington!"

"Hold up," said Jylling, "that statue said something about him losing to Napoleon! Figures. Angry old dude's just a sore loser."

"If you can't be angry when your life's greatest achievements has been retroactively ruined, when can you?" Dhlara asked Jylling.

"Abducted us, Dhlara! Has been nothing but a jerk to us! If I can't be angry about that, when can I?!"

"What if we wanted to find more people like us, Melvin? Can you remember where any of them went?"

"Hmmm... Oh! I know! There was a guy who came through here a few times. I liked him! Had a fun name! He went off through door eight-ten! Haven't seen him for a bit."

"Alright, thanks, Melvin. Will we see you again?" said Dhlara.

"Yep!" he said. His legs carried him out of the hallway, his forehead knocking the door ajar with a bonk.

"That was super weird," said Jylling.

"I agree. I'm beginning to suspect that's not unusual for this place."

"Let's go find this guy in eight-ten."

"You're not curious about why we just got shot at?"

"Curious, sure. But I'm not interested in giving him an opportunity to try again. Maybe this guy in eight-ten knows something. Maybe he has food. Or maybe we can just take food from eight-ten, and get away with it, because they didn't have guns then."

"Or at least they didn't. Who knows, now."

"Right. Crap."

"Well, still, you're right, let's go find this guy with the funny name and see what he knows. He's been here longer than us, so maybe he knows more about what's going on."

They started walking further down the hall, heading for a door one thousand doors away. Moments after they started, however, Jylling grabbed Dhlara's arm.

"Eight-hundred," he said, pointing to the left. Dhlara's brow furrowed. She looked back the way they had come. The entrance doors were far away down the corridor.

"That's very strange," she said. They looked at each other for a moment, then shrugged. They walked over to the door marked *810*. Dhlara gripped the doorknob, turned it, and pushed the door open.

III

A Pagan Storm

Dhlara and Jylling stood on a white beach. They watched the waves of a dark blue sea crash onto the shore. Behind them, the doorway stood open in the sand. The orange light of a cresting sunrise filtered through a thick morning fog. Dhlara wrapped her arms around herself and Jylling stuffed his hands in his pockets; both of them shivered from the cold.

"This is not promising," said Jylling.

Dhlara looked around, trying to peer through the fog.

"Well... what if we walked along this beach some?" she asked. "Maybe we'll find something. But we can't stay here; we need food and warmer clothes, first."

"Yeah alright."

"Inland or along the beach?"

"Let's just follow the beach. We have no idea what's out there," he gestured away from the water. Dhlara picked a direction and they trudged along the shore, sand kicking up from their shoes as they walked. A few minutes passed in silence.

"Okay, I'm done with being cold," Jylling announced.

"Give it a couple more minutes."

Dhlara heard him grumble something behind her.

Silence pervaded a little longer as they continued on. And then, through the fog, Dhlara spotted something long and dark on the beach.

"Look," she said, pointing.

Drawing closer, the veiled shape became clear, and it wasn't alone: at least five narrow, shallow wooden vessels lay in the sand. Leaning to one side due to the protrusion of the keel, each had a mast at its center with a furled sail and the shape of a toothy, fierce-looking bestial head jutting out above the prow. The pair halted.

"Aw, crap," said Jylling. "Vikings. Awesome."

"Hold on... I don't see anybody."

"Yeah, we've probably caught them mid-rape and pillage."

"Right." Dhlara approached the ships.

"No, I mean that's why we should leave their boats alone!" She went on. He reluctantly followed.

When she reached the closest ship, Dhlara examined its interior. Fifteen wooden benches, each spanning the width of the ship, were spaced at intervals along the length of it. Jylling walked over to the next ship.

"Ooou!" he went. Dhlara saw him throw a large, furry hide around his shoulders.

"Oh man," he said, running around to a third ship, "I wonder if they've got any of those helmets with the horns!"

She started to shake her head, but stopped suddenly to cock her ear at the sea. She remained motionless, waiting. The faint sound of voices drifted across the plane of water. It sounded like... singing.

"...we sail by the light of the northern star!" sang a distant group of bellowing men.

Jylling ran back to her.

"See? Vikings! Famously bad tempered people, let me remind you! We need to leave!" he hissed.

"I want to see if they know anything about the guy Melvin was talking about!" she whispered.

Jylling ran over to another boat and kneeled down, hiding himself behind it. "If you get axed, I'm leaving!"

"Why don't you put their fur back?"

"No way! This thing is warm. Screw 'em! I've got my watch!"

Dhlara walked out to the edge of the water. The prow of a longship broke through the fog. A man wearing chainmail and a metal helmet that covered part of his face stood behind the dragon head. He planted his foot up on the edge of the hull as he looked at the shoreline. Long yellow hair covered his shoulders and a bushy yellow beard draped over his chest. When he spotted Dhlara, he turned around, speaking to the few dozen men rowing behind him. The singing stopped and the longship veered toward her. She put her hands in the air. As the hull ground into the sand, the Viking jumped down with a splash.

"Who are you?" he asked her suspiciously.

"I am Dhlara. I mean no harm. I am looking for someone very strange to you."

"You speak my language?"

"No, I... Well, apparently I do."

"Then you are very strange to me."

"I— Yes, well... I'm looking for somebody else like me."

"There he is," he pointed behind her. Turning around, she saw Jylling peering out from behind a ship.

"Yes, you're right, I know him. But I'm looking for somebody else."

"Someone who wears one of those?"

"One of what?"

He nodded at and pointed to her arm. She looked down.

"Oh," she said, holding the watch out towards him. "Yes! Wearing one of these."

"Hmmm. . I will have to take you to King Good Fred."

"Why? Who is 'King Good Fred'?"

"Come. I will take you to him," he said, climbing back into the longship. Dhlara started to follow.

"You can't be serious," she heard Jylling say from behind her.

"He seems to know something," she replied.

"Vikings! Murderous villains! The world's most famous seaborne arsonists! What's wrong with you?!"

Dhlara could hear the sound of laughter coming from the ship.

"What's wrong with *you*?" she retorted. "Do you have a better idea? Or are you just going to be hysterical?"

"I don't have to have everything figured out to know that hanging out with a crew of Vikings is not something you do when one of your life's goals is to not die!"

"We have an opportunity here to do something no one else has ever done *and* we have an easy way of staying safe," she said, pointing to her watch.

"And how reliable is that? How many times have you used it? Because if it doesn't work exactly how you expect when you expect, you're dead. I'm not betting my life on this *thing* that we know nothing about!"

"Well what do you want to do, then?"

"Not get chopped into bits on account of being stupid, for starters."

"I got that part, Jylling! That's not an answer!"

"...I don't know."

"Grand."

The Viking splashed back onto shore and approached them. "If your friend is afraid of our reputation, he can stay here if he likes," he said.

"I don't think that's an option," said Dhlara. He shrugged and walked back.

"See?" Jylling hissed. "See what he's trying to do? He and his gaggle of muscled friends would just love it if you got in their boat with them."

"Listen, you come up with a better plan, or I'm going to trust this *thing*," she said, pointing to her watch, "and get in that boat."

Jylling threw up his hands in exasperation and looked around. As his gaze passed over the row of ships along the shore, he suddenly jerked his head in a double-take.

"Hey!" he shouted to the Viking. "Hey! We'll go along if we can take one of your extra ships!"

Looking at the ships, the armoured man replied, "Do you know how to sail it?"

Jylling waved dismissively. "Splish, splash, starboard, port, first mate, whatever. Can we take one?"

The Viking whistled at his own ship and pointed to the empty one on the beach. Half his crew jumped out and pushed the other ship into the water. A few climbed aboard to raise, unfurl, and rig the sail. Jylling turned to Dhlara and held out his arms.

"A better plan."

"We do not, in fact, know anything about sailing, Jylling."

"So we learn. Watch how Captain Beardo does it."

As his men clambered back into their ship, the Viking called to them, "Now you will follow us to King Good Fred. And don't try to steal our ship, because you won't get very far with it."

The pair waded into the water and hoisted themselves into the longship.

*

Hours later, the fog had cleared and the morning sun was ascending. The dragon head of a longship rode above the calm sea, propelled onward by oars that cut into the water and swung backwards together. The sail remained furled, as the air was still stagnant. A man in chainmail with an axe at his hip strode across the deck of the craft between rows of men sitting on chests pulling the oars. After every pull, there was a wooden sound of "THUNK" and the ship jerked forward, returning to normal motion after a few seconds. As he walked, the man braced himself against the mast or parts of the hull, anticipating each sudden movement. Reaching the front of the ship, he stepped onto a platform and removed his helmet, holding it in the crook of his arm. He gripped the face of the dragon head as he looked up at the sun. There was a THUNK and the ship jolted. The Viking's arm flexed as he held himself in place. Relaxing, he studied the shoreline to his right a few hundred yards away. Tens of ships were sitting in the water of the rocky shoreline and columns of black smoke rose in the distance somewhere beyond the thick forest. He looked back at the rear of the ship, where another man sat on a platform tucked into the narrow space where the hull converged to make the stern. His hands held a piece of wood that connected to the side of the hull. The prow Viking cupped his mouth with his hand and shouted something to the sitting man. He nodded and pulled on the wood. The ship turned toward the shore. THUNK. The captain caught himself on the gunwale to stop his fall as the deck lurched under his feet. His Norse curses drifted across the water.

Behind the head of the aft-most man was a rope coiled around the stern. The rest of the rope extended out across the water and wrapped around the prow of another longship. The sail and yard of this ship were missing entirely. At the rear, holding a piece of wood, sat Jylling, looking dejected. Dhlara stood with her arm around the mast. She had also found furs to wrap around herself. The oars of the ship in front of them dipped into the water and pushed the ship forward. The connecting rope strained taught, then relaxed as the second ship was pulled forward. With a THUNK, the hulls of the ships collided.

The ships slowly made their way to the shore by this accordion action. The leading ship's hull ground against the rocks a few feet under the water and came to a halt. The Viking, helmeted again, stood at the stern and yelled to the ship still in tow.

"Out!"

Then he went to the opposite end of the ship and jumped into the shallow water.

The pair walked across the deck towards the prow. They looked over the edge of the hull at the undoubtedly very cold water. Jylling sighed.

"We're going to get real wet," he said.

"Yeah, that's probably the idea," said Dhlara as she discarded her furs onto the deck. "He's clearly pissed at us. For all of your quivering fear of Vikings, you're apparently pretty good at making them mad at you."

"I didn't *mean* for that stupid sail to fall into the water."

"I don't think it matters what you meant."

"Look, I didn't see you helping."

"I didn't tell him we could sail the thing, Jylling. Maybe because I know that we *can't*, and if we try, we'll end up dumping something important overboard."

"Whatever. Next time I'll just let you hang out with a boatload of Vikings. I'm sure they'll treat you with respect and dignity and it'll be a whole lot better than swimming in a little bit of water."

"Okay," Dhlara laughed. "Now let's go see what your friend's up to."

She vaulted over the edge and there was a splash below. Jylling leaned over and saw her swimming to shore. He let the fur cloak fall off his shoulders onto the deck and jumped down.

Dhlara hauled herself out of the gently breaking sea. Water poured from her clothes. Shivering, she folded her arms and tucked them into her stomach. She could hear Jylling splashing and complaining behind her.

"Frick, frick, frick!"

He ran past her and hopped in place and rubbed his arms.

After a stretch of shoreline consisting of small rocks, the ground rose up a few feet and turned into a grassy field for about fifty yards inland, ending at the feet of a forest. Dhlara could see the frustrated captain jogging across the grass, heading to the forest. The crew of his ship had disembarked and were busily securing the two vessels and attending to various other tasks she could not discern.

"Frick!" continued Jylling.

*

A few hours later, a large wood fire had been built on the grass by the crew, which Jylling and Dhlara used to dry off. They were warming themselves, huddled in wool cloaks that had been offered to them, when Dhlara spotted figures on horseback emerging from the forest. She stood up, watching about a dozen riders as they approached the camp. In the lead was a tall, red-haired man on a stumpy horse. His hair was long, whipping about in the air behind him. Men clad in chainmail carrying spears rode behind him, followed by the familiar captain. The group galloped up to the fire and dismounted. The red-haired man, also fully armoured in chainmail and armed with a sword at his hip, strode over to where Dhlara and Jylling were sitting. The rest of the group gathered around him.

"I am King Good Fred!" he announced, raising his arms. He had narrow shoulders, yet big, thick hands. His face was clean-shaven.

Dhlara bowed her head. "I am Dhlara, and this is Jylling." Jylling nodded.

"It is good to be meeting you! Welcome to my kingdom, travelers! Come, we will have a feast in honour of our good fortune this day!"

"What, here?" Jylling asked, looking around.

The King laughed. "No, no, not here! At Hedeby! Our friend Hasdrubal is there, and so we will go on to meet and feast with him!"

"Is Hasdrubal another traveler?" inquired Dhlara.

"Yes, of course! Just like yourselves! But surely you knew that already? Do you not know him?"

"Well, we know of him."

"Gods! How many of you are there?!"

"What do you mean?"

"Travelers from distant shores, like yourselves and Hasdrubal. How many have you met?"

"Uh, none, I guess. That's why we're looking for Hasdrubal."

"Interesting... I am sure he will want to meet you right away. And if you are anything like him, I am very glad to have you in my kingdom! Now we shall sail for home!" A man at his side walked off and began issuing orders to the crew bustling among the ships.

"Tell me about the place you come from," said the King. "Hasdrubal has told us much of his land, and it is fascinating! Have you heard of elephants?"

"Yeah."

"Have you seen one?"

"I think so... in a zoo or something, I guess."

"And you, have you seen one?" he asked Jylling.

"Yeah."

"Did you face them in battle?"

"What? No."

"Do the kings of your land use elephants in battle where

you're from?"

"Not so much."

"Have you been to Carthage?"

"I've never heard of it."

"Really? Hasdrubal has told us much about Carthage. It sounds like an incredible place. I am sure he can tell you about it. But tell me about where you are from."

"I don't really know where to start."

"You speak our language; do my people live in your land?"

"No one speaks it where we're from."

"Hmmm... have you heard of us, then?"

"Only in opera, and you guys had a lot more horns and wings on your helmets than what I'm seeing right here."

"Huh. That's odd. Why would we have horns on our helmets?"

Jylling shrugged. "I don't know. Sure looks cool though."

"I see..." said the King, staring at the ground in thought. Then he looked up and asked, "What is 'opera'?"

*

Jylling sat on the deck of a longship, gnawing on a piece of bread and looking up at the sky painted red and orange by the setting sun. The crew sat on chests lined along the interior of hull, talking amongst each other. The sail billowed above him as the ship rode on the water. He was still wrapped up in a wool cloak as he leaned against the mast. Dhlara walked over to him and sat down, leaning against another part of the mast.

"He finally had something else to do. I've gotten pretty sick of his questions."

"You shouldn't be telling him anything. That's why *I* stopped answering them."

"What? Why not?"

"He's some guy we don't know that can have us killed. Having people killed is mostly what kings do, and also mostly what Vikings do, and he's a Viking king. I think that's reason enough not to trust him."

"Oh come on. He seems pretty happy with us."

"Because he thinks we'll help him. Who knows who this Hasdrubal is or what he's done for them."

"We'll see."

"And besides, how about the whole 'screwing up history' sort of thing? Giving people in the past information about the future is never a good idea."

"We live in a completely different millenium. I don't think there's that much that means anything to him or that he can even do something about."

"That's not the point! Even just talking to him is changing history. Maybe you'll give him some ideas and then later we'll come to find the United Vikings of America."

"Well it sounds like this Hasdrubal has already been actively changing history. He's apparently a general from a long time ago—"

"Everybody here is from a long time ago."

"Even longer, I mean. He's been some sort of military advisor for the King for a few years."

"That isn't good. Somebody ought to fix this."

"I'm sure that British guy would be glad to hear you say that, though."

"Hey!"

"Just saying."

"He's a loud, incompetent moron who's shuffling people up all throughout time. He's the reason we're here right now and he's the reason Hasdrubal is here screwing everything up. Just because he shouts about fixing history doesn't mean he actually cares about it. And just because he shouts about it doesn't mean it's the wrong thing to do, either."

"I know. I understand. I probably shouldn't say as much to these people. But I don't think there's a whole lot we can do about setting things right, and things are already messed up and messing up."

"Yeah..."

A crewman in leather armour strolled over to them and offered a drinking horn. When both refused it, he sat on a chest nearby.

"The King's been very curious about the two of you," he

said.

"What, are you here to ask questions too?" said Jylling.

The man laughed. "No, I am not. Frankly, I don't care about where you are from."

"How can you not care about that? We're from the future!"

"I grow food and raise my family," the man shrugged. "I don't have much use for places far beyond when I am and I don't think they have much use for me. I am a man of my own time."

"Well what are you doing over here, then?"

"Perhaps I'm curious about *who* you are. Surely where you are from isn't the most interesting thing about you."

Jylling snorted. "I live in a place you wouldn't understand even if I tried to tell you about it," he said, "and everyday items would seem like magic to you. How are you supposed to understand who I am?"

"I think there's more to someone than what they have in their pockets."

"He's Jylling," said Dhlara. "And being cantankerous is part of who he is."

"Hah!" the crewman laughed, reaching out and slapping Jylling on the back. "Don't you sound like a Northman!"

Jylling scowled.

They fell silent, watching the sun set. A commotion had developed among the crew; they slid oars through holes in the gunwales and sat holding the ends, preparing to row, and a few busied themselves with the rigging attached to the sail. Dhlara and Jylling stood up and made their way to the front of the ship, clearing the area around the mast for the sailors. Looking beyond the prow, they could see they were headed for a white beach shoreline.

"There, the Jutting Land!" the King said to them. "We will go to a mighty city raised up by my hand. You will come with us and feast and you will meet the man you have been looking for. And then we shall talk of the future!"

*

A few hours after sunset, Dhlara and Jylling were riding on horses, following the King and at least twenty other Vikings. Some of the other riders carried torches to enlighten the darkness. The group rode through a grove, then out onto a level field of spring grass. By the moonlight, Dhlara saw a long wooden wall. The grassy field sloped up several feet and the wall itself sat atop the mound. It angled obliquely from her right to directly in front of them and beyond. Intervals of burning torches dotted its length far into the distance on either side.

When they drew closer, the King reined in his horse and fell back to ride alongside his guests. He held out an arm and pointed at the wall ahead.

"With the help of Hasdrubal, I have made this land strong! No matter who may gather armies in the south, they will not tramp upon our lands!"

"It is impressive," said Dhlara, studying the wall.

"And this Danish work will be but the least of my feats! The Danes have much in store for the world!"

No one made any reply to this, and the King rode forward again, appearing not to notice.

Soon they passed through a gate in the wall and rode on. After another hour, the walled city of Hedeby came into view in the distance, and riders bearing torches approached from the right. The King signaled a change of course to meet them.

"Emissary at the gates, my Lord!" one of them yelled as he drew close.

"Ha-hah! Have they come to cry at the feet of the Danes, my lads?!" hollered Good Fred.

"He is anxious indeed!"

"Let us see what he has to say, then!"

The dull thud of galloping hooves resounded as the King and his entourage rode south to the wall. They rode through another gate, then came to a stop at the next one. The area was bright with torchlight and men stood gathered around the doors.

"King Good Fred! I must speak with King Good Fred!" a shrill voice yelled from the other side of the wall.

36

The King and his bodyguards dismounted, Jylling and Dhlara following suit.

"The King is busy taking your lands and killing your kin, little man," replied a voice from the dark ramparts above the gate. "If your message is that you hate our ears, message received."

"I must speak with the King, by God!"

King Good Fred strode over to the men standing near the doors of the gate and shouted up to the ramparts of the wall.

"Hasdrubal! What does the cowering worm have to say?"

"Oh, good evening, my King! Nothing, as yet," came a male voice from the darkness above the gate.

A figure jumped down from the ramparts. The man crouched as he landed, then straightened upright. He was olive-skinned with a black beard and his green eyes shined beneath his chin-length, slightly curly black hair. What caught Dhlara's eye first, however, was the red fez, with a gold tassel draped over the side, on top of his head. The sides of his short, dark blue jacket with red trim hung open, just above a light blue sash wrapped around his waist under his belt. His baggy red trousers were tucked into white gaiters over black shoes.

"He is rather hysterically refusing to speak with me," he said, grinning broadly.

Good Fred laughed, slapping him on the shoulder as he passed to push open the gate. He strode out onto to the grassy field beyond the doors; a group of ten men stood a few dozen yards away beside their horses. Several hundred yards behind them was the treeline of another forest. The King held open his arms towards them as his bodyguards, Hasdrubal, and Dhlara and Jylling followed out onto the field.

"Well then, messenger!" the King yelled. "Get on with it!"

One of the group across the field with a gold tunic and a shield strapped to his back stepped forward.

"I am an emissary of Karl the Big," he yelled, "Emperor of the Romans and King of the Frank folk! Your invasion of Frisia must cease, or Karl the Big will visit war upon your lands!"

"We are already at war! Why are you here? Defend your

shores or die! Frisia belongs to me and I shall have it!"

"Surely you can see how hopeless it is to rely on the arms of sailors and merchants from this puny land to contend with the armies of a mighty king crowned by the hand of God!"

"I think you will soon find it is not your king the gods favour!" Hasdrubal interjected.

"I have come to speak with King Good Fred, not his lackeys!"

"I am Hasdrubal! Do you know what that means, petulant child?"

"King Good Fred, we have come in good faith to reach reasonable diplomatic accord. I beseech you, remove this man—"

"That means before even the most distant of your fathers were ever born, I was killing Romans! Before your God was even known to the world, I was killing Romans! I am a curse upon the throne of Rome!"

"I will not stand here and listen to lies!"

"Lies?!" bellowed Hasdrubal. He retrieved two flintlock pistols from his sash and discharged one into the night air in front of him. Sparks and smoke billowed out from the muzzle. A member of the messenger's party fell to his knees, then thumped the ground with his face. Hasdrubal advanced several paces, extended his other arm, and fired again. The remaining men and horses bolted in panic.

"Let the world know: the wrath of the Norsemen is coming for the pretender of Rome!" King Good Fred yelled after them.

Hasdrubal and the King laughed heartily as the envoys scampered away.

"That was quite a show, my friend! I believe our message is safe in his hands," the King said, slapping Hasdrubal on the back.

"It is about time we got to do that."

Dhlara watched Hasdrubal's wrist as he returned his pistols to his sash; wrapped around it was a timepiece that very much resembled the one on her own wrist. Noticing this, the King started.

"Ah, Hasdrubal! This is Jylling and Dhlara; they are travelers like yourself."

Hasdrubal jerked his head.

"Are you now?" he held his fist over his chest and bowed slightly to them. "You have passed through the junction of history?"

"Yeah," Dhlara answered.

"How is Melvin?" he asked with a grin. "I haven't seen him for some years."

Dhlara's face scrunched up for a moment.

"I don't really know... Good? I guess? Or maybe really bad? Has he always been, well, deheaded?"

Hasdrubal shrugged. "I suppose so. I haven't seen him otherwise."

"How many of us," Jylling cut in, gesturing to the three of them, "are there?"

"No idea. I saw a few, when I was still there. But I didn't stay long. That man Wellington is pushy and I have better uses for his mechanisms."

"What sort of better uses?" Jylling gave him a sidelong look.

"Raising an army!" proclaimed the King.

Hasdrubal nodded and grinned, "I've decided to make a bit of trouble."

"What exactly does that mean?" Jylling asked.

"We have gathered to my banners," answered the King, "a thundering force of Norsemen to destroy the kingdoms to the south! You have seen my invasion of Frisia, and we conquer many lands more!"

"King Karl declared himself Emperor of the Romans," said Hasdrubal, "and I am not overly fond of Romans. And, after having done some reconnaissance through time, I have learned that this is where the French people originate, so if Karl's empire is destroyed, there are no French troublemakers in time."

"That's your solution?" asked Jylling. "Get rid of the French?"

"Yep," said Hasdrubal. He looked proud of himself.

"You can't do that!"

"I can do whatever I like."

"Hold on!" Dhlara moved between them. "Hasdrubal, we have been looking for you because we don't know anyone else who is... like us. We were hoping we could speak to you and maybe learn something about what is going on here."

"New to this, are you?"

"Yes. Wellington dragged us here today."

"Is he still terribly hysterical about Waterloo?"

"I would say so, emphatically," Jylling scoffed.

"When are you from?"

"The twenty-first century," said Dhlara.

"How surprised were you to learn Napoleon actually lost the Battle of Waterloo?" Hasdrubal smirked.

"Well, not very. He did."

"What?" Hasdrubal's brow furrowed.

"The first we heard he'd ever won was from the Minister."

"That can't be possible."

"We had always learned he lost."

"No, that doesn't make any sense. Are you sure? Are you only repeating what Wellington told you?"

"No, that's what happened."

"That isn't right. He was victorious; I saw it. Why did you not know that in your own time?"

Dhlara shrugged.

"I need to find out what is going on here. Maybe all of this," Hasdrubal gestured vaguely at the Viking settlement, "won't work. If your time has not changed with the past, maybe this past cannot affect its future either. I must look into this."

"What are you saying?" the King asked.

"It is necessary for me to leave for a short while, I'm afraid."

"No!" the King cried. "Hasdrubal! You cannot! What we are about to do here will change the world!"

"I am not entirely sure that it will."

"What are you saying?! Of course it will! How does war not change the world forever?!"

"I need to see that it does," Hasdrubal turned, holding out his hand to the King. "I will return, King Good Fred. I intend to return momentarily! Perhaps it will seem like I never leave at all. I do not know how things will go, but I swear to return. I will finish the work we have started."

"You swear?"

"I do."

The King grasped Hasdrubal's hand with both of his own.

"I hope I will not need to depend upon that. I do not wish to see you go, but you have helped us immensely as it is. If we do not meet again, let us happen upon each other feasting and drinking in Valhalla."

"May Oden be with you, good king."

With that, Hasdrubal walked away, out into the field. Dhlara and Jylling trailed behind him. King Good Fred stood staring after them with a puzzled look on his face while running a hand through his hair.

IV

Midnight Sun

Dhlara trotted to catch up with Hasdrubal. "That was a bit abrupt," she said.

"Life is abrupt."

"You aren't *life*."

"I live in it, so I know what I'm talking about."

"Where are you going?"

"Preparing to ruin sometime else, no doubt," Jylling muttered.

"There," Hasdrubal answered, pointing to the treeline at the end of the field. "I wish to avoid demonstrating how exactly my method of travel works to people who are not already familiar with it."

"That makes sense," said Dhlara. She was silent for a moment. "So you're from Carthage?" she asked.

"I am."

"What exactly is that?" asked Jylling. "I've never heard of Carthage."

"Of course you haven't."

"Hey! What's that supposed to mean?"

"It's supposed to mean that you'd have little reason to hear of Carthage."

"Okay. Why is that, then?"

"My city ceased to exist in what you refer to as one hundred and forty-six B.C."

"What happened?" asked Dhlara.

"It was destroyed by Romans."

"Well I've heard of them," said Jylling.

"Of course you have."

"We haven't met anyone else Wellington has brought in

aside from ourselves," said Dhlara.

"I haven't, either."

"What was it like for you? When he showed up, I mean."

"I was in Iberia planning campaigns against Rome and he appeared out of thin air. He looked at all of my generals, then looked at me and said, 'You. You're the man for the job'."

"Did you agree to go with him?"

"No, he grabbed me and suddenly I was in his metal machine."

"How long ago was that?"

"About six years ago, now."

"Whoah! That's some time ago."

"Yes it is! I've spent most of it here, though, and these northern people know a drinking song or two. Time flies when you're singing drinking songs."

"Six years of drinking songs?" Dhlara laughed.

Hasdrubal grinned, "What does that mean? Are you saying I should tire of them after a certain number of years? That I should spend my time on more important things?"

"I don't... I guess I wouldn't really know."

"There is nothing more important in life than a drinking song. When we come to stand in the halls of the gods, what will we do, but sing? Any gods who do not sing are no gods of mine."

"I wouldn't really know about that either."

"Who asked you to know?" Hasdrubal threw out his arms. "I asked what you think!"

"I don't think much about something I know nothing about."

"What else is there really to think about? If you know it, why do you have to think about it?"

"I... I don't know, man. I was just trying to find out what you're about."

"And I'm finding out what you're about," Hasdrubal smirked.

"We're about hanging out with old timey drunkards, apparently," they heard Jylling say from behind them.

Hasdrubal turned around to face Jylling while walking

backwards.

"I have not said a thing about drinking, have I?"

Jylling scoffed, "I'm going to guess Vikings wouldn't be pals with a teetotaler."

Hasdrubal laughed and spun back around. "Maybe not! But I am no drunkard. And I'm not as stuck in the past as you seem to think."

"Yeah, we can see that. Where did you get the guns?" Dhlara asked.

"After being brought to the Ministries of Time, I spent a few months researching many of the events that happened beyond my own time. There is a long amount of human history, it turns out. In the course of doing reconnaissance on the French army, I encountered a unit dressed in this quite dashing outfit," he gestured to his clothes, "and I helped myself their regalia. As well as their arms, of course."

"How did you learn how to use them?"

"The clothes? We did have clothes in Carthage, you know."

"No, the guns."

Hasdrubal chuckled. "I trained with the French unit," he explained.

"Uh… hey guys…" Jylling cut in.

Dhlara continued questioning Hasdrubal. "You speak French?"

"Apparently I do," he answered.

"What does that mean?"

"I mean to say that I never learned it, and yet I understand them perfectly."

"Oh! So you also have whatever implant the Minister put in our heads, too?"

"That's what he said. Who knows what's really going on. All I know is I understand every language and everyone can understand me."

"That's so weird."

"There's something up there…" said Jylling.

Hasdrubal shrugged. "Considering all the things going on right now, that is one gifted horse whose mouth I will not be looking into."

Dhlara raised an eyebrow.

"What?" said Hasdrubal. "I'm trying out your idioms! Don't look at me like that. It's you future people's nonsensical saying."

"Fire in the sky, you guys!" Jylling persisted.

"Huh?" Dhlara looked back. Jylling pointed up at the sky in front of him. Following his finger, she turned and looked up at the sky. There was a small yellow glow emanating from within a few clouds in the night sky. A ball of fire fell out of the bottom of one of the clouds and kept plummeting toward the ground.

"What is that?" Dhlara wondered aloud.

The light from the fire grew brighter as the ball fell, until it was brighter than the moon and lit up their upturned faces. Its glow flickered as the swirl of fire swelled and dimmed seemingly at random.

"What is that?" Dhlara wondered aloud.

"Crazy crap has happened all day," said Jylling. "That right there is more incoming crazy crap."

Hasdrubal laughed. "Then let us go meet it!" he said, sprinting closer to the light.

Dhlara trotted after him. Jylling stopped in his tracks and threw his hands up, exasperated. Keeping an eye on the fiery mystery as she chased after Hasdrubal, she saw the fire lessen for a moment. It was hard to make out in the distance, but something large was at the center, inside the fire, and moving within it. Something was... thrashing around. Before she could make out what it was, though, the flames roared to life again and fully obscured the shape again. The fire and whatever it surrounded continued to hurtle downward in complete freefall despite the rapidly approaching impact with the earth. Dhlara realized, as it steadily came closer, that what had been a distant oddity in the sky was in fact something very large, much larger than her, and about to land very close to them. Moments before it hit the ground, the fire suddenly dissipated, and in the moonlight she glimpsed two massive wings splay out from within the smoke left by the inferno. And then, with a resonant thud, the thing slammed into the dirt near the treeline across the field. Dhlara broke into a run.

As she drew closer, she saw that what had landed was a creature; it thrashed about violently, belching flames from a narrow mouth with huge fangs.

"Dragon!" shouted Jylling far behind her. "Come on, Dhlara! You don't mess with dragons! This one is an easy call! Stop!"

Dhlara trotted to a halt as she came up alongside Hasdrubal. She saw an enormous, scaly beast with its wide wings wrapped around its body. It rolled over onto its back, then curled its very long neck so that its head looked down at its own chest. Its wings unfurled, revealing another figure: a tall, thin man standing rigidly upright upon the dragon's chest. The dragon opened its jaws with a roar and fire erupted from its mouth. He leaped clear of the approaching flames and landed beside the dragon's head. Dhlara felt heat on her face and squinted her eyes against the bright orange light emitted by the roiling waves of fire. In a calm motion, the man placed his hand over the dragon's massive throat and the flames immediately diminished into nothing more than a strangled wheeze. The giant creature beat its wings against the ground and strained against the man's hold, but it could do nothing to even move his hand.

The man choking the dragon was six and a half feet tall, narrow shouldered and slim, and very pale. His blonde hair appeared to be greased back, yet not one hair had been disturbed in the act of plummeting from the sky while fighting a dragon. A black pinstripe waistcoat was neatly buttoned over his white dress shirt, the sleeves of which were rolled up to his elbows. Below, he wore a matching pair of pinstripe trousers and a shiny and rather pointy pair of black dress boots.

He reached into his waistcoat with his free hand and pulled out a coil of thin wire. He swiftly clapped the dragon's mouth shut with both hands, then started wrapping the wire around its snout. While his hands worked, his narrow face turned to look at Dhlara. His irises were a pure green, and she almost thought they glowed. Even the whites of his eyes were particularly white. He glanced at the watch on her wrist, then smiled at her, revealing a perfectly aligned row of stark white teeth.

"What time is it?" he asked her, looking up at the sky.

"Time? I… I don't really know."

"Your watch," he nodded.

"Oh, this? This just tells the year."

"Right. What time are we in?"

"Ah, eight ten. But, uh, that's a dragon."

"It is."

"How?"

"It was born one."

"No, I mean how are there any dragons at all?"

"The Ministry of Planning made them."

"Why is it here?"

"It escaped."

"So you're a dragon-hunter, or something?"

"I'm more of a wrangler. And it's more than just dragons," he said as he finished wrapping the wire around the dragon's mouth. He took something out of his trouser pocket and slapped it onto the scaly flank of the beast. The dragon beat its wings, lifting itself up into the air, and flew a few dozen feet away, but then there was a brilliant flash of light, and it disappeared.

Behind her, Hascrubal laughed and clapped his hands. "That's a fancy trick, sky-man. Have you got a bunch of these," he said, lifting his wrist and pointing to his watch, "in your pocket?"

"Basically. They're not the same devices, but close enough. I used one to recall the dragon back to the Ministry of Planning."

"What sort of plans call for dragons?" Jylling cut in as he walked up.

The man shrugged. "I don't do the planning. But I guess it's a matter of having them if you need them."

"Do they make any plans to not lose their fire-breathing monsters somewhere in time?"

"That isn't their job," he said as he turned his back to the group and started to walk away.

"Who are you?" asked Dhlara.

He stopped and turned halfway back around to look at her. "My name is Gordon," he said. He pulled a pocket watch out of his waistcoat and held it flat in his hand. With the press of a button, the cover flipped open. A door appeared next to him.

"Where are you going?" Dhlara asked.

"Back to the Ministries of Time. You're free to come along, if you like," he answered, returning the watch to its pocket. He grabbed the doorknob and pulled the door open. Hanging in the doorway was an upside down head with a blank stare and mouth agape in an eerie smile.

"AUUGH!" Jylling yelled.

Hasdrubal laughed.

"Hey guys!" the head said excitedly, his hair waving in the air beneath him as he spoke. His metal legs were splayed out so that the pointed ends braced him at the top of the doorway. Without changing his expression, his eyes darted over to Gordon. "Gordon! What's up, man?"

"Caught another one," Gordon answered.

"That's swell!"

"Melvin! How are you doing?!" Hasdrubal hailed the head.

"Hey, brother! You didn't die!"

Hasdrubal threw back his head and laughed, "No, I didn't!"

"Hey, and you two didn't die either!" Melvin continued, looking at Dhlara and Jylling. "Good job!"

"Melvin, what the heck are you doing?" Jylling pressed. "Were you hanging on some door hoping somebody would open it?"

"Yes! Also, you went out this door, like, two seconds ago!"

"So you just hang in doorways that people go through?"

"Yes!"

Gordon held his hand out underneath Melvin. The happy head fell into his palm, his metal legs still splayed out in the air. Gordon turned him over and bent down to place him back on the floor. Melvin's legs skittered wildly in the air until they touched the floor and he took off down the hallway.

"Keep doin' what you do, Gordon!" he shouted back over

the clatter of his metal legs.

"You got it, boss."

"Boss?" Jylling looked at him incredulously as the group entered the hallway.

"He's the Minister of Maintenance. Keeping the Ministry of Planning's prototypes from getting out of control is our job."

"What does *that* mean?"

"Well, like dragons, for instance."

"Does that happen a lot that they need a whole Ministry for it?"

"We maintain all Ministries, not just the one of Planning."

"What? Isn't the whole reason we're here is because some buck-wild nonsense is being perpetrated by some other stupid Ministry?"

"The actions of the Minister of Chaos have caused us significant problems."

"Sounds to me like you guys asked for that problem by having a Ministry of Chaos at all."

"I didn't make those decisions," Gordon shrugged.

"Well whoever did doesn't seem to know what they're doing."

"If part of your job is to fix what has happened with Napoleon," said Dhlara, "maybe we can work together on that."

"Is that what we've decided to do?" Jylling asked her.

"It's what I've decided to do."

"Just because some doofus in a red jacket claiming to be a dead guy told you to?"

"That really has nothing to do with it."

"Doesn't it though? I don't like that guy."

"What does that have to do with history? Weren't you saying we needed to set things right again?"

"No, I said *somebody* should fix this mess. I did not say you or me, because I am not in the business of cleaning up after some raging British buffoon. Why us? Why not someone more capable?"

"Who would that be? Who is there? Who do you trust that

much?"

"Yeah…" Jylling frowned and stared at the ceiling as he thought.

"So would you like to work with us, Gordon?"

"That may be too big picture for me," he answered. "Collecting wayward creatures is more my kind of work."

"Napoleon does have that huge walking squid," said Hasdrubal, holding his fez in one hand and spinning the tassel around, "if you're looking for more things to wrestle."

"All I'm saying is if you'd like to help us, in whatever ways you can, we'd appreciate it. We're new to this place, so even if you could only tell us about what's going on here, that'd really help us."

Gordon smiled. "Yeah, I could do that."

"Hey, how about, before we get too ahead of ourselves," said Jylling, "we figure out what we're going to do about the necessities? I mean, we need to sleep. Where are we going to do that? What are we going to eat? I don't see this madhouse providing reliable answers to those questions."

"I can't say I've ever seen anyone here eat or sleep," said Hasdrubal.

"What do you eat?" Dhlara asked Gordon.

"Most of the time my dietary needs are supplied by my quarry."

"Huh?"

Gordon reached into his waistcoat and pulled out a strip of dried meat.

"Owlbear jerky," he explained, holding it out as he offered it to the group. When no one reached for it, he shrugged and returned it to the interior of his waistcoat.

"Hmmm… let's see if Wellington has anything prepared for us," said Dhlara. "If he wants us to stop Napoleon so badly surely he must have thought to provide us with these sorts of things."

The group followed Dhlara down the hallway and through the doors leading to the Ministry of Order. The Minister of Order was marching around his desk, waving his hand around as if he was talking about something, but there was no one around him. Dhlara, Gordon, and Hasdrubal headed for him, but Jylling heard a clatter. Looking around, he saw Melvin, who had climbed up onto a wall, ripped off the metallic grate of what appeared to be an air duct with his claws, and discarded it onto the floor. He shoved his head entirely inside the duct as Jylling approached.

"What are you doing?" Jylling asked.

"Checking for time termites!" came the muffled reply from within the duct.

"What?"

"They're a serious problem, don't you know!" The metal legs sticking out of the wall waggled back and forth.

"No, I don't think I do know."

"Well watch out for them! They'll eat the time right out your bones!"

"Melvin, you're a weird little dude, do you know that?"

"Yep!"

Jylling laughed.

Dhlara approached the Minister of Order. "Is there somewhere we can sleep?" she asked.

"Heavens no! No time for sleep!" he shouted. "Go out and make war, sir!"

"How about food?"

"I subsist purely upon a diet of love of king and country, and I expect the same from all men of the ranks!"

"I don't think that has ever stopped anyone from starving."

"It does for me, by God! Don't come to me and whine about your contemptible inadequacies, sir! Go forth and do your duty!" The Minister's face grew red with the force he applied to every word.

"This is the essence of his character," said Gordon.

"And I find the character of your essence to be lacking!" the Minister retorted.

Gordon just stared at him impassively.

The Minister resumed marching around his desk.

"Do you see why I chose to ignore this guy?" Hasdrubal asked her.

"Oh I understood. Figured it wouldn't hurt to see if he'd

made any preparations whatsoever. Well, now we have to figure out something on our own. I don't suppose you've got a lot of that kind of... food, do you?" she asked Gordon.

"Not really. Usually there is just enough for what I need. I've only been catching dragons lately, so I've been running low even for myself."

"You don't eat dragon?"

"It is more so that the Minister of Planning is insistent that I return all of them to him alive."

"This area serves as well as any other for quarter," said Hasdrubal, surveying the room. "We would only need to collect proper equipment, which is easy enough. As overblown as our distinguished red gentleman here is, I can't say that Napoleon, whoever he is, is any less so, and at the very least it seems that this Minister doesn't intend to kill us in our sleep. What's more, he has something of an armed force, and appears to have maintained this position in spite of Napoleon's intention to defeat him. Whatever each of us decides to do, here we will have protection against an unknown and possibly hostile party of substantial power."

"Yeah, that makes a lot of sense," said Dhlara.

"I could go into a year and hunt something for everybody to eat," offered Gordon.

"That'll work."

"Where's Jylling? He ought to know what we're doing..." Dhlara looked back and saw Melvin climbing onto Jylling. While she walked over, Melvin climbed onto Jylling's chest, pulled on Jylling's shirt collar with his claw, and put his face inside the shirt and looked around. After a moment, Melvin released the shirt collar and patted it carefully with his claw against Jylling's chest, then scurried around Jylling's waist to his back.

"What's going on here?" asked Dhlara.

Melvin's head popped up over Jylling's shoulder, "Time termites!"

"They're a serious problem, don't you know," Jylling grinned.

"Alright... So we're basically going to set up camp here."

52

"Ack! *That's cool...*" Jylling replied in a constricted voice as Melvin tugged on his collar from behind.

Before she was even aware that he left, Gordon returned from the hallway with armfuls of jerky.

"I thought you said you didn't have enough food?"

"I made some."

"That was fast. Wait, you're saying you made that from an animal?"

"Yeah."

"Why jerky, then? What's wrong with just cooking it?"

"I don't know," he said, shrugging, "This keeps longer."

"And it tastes awful."

"If this is not acceptable," he turned and headed back to the hallway, "I will make something else."

"No, I'm not saying it's unacceptable! I appreciate it, Gordon."

He continued on and passed through the doors into the hall.

Hasdrubal sidled up to her, his hand inside his fez, idly twirling it on his finger. "That guy was wrestling dragons," he said.

"Yeah, he was..." she looked at him quizzically.

"And now you're turning your nose up at the food he tried to make for you." He held his fez above his head by the tassel and dropped the hat onto his curly black hair.

"That's not what I said!"

Hasdrubal chuckled. "I will go fetch some bedrolls," he said.

Soon enough, Gordon returned with several plates of steak in his hands and balanced on his arms. Dhlara could see steam still wafting from the meat.

"Wow, you didn't have to do that!"

"You said you wanted something better," he said. He set them down on the long table in the center of the room.

"Do you mind if I—" she started.

"Eat. That's what I brought it here for."

She looked around. "I don't—"

"Ah, right," he reached into his waistcoat and produced a

fork and knife.

She cut off a piece and put it in her mouth. Her eyes widened.

"Gordon, this is incredible! Where did you get it?!"

"I made it."

"That's impossible. You were hardly gone at all."

"I made it," he repeated. "I can show you, if you would like."

"No, I'm not— Thank you. I didn't really realize how hungry I was."

"It was no trouble."

"Oh cool," Jylling said behind her, "food!" He walked over and sat down across from her. Dhlara's eyebrow lifted when she saw Melvin atop Jylling's head, his metal appendages gripping him firmly in place. His face was blank and expressionless, turning and bobbing with every movement of Jylling's head.

"Wait a minute," said Jylling, looking suspiciously at Gordon. "How do I know this isn't going to kill me or something?"

"It won't," Gordon answered.

"What is he doing?" Dhlara asked, looking up at Melvin.

"No idea," Jylling grinned. "Hey Melvin, you want some steak?" he asked, his eyes looking up as far as they could go.

"Okay!"

Jylling cut off a piece of meat, speared it with a fork, and held it up. Melvin's mouth popped wide open and Jylling maneuvered the fork up into Melvin's mouth. Melvin's jaw snapped shut and he swallowed the piece whole. Jylling's face abruptly changed to an expression of consternation.

"Melvin, get off of my head," he said slowly and deliberately.

"Okay!" Melvin hopped off. The points of his legs clicked along the table and then onto the floor as he scurried off. The same — though now somewhat slimier — piece of steak Jylling had cut off was sitting on top of his head, nestled in his hair.

"Of course it didn't have anywhere to go but back out," he said. "I should have seen that coming."

Hasdrubal, meanwhile, had re-entered the room with bedrolls under his arms. Soon, after Dhlara and Jylling finished eating, they set up their bedrolls in-between a pair of shelves of books and went to sleep.

V

Paranormal Mysteria

Dhlara blinked as she awoke, clearing her bleary eyes. She sat up and looked around her. She had no idea how long she had slept; everything looked exactly the same as it had when she had fallen asleep. The sunlight coming in through the roof of the library was still the same colour and coming in at the same angle as when they first arrived. She could have slept for ten minutes or ten hours; it was impossible to tell. The shelves of books obscured most of the room from her view. No one was at the section of table beyond her feet. She twisted around and looked over at the bedroll that Jylling had laid out to sleep in, but it now lay flat and empty on the floor. She crawled out of her sleeping sack and stood up. Stifling a yawn, she adjusted her clothing to fix all the bunching up and jamming into awkward places it had done while she was unconscious. She walked out from between the bookcases toward the table. Another empty bedroll lay in a corner to her right. The lamps near it had been extinguished; whoever slept there had apparently wanted a darker area to sleep in.

As she wondered who had slept there, she realized there was a pleasant smell in the air. It was… bacon? She spotted several plates of sausage, eggs, French toast, and, indeed, bacon at the end of the table. She walked over and sat on the long bench seat. She pulled the plate of bacon toward her to grab a crisp piece and chomped on it; it was still somewhat warm. There was a stack of empty plates nearby, so she grabbed one and started piling food onto it.

While she was in the process of pouring syrup onto her French toast, one of the doors to the hallway opened and Hasdrubal strode into the room with nothing but his baggy trousers on. A towel hung around his neck and over his hairy chest and arms.

"Good morning!" he said as he walked toward her.

"Morning!... Is it morning?"

He shrugged. "It can be any time you want it to be," he answered. "Seems like morning is a good time for waking up, though, and I just came from a morning, so to me it is morning."

He swung his leg over the bench and sat down across from her. Dhlara noticed his curly head of hair was wet.

"What have you been doing?" she asked.

"A twentieth century beach on a summer morning! We have any option of how to wake up as we want, in there," he said, motioning to the hallway as he grabbed an empty plate.

"Why the twentieth century?"

"I like the feeling and bustle of people being around, and the twentieth century has some spots that suit me very well. Where'd your friend go?"

"I don't know. He was gone when I woke up."

"This man Gordon makes delicious food, I'm inclined to say," said Hasdrubal, chewing a bite of sausage.

"Did he do this?"

"I figure so. Can't think of who else would. Our hospitable host, perhaps?" he grinned and waved to Wellington's desk beyond the opposite end of the table. The old soldier was still standing there, engaged in a cycle of marching back and forth past the desk, stopping to adjust his bicorne hat, taking it off, and setting it back down on his head before marching around again over and over.

"This particular kind of bread here," Hasdrubal said, pointing to the plate of French toast, "you call that French toast, correct? I certainly don't think he'd be putting that out."

"I doubt that food has allegiances," she laughed.

Hasdrubal stopped chewing and cocked his head. "Wait, do you hear that?" he wondered.

Dhlara sat still and listened. Then she heard it as well: coming from behind the doors to the hallway was a metallic sound... a sort of... jingling. One of the doors was pushed open and Jylling stepped through. He held the door open with his foot while shaking a chain of bells in one hand. He puffed out his chest and held out his free arm. *"Oh! Chi è che giunge?"* he sang. *"Ragazza, guarda! Odo i sonagli…"*

With a clatter of pointy metal feet, Melvin ran past him. He held his little pincer hand up to his brow, looking at Dhlara and Hasdrubal. *"E un baroccino…"* Melvin sang. *"I vostri amici! Beppe, il Rabbino…"*

"E Federico!" Jylling cut in. *"Visto il bel cielo, Vengono qui."*

"Scesi son già."

"Incontro andiamo!"

Melvin climbed up onto the table and walked in front of Dhlara. He gripped the front of her shirt with his pincers and pulled her forward. Their foreheads bonked together. He raised his incredibly close eyebrows as he stared straight into her eyes. "We went to the opera," he told her. With that, he scurried off.

Jylling smiled in amusement at a flabbergasted Dhlara. "Might as well culture the little guy," he said.

"You went and saw a whole opera with him?" she asked.

"Indeed I did." Jylling sat down at the table next to Hasdrubal and reached for a piece of bacon.

"It would seem you slept for quite a while," said Hasdrubal.

"I must have…"

Jylling's brow furrowed. "Did you heat this up or something?" he asked Dhlara.

"No. Why?"

Jylling looked around the room. "It's just that… this is warm. It was warm when we left…"

"Maybe somebody brought in fresh food."

"I guess… but Gordon said he was going out. And these plates look about the same…"

"Well, are you going to eat it?" Hasdrubal pointed at the plate of bacon.

"Not the whole thing," Jylling answered.

"Alright then," Hasdrubal pulled the plate over to himself.

"Is that not weird to you?"

Hasdrubal crunched happily on the strips of meat as he

gave Jylling a blank look. "Is what weird?"

"This here food is still warm! It was here hours ago!"

"Okay. What about this place makes sense to you?"

"Not much, really."

"So why does this one bother you?"

"It doesn't, exactly, it just seems weird to me."

"There is food here, and it still has the heat of being cooked. I don't have much of a problem about that. That is how I like it."

"That's not the point."

"I understand what you're saying, Jylling," said Dhlara.

"We have larger issues to deal with," Hasdrubal reminded them. "It would only make sense that the two of you, in coming from a later age, should have been aware in your own time of the changes made to past sequence of human events. And yet you were not."

"Well the obvious question is did those changes really happen," Dhlara posited.

"Whoah, hey," Jylling started. "I don't think there's any doubt that someone has drastically altered history. I think I'd know about it if our time believed there was a gigantic squid wrecking shop in any war."

"Yeah, we did see things with our own eyes that don't seem like they should have happened. Maybe we should find out what these records," she waved at the bookshelves around them, "have to say should happen. If we're going to try to set things right, we ought to know what right is. But there's two separate things here: what happened, and what passes down to us in our time as what happened. Maybe something occurred later in time that changed what we learned."

Hasdrubal frowned. "That is very convoluted. I don't think this is that complicated. There is clearly a man trying to increase his power over the peoples of the world, and it is our duty in general to oppose such a thing. Whatever these records say is not my concern. What we do is for ourselves to decide, not a set of writings."

"Isn't that the whole reason we're here in the first place?" Jylling rejoined. "Somebody decided the way things are wasn't his concern and what he was going to do was for him to decide?"

"Of course it is. Nobody's obliged to be as others say he should be, and everybody has the ability to make of themselves and their time what they can. The difference is what this French man decided to do with that."

"I'd also like," said Dhlara, "to ask Wellington about some of the things we saw."

Jylling scoffed. "Well you can have that special pleasure all to yourself."

"I'll go do that and see if I can learn anything from him." She got up and walked all the way down the length of the table and up the stairs to the Minister's desk. He appeared to take no notice of her as she approached, staring sternly down at the medals on his chest, carefully adjusting each in turn with his hands.

"So we went to the Battle of Waterloo," she said. "And there really was a great big squid there. Do you know how it got there?"

"Some dastardly plot of old Boney's, I suspect!"

"Yes, of course, but what plot exactly? How did it get there?"

"Pure Frankish villainy! They have, in their despicable and malodorous moral depravity, corrupted even the very finest of the King's oceanic subjects!"

"Yes, well, we did see a smaller squid pulling a cart, too."

The Minister jolted upright. "WHAT?!" he roared.

"One of them was pulling a cart."

"BY GOD, SIR! DO YOU KNOW WHAT THIS MEANS?!" His face reddened as he yelled.

"...I don't know that I do."

"THEY HAVE UNLOCKED THE SECRETS OF ALL MANNER OF SQUID-BASED TECHNOLOGY! SQUID-DRAWN CARTS! THE DEVILS!"

Dhlara's mouth fell open. "Uh... I don't think it's that important, comparatively. Seems less efficient, actually."

The Minister stomped over to the wall behind him where an upside down map of India hung. "WE'LL HAVE TO

GIVE THEM THE BAYONET! CHARGE STRAIGHT UPON THEIR WORKS!" He pounded a finger into the Indian Ocean.

"Charge what, exactly?"

"THE SEA, OF COURSE! ONWARD, STRAIGHT ON INTO THE BRINY DEEP, UNTIL THERE IS NOTHING LEFT BUT A PILE OF DEAD FRENCHMEN ATOP A PILE OF EQUALLY DEAD FRENCHCEPHALOPODS!"

"Okay. So you don't have any idea how they got there, I guess. Some random person shot at us while we were in France. Would you know anything about that?"

"A betentacled agent of the little corporal, no doubt!"

"No, it was just a regular person, not a squid. Or a squid person."

"So far as you could see, sir! Only the trained eye can tell a genuine Frenchman apart from other spineless creatures!"

"Uh-huh. So this went well." Dhlara turned and walked away as the old man's blazing eyes stared menacingly at the map. Hasdrubal had brought a chair over to the end of the table and was leaning back in it with his feet on the table. He smirked at her as she returned.

"Looks like you worked him up into a fit," he said.

"He is quite actually a crazy person," she sighed.

Jylling carried several thick books in his arms over to them. He dropped them with a thump onto a stack of books on the table. He ran his finger down the spines until he came to *1814: Being in Large Part an Abbreviated History of the Events of the Year 1814*, and pulled that book out of the stack. He set it down, opening the covers to a random set of pages, which were lined with hand-written scrawl.

"It's entirely possible this is nothing but his deluded idea of what occurred — or should occur, or whatever," said Jylling as he thumbed through page after page, "but either way, he certainly is fastidious in recording it. Ah, here we are. It says Napoleon was exiled to the island of Elba in May of eighteen-fourteen and… it looks like he stayed there through the end of the year."

He scanned the stack of books and pulled out the volume

about 1815, setting it next to its earlier counterpart. The binding crackled as he spread open the covers and rustled page over page again.

"Hang on," Dhlara interrupted as she looked at the pages from across the table. "Isn't the handwriting different in this part here, about Napoleon at Saint Helena?"

"I don't think so," said Jylling.

"No, go back to the beginning."

Jylling flipped *1814* back to its early pages. "Oh yeah, it does look different. Huh."

"If these are Wellington's records, why is someone else writing in them?"

"We don't really know who wrote these," Hasdrubal shrugged indifferently as he crunched a piece of bacon. "Could just be different clerks he dictates to. Or maybe he didn't write any of this and he abides by the content inside them."

"Hmmm. So, anyway," continued Jylling, "this other one says he then escaped February twenty-fifth, eighteen-fifteen. He went to France, became Emperor of France again..." thick paper pages scraped against each other as they were turned. "Yada yada yada... Fought the Prussians and English in a series of battles... uh... ending with the Battle of Waterloo, which he loses, then gets exiled to St. Helena." He looked up from the books. "Well, as far as we know, this is all still accurate up until Waterloo."

"So somewhere in there," said Dhlara, "he did something that changed the past."

"Or so I thought," Hasdrubal appended.

"Are you suggesting that warsquids were just part of the regular course of history?" said Jylling.

"The fact that these changes happened before you came to this place, and yet word of them never came to either of you in your own time suggests that history was not, in fact, made to be any different than it was before."

"That's impossible. There is no way what we saw was what had always happened then."

"I haven't seen anything that makes me think as you do. Somebody writing it down in a book doesn't make it true."

"I *know* what we saw is different from actual history."

"Why? How do you know that?"

"Because that's not what I learned. Nobody has ever said that Napoleon won Waterloo, especially in this ludicrous way!"

"The truth isn't subject to a vote. It either is or it isn't."

"What would be proof to you that something *was* changed, then?"

"Actually seeing the act of it being changed. If he went back to alter events, he must have entered the past at some point and introduced something new to the situation. If we can actually see him do that, then he did change history."

"How are we supposed to catch him doing it? He already did it! It's done!"

"But he did it somewhere in time," said Dhlara. "So if we go to that time, we'll see him do it. And it'll be a lot easier to undo what he did if we know where he started."

"Alright then," said Jylling. "Well, sometime between Elba and Waterloo is where something must have changed."

"If we start at Elba and work our way forward, we will find whatever he did that caused what you witnessed at Waterloo," said Hasdrubal.

"That's months!" Jylling objected.

"I spent years on a plan that apparently won't work, so it's not that long. We could start at Waterloo and work backwards, but we'd need to get close to that squid and all other forces under Napoleon's command. And perhaps it still would take months. My way is safer."

"Alright, so we'll go check out Elba and if everything looks to be the way it should be, then we'll move forward until we find something amiss."

"If we find something amiss."

"Yes, yes, *if*."

"We should find clothes that are less conspicuous first, though," said Dhlara.

Hasdrubal's face lit up. He brought his black boots down off the table and sat upright. "I can help you with that! They have some very elegant dresses with a wonderful sense of colour—"

"No dresses."

"What? Why?" He frowned.

"They aren't practical for what we are going to be doing."

"I agree, but it's the regular attire of the time. And their men take to awfully drab fashion."

"I don't care so much for how it looks, honestly."

"Ah, I see. For my own self, if I'm going to do something important, I want to look good doing it."

"Is that uniform even accurate to the time?" She looked down at his baggy red pants.

"My uniform," he stood up proudly, "is not up for negotiation."

"Fair enough, but we will still have to find something for ourselves."

"I know just what to get."

*

Some time later, Dhlara and Jylling were donning outfits that Hasdrubal acquired for them. Dhlara wore a frilled white shirt with a white cravat and gray trousers. She put her arm into a black overcoat and swung onto her shoulders, then put the other arm through. Her hair was tied back into a ponytail. Jylling buttoned up a dark blue overcoat; a high light yellow collar stood up from underneath it over a white cravat. His pants were brown, and Hasdrubal put a top hat onto his head.

"I said no," he objected and took off the hat.

"That's not very fashionable," said Hasdrubal. He was again wearing his full French uniform.

"Hats are dumb. Any sort of wind takes them off."

"In my time, there was not such a fantastic variety of hats as the future has."

Jylling scoffed. "I'm not going to wear a hat because back in your day you didn't have any."

Hasdrubal smirked. "Whatever you like."

"Alright, let's go to Elba on February twenty-fifth, eighteen-fifteen."

CLANK.

Melvin popped out from the ceiling. One of his metal pincers held open a metal hatch.

"Are you all going on an adventure?!" he asked. His mouth hung open excitedly, his chin touching the ceiling.

"I suppose you could say that," said Jylling.

Melvin's face straightened into a blank expression; he pursed his lips and stuck his chin out. He held his pincers out in front of his face and clinked them together twice. Behind the Minister of Order's desk came the sound of a door slamming. Jylling turned to look.

"Whoah!" He jumped as he found Gordon suddenly standing next to him.

"My apologies," said Gordon. "You called, boss?"

"Hey Gordon! These guys are having an adventure! I think it's time you moved out and had an adventure of your own. Go do whatever it is they're doing!" And with that he retracted back into the ceiling and closed the hatch behind him.

"Is that something you would be agreeable to?" Gordon asked.

"Of course," Dhlara answered.

"That getup isn't very Napoleonic, though," Jylling nodded to his pinstripe waistcoat and trousers.

"Yes," said Hasdrubal, "but I think we'll find that Mr. Gordon here can handle any problems that might come up. He's already shown us to be a remarkably talented individual."

"Well, fair enough."

Soon they were all in the hallway of doors. Dhlara opened door *1815* and a gust of cold air blew in from the dark of night beyond; lights of a village twinkled in the distance. The group filed through the doorway. Dhlara smelled seawater and heard waves crashing. To her left, she saw a sandy coastline below her, down the hill they were standing on. Far beyond the coast, more lights hovered just above the water. She peered at them, but her eyes were not yet adjusted to the dark, and all she could make out was darkness. She stuffed her hands into the pockets of her overcoat to protect them from the bite of the cold air.

Hasdrubal climbed up some boulders to the right, looking at the village. "Seems to be some sort of settlement down there," he said.

"It is," said Gordon. "There are many people there. Many of them are soldiers. Some are on patrol."

"Have you been here before?" Hasdrubal sounded surprised.

"No."

"How do you know these things, then?"

"I can see it."

All Dhlara could see was flickering lights and the silhouettes of buildings against the light. She squinted to see if she could make out the silhouette of a person, or movement, but couldn't see either.

"What?" Jylling was incredulous. "I can't see anything down there."

"I can."

"How?"

"I don't know. I see it. How do you see anything?"

"Do you understand that that's unusually good eyesight?"

"Well, it isn't unusual for me."

"What can you see out there?" Dhlara asked, pointing to the lights out on the water.

"It's a sailing ship. Appears to be anchored."

As her eyes adjusted to the dark, she could indeed see a ship.

"So we're looking for something weird," said Jylling. "Something non-historical. Or what used to be non-historical, but now is, I guess. Where should we start?"

"Is that what you're doing? Are you looking for something specifically?" Gordon asked.

"This is the island of Elba," Jylling explained, "in the year eighteen-fifteen. We're looking for anything Napoleon — er, the Minister of Chaos may have changed."

"I see."

"If there are military units down there," said Hasdrubal, "we ought to stay clear of them if we can."

"What should we do, then?" Dhlara asked him.

"You and Mr. Gordon should move closer to that settlement and keep an eye on the area. Just lay low and watch.

What we're looking for may not be here, or it may be hard to find. So our best course is to gather information about the forces on this island."

"What about you?"

"Mr. Jylling and myself shall go down to the coast. There's probably a dock here, and if we find it we can scout it out, but if not we can find another vantage point to survey the village That is, of course, if Mr. Jylling is amenable to the idea." He looked at Jylling for his assent.

"Yeah alright."

"Splendid!" Hasdrubal grinned and rubbed his hands together. "Remember, if you find yourselves in any danger, just leave," he said as he pulled up his shirt sleeve to show his watch. "Now, let's see what we can find!" And he marched off down the hill toward the beach. Jylling trotted after him.

Dhlara turned to her right. The hill they were standing on extended out in that direction, obliquely drawing closer to the lights of the village as it sloped up and down.

"Come on, let's follow this to a better vantage point for you," she said to Gordon.

He nodded.

She felt the soft press of grass and moss against her shoe as she walked along the crest of the hill. The night air nipped at her face as it blew over her in gusts. She twisted her head to look at Gordon. She noticed he still had his white shirt sleeves rolled up to his elbows.

"Aren't you cold?" she asked as she hunched her shoulders so that the collar of her overcoat would cover more of her face from the wind.

He shook his head. "It is cold, but I am not cold."

"Where do you come from?"

"The Ministry of Maintenance."

"Is that where you've always been? Your whole life?"

"Well, no."

"So where are you originally from?"

"America in the early twentieth century."

"Oh yeah? Where in America?" She looked at the ground as rocks crunched under her shoes.

"The West."

"How did you get to be so… unusual? Did joining Ministry of Maintenance change you?"

"No, not at all. I've been however it is I am for as long as I can remember."

"Really? I don't think other twentieth century Americans can wrestle dragons out of the sky."

"No they can't. It's just me, as far as I know."

"And you don't know why that is?"

"I don't."

"Huh. What else can you do?" she asked as they came to the edge of a steep slope on the side of the hill facing the village. She crouched down and laid out flat on her stomach.

"I'm not sure what you mean by that." He lowered himself down onto the ground as well and crawled up next to her elbow over elbow.

"It looked like you have a lot of physical strength and speed when we saw you before, and apparently you can see extremely far. Is there anything else exceptional about you?"

Gordon smiled to himself. "I don't know that I am exceptional. I simply corral wayward rare animals. I don't make them, or use them, or command them. I am just me. I might be able to run faster than some, but one individual is only ever just one, and that is small compared to the numerous whole."

"We're all individuals."

"We are, but many people are a part of many groups. Families, friends, companies, states, cities, nations, everybody is a part of something. Those are what make the world. I am just me."

"That's overstating things, don't you think? Who you are means something."

"In small ways, I suppose."

"So what can you see down there?" She nodded to the illuminated little town.

Gordon turned and surveyed lit streets, small one-story homes, and a several stories tall mansion on another hill in the center. The dark profiles of trees obscured much of the view.

"Not a great deal. Some guards patrolling the streets,

people sleeping in their houses, dogs... things look normal. Hang on, though..." he squinted at a two-story mansion on a hill across from them. "There is something... odd in that place over there." He pointed.

"What is it?"

"I don't know..."

"What does it look like?"

"I can't make it out, exactly. But I can see that there is something strange in there."

"What does *that* mean? If you can see it how can you not know what it looks like?"

"I can't see whatever it is, but I can see that it's inside that mansion."

"How? I don't know what that means."

"I can see that there is something in there that is out of place. I don't know how to describe it. It is as though I can see a glow of light coming through the walls."

"Well, I can't see anything unusual."

"There is something in there, trust me."

"Dhlara!" A voice hissed from the darkness behind them. Her head whipped around at the sound of her name.

"Who's there?!"

"It is your friend," observed Gordon.

"Yeah, it's me!" Jylling came running up to them. He bent over, putting his hands on his knees, his chest heaving from being out of breath. Dhlara hoisted herself off the ground.

"What's up? Why are you back over here?" she asked.

He pointed toward the sea. "There's something..." he panted, "in the water... the ship..."

She ran back to where they had started and then down to the beach. Hasdrubal was standing in the sand. Looking at her, he pointed out at the dark horizon. Drifting in over the lap of waves were the sounds of a distant drumroll and shouting. Her eyes searched for the source, but, at first, all she could see was darkness.

Then flashes of light pierced the night; the ship she had seen earlier was firing its cannon. The bright flash of a broadside from the far half of the ship outlined the vessel.

Shortly after, the thump and boom of the guns reached the spectators on the shore as the ship was enveloped in darkness again. Another volley of cannon lit up the night, but this time there were silhouettes of long, curling tendrils as tall as the masts of the ship in the billowing gunsmoke.

Dhlara quickly turned to her companions. "Was that— Did you—"

Gordon nodded. "There is some manner of large creature out there."

Soon, the cannon fired again, and in the flash, dark against the diffuse light in the smoke, Dhlara saw the mainmast falling and the tentacles striking at different sections of the ship. Small jets of fire, smoke, and sparks started shooting up from the top decks. Dhlara heard the roar of the cannon reach them, and then she heard screams, the crack and crash of timber, and the popping of small arms fire. The cannonfire died down as fewer and fewer guns fired with each volley, until the firing stopped altogether. The deck continued to pop and flash with sporadic shots of muskets and pistols, but these soon ceased as well. The ship returned to darkness and once again all that was heard on the beach was the lap of waves.

"What just happened out there?" Dhlara wondered aloud.

"An unnaturally large cephalopod attacked that sailing vessel," stated Gordon. "It has wrapped its tentacles around the hull and turned the ship on its side and is pulling it under."

"Okay, see? Not normal!" Jylling said from behind them.

Hasdrubal shrugged. "Maybe that always happened."

"What?!"

"I don't know what happened to that ship in 1816. Maybe that always happened."

"That is ridiculous. You are ridiculous."

"The future is ridiculous. Maybe there exists really big animals sometimes. That is not so hard to believe."

"Nope. Nope. There aren't sea critters that big that just attack ships! That's time travel sea critters and if that one's around here Napoleon's around here somewhere."

"Well he's supposed to be here," Dhlara reminded him.

"Yes, no— you know what I mean. He's here *again*, I

guess. Let's look around and see if we can find any more things he's changed. Should we split up again?"

"No," said Hasdrubal. "What happened to that ship out there is unusual, and if you take it as a sign that there is somebody here trying to change history, we ought to be careful."

"There is someone on this beach with us," Gordon interjected.

"What? Where?" Jylling looked around.

Gordon pointed down the beach to his right. "There. It's someone in a military uniform."

Hasdrubal nodded to a cliff face that bordered the beach. Clusters of rocks were clumped up near the base. "Here, let's take cover near this wall."

Hasdrubal led them single-file along the cliff, the group ducking down to obscure themselves behind the rocks and piles of sand.

After a few minutes of crouched walking, Gordon said in a low voice, "Stop. This is about where he was." Hasdrubal halted and turned around.

"Can you see him now?" Jylling whispered, looking back at Gordon. Gordon shook his head.

"There's rocks in my way." He pointed at a big boulder they were squatting down behind.

"You seem really good at seeing stuff. Maybe you had X-ray vision or something, I don't know."

"X-ray vision would mean I could see X-rays. X-rays don't wear military uniforms."

"Ah whatever."

Dhlara stood up slightly and peered over the top of the boulder. A lone figure stood in the sand a few yards away. He was wearing a long, dark overcoat and the ends of a bicorne hat extended out above his shoulders. He turned to his left, gazing at the beach. She saw the profile of his face, and she recognized it from paintings: he was Napoleon. She ducked back down.

"That's Napoleon!" she hissed.

"What?!" Jylling started.

"Shhhh… That guy looks like he's Napoleon."

"Well let's get him!"

"Hang on! Let's not do anything until we're sure of what's going on."

The four of them peered up over the boulder. Napoleon had put a telescoping spyglass up to his eye and was scanning the sea. His head slowly swiveled back and forth as he surveyed the horizon.

"What is he looking for?" Jylling said to Dhlara out of the side of his mouth.

Suddenly, Napoleon jerked his spyglass back to the left in a double-take, then lowered it and stared out at the dark sea. Dhlara looked over at the waves hitting the beach and was startled by the sight of a gigantic squid that had risen halfway out of the water. In the moonlight, she could see another man in uniform hanging on to the back of the creature. Water poured off the animal as it shuffled up the beach on its tentacles. Napoleon took a couple steps back and looked around him.

"By God…" she heard him say aloud as he watched the squid approach.

The squid stopped in front of him and the man on its back jumped off into the sand. He was wearing a soaked blue officer's uniform with tasseled and gold epaulettes and medals on his chest, as well as a bicorne hat fixed longways from ear to ear on his head. As she looked at his face, her eyes widened. This man also looked like Napoleon. He was much older, though, and fatter. His gut stuck out inside his jacket and his face was puffy and bloated, but he was Napoleon, too. The oceanic Napoleon squelched in his boots as he strode toward his counterpart with his hand held out. The overcoated Napoleon laughed as they shook hands.

"I've accomplished the incredible, I see," he said.

"More than you can imagine," the older Napoleon affirmed. "And we will do even more." He clasped his hands behind his back and started walking along the beach away from the hidden group of eavesdroppers. The other Napoleon followed alongside. They leaned their heads in toward each other and took turns talking to one another, but what exactly was being said was lost in the noise of the waves and wind. Jylling lowered himself behind the rock and pulled Hasdrubal with him. Dhlara watched the two of them.

"So that right there is some time travel shenanigans, yeah?" Jylling pressed.

"I don't know. Maybe that's his dad," Hasdrubal answered. Jylling scowled in disbelief and frustration. Dhlara chuckled to herself. "I'm joking," Hasdrubal laughed. "Yes, a man talking to himself sufficiently proves the existence of shenanigans."

"Alright, now let's take this bloated squid-surfer out." Jylling spun around on his heel to look up at Gordon. "Hey, Gordon, go punch his lights out."

"I'm not sure that's the best idea."

"He— They do have a really big squid." Dhlara pointed out. Jylling spun back around and arched an eyebrow at her as if she'd said something crazy.

"You saw this guy choke the crap out of a dragon! What the heck does a limp, wet squid matter? Dragons have huge jaws full of razor sharp teeth and breathe fire! Squids are squishy and their primary evolutionary advantage is firing a cloud of goop out its butt so that it can swim away. Gordon, can you take out that squid?"

"I believe I am capable of subduing it, yes."

"See? Let's do this. All this business will be solved right here!"

"We should know more about what's going on here first," Dhlara argued. "Maybe this is a trap. Maybe there's more to him or *other* him or that squid than we think. If the solution is to apply punches liberally we can always come back to this time whenever we want and do exactly that."

"And by that you mean have *me* do exactly that, I take it?" said Gordon.

"Well, not have you do it. If you wanted to do it, I mean."

She looked back at the Napoleons. They shook hands again, and then the older one vanished. The younger one in the overcoat climbed up onto the squid's body and the creature shuffled back into the sea and swam out into the darkness.

"That was weird," Jylling remarked as he stood up.

"Let's go back to the Ministry of Order and sort out where we go from here," said Hasdrubal.

"Yeah, that's a good idea," Dhlara agreed.

"Hold on, I saw something odd in that mansion back there," Gordon cut in.

"Oh yeah!" Dhlara remembered.

"I'd like to go find out precisely what is in there. It was very strange. It clearly didn't belong here."

"Alright, let's go check it out."

They backtracked until they stood on the overlook Dhlara and Gordon had been on.

"See?" Gordon pointed at the mansion. "It's in there."

"What is?" Jylling asked.

"I don't know."

"...Alright."

"I suppose you can't see it, but things in the Ministries of Time look different. They don't look normal. There is something in there that is from the Ministries."

Jylling's eyebrows raised. "That has to have something to do with what Napoleon has done."

"Undoubtedly. I am going to find out what it is." The group followed as Gordon walked down the hill and across a small field of grass and trees up to the back of a brick building. He touched the wall as he continued along it to a corner. A dirt road lit by streetlamps lay a few yards away from the building. He faced the brick wall and leaned his head sideways to peer around the corner and pulled back immediately. With a wave of his hand he motioned to his companions and crossed the road in a dark area between streetlamps. Treading softly, the group followed one by one.

As she crossed, Dhlara looked down the street where Gordon had looked; a cluster of soldiers stood in front of another brick building talking amongst themselves. She heard the sound of laughter drift over as a couple of them threw their heads back and slapped each other on the back.

They passed several more buildings in this way and came to another road that ran across the front of the mansion. Several soldiers were patrolling the grounds around the mansion and a pair stood guard at the front door. The road and the path up to the mansion were well-lit by streetlamps.

Hasdrubal moved up next to Gordon. "I'll make a distraction and then all of you can go in without me; I'll get back on my own." Gordon nodded and Hasdrubal jogged away in the darkness just beyond the light of the streetlamps. They waited a few minutes, crouched next to the side of a house, until a gunshot rang out from a wooded area left of the mansion. Many of the soldiers turned and ran toward the sound, but one of the guards remained standing at attention at the entrance.

In a blur of motion, Gordon bolted across the road and knelt behind a bush near the front door before Dhlara even realized he was moving. The guard jerked in surprise and craned his head forward, staring at the spot where Gordon had been. He gripped his musket with both hands, leveling the bayonet out in front of him, and walked down the set of stone steps to investigate.

When he neared the shrubbery lining the path, Gordon's hand shot out and grabbed his arm. Gordon pulled him closer and put his other hand around his neck. The man dropped his gun in shock and struggled uselessly with his one free hand against the firm grip around his throat, silently panicking until he passed out and went limp. Gordon caught him as he fell and laid him down behind the bushes, then motioned for Dhlara and Jylling to come up.

The trio ascended the stone steps and filed into the foyer of the mansion after Gordon opened the unlocked door. The building was dark inside; the rooms around them were dimly lit by the ambient orange light from the streetlamps outside.

"This way," Gordon whispered, and headed straight into a sitting room on the right. As he led them around a series of couches and chairs, a loud crash abruptly filled the room. Jylling lay sprawled out on the floor on top of a pile of broken pieces of an end table that had been particularly well obscured by shadows. Jylling lept to his feet and stood still, as if he was waiting for something. And then something came: the clomp of boots on the floor above them.

"Hurry!" Jylling hissed. Gordon wheeled around and rushed over to a closet door. He flung it open and bent over as he rapidly rifled through various objects in the closet, looking for something specific as the tramping grew louder. Dhlara watched Gordon anxiously as she heard the oncoming feet descend a staircase. Jylling ran his fingers into his short hair, gripping his head with both hands. He looked around the room, as if he was out of ideas and looking for one.

"Halt!" a voice yelled behind them. Dhlara and Jylling instantly raised their hands over their heads. Dhlara looked behind her; four French soldiers stood in the foyer with muskets pointed squarely at her and Jylling's backs.

"Don't move!" the burly one with a bushy black moustache shouted. Glancing back at Gordon, she saw him calmly stand up straight, close the closet door, and open it again. This time, there was no closet behind the door; instead, Dhlara could see the hallways of doors in the Ministry of Order. He turned around to face the soldiers, also raising his hands over his head. He looked Dhlara right in the eye, looked up at her arms, then looked her in the eye again and raised his eyebrows. She nodded slightly.

"Screw it," she heard Jylling mutter, and he disappeared. The soldiers shouted in alarm. They all pointed their guns at her.

"You! Where did he go?! Answer!" one of them yelled.

She slowly put her hands up in the air and onto her head. When her hands neared each other, however, she calmly pushed the button on her watch with her forefinger.

VI

Guardians of Fate

Dhlara was enveloped in complete darkness. All she could hear was the muffled sound of steam hissing. She put out her arms to feel around her and she felt her forearm collide with something soft.

"Augh, god! Why?!" she heard Jylling's voice exclaim.

"Eeesh, sorry, did I just hit you?" she apologized.

"Yeah, right in my side!"

"So," another voice intoned behind them, startling both of them, "what happened in there?"

"Hasdrubal?" Jylling asked.

"That is me."

"Some soldiers were in the house and they caught us," explained Dhlara.

"Did Gordon find what he was looking for?"

"I don't know."

Loud metallic clanking noises resounded through the bronze oval they were in. The door swung open and the light of the Ministry of Order flooded in.

"We ought to see if he made it out of there," said Hasdrubal, stepping out.

"Before I left he'd opened a door back to the hallway," Dhlara recalled.

"Let's see if he's there."

They left the time bathysphere, passed through the shelves of books, and opened the doors to the hallway. Gordon was standing in front of door 1816 holding a plain blacksmith's hammer in his right hand. The others joined him in front of the door while he held the hammer in front of him and examined it. Dhlara noticed there were bullet holes in the wall across from door 1816.

"Is that what we went there for?" Jylling asked.

"It is," Gordon answered in a distracted voice, turning the tool over as he examined it.

"Doesn't look like much," Hasdrubal stated.

"It's more than it appears to be. This is not an ordinary object."

"What is it?" Dhlara asked.

"I don't know. But as I said before, things that come from these Ministries have certain properties; they aren't made of substances from the normal world. I can see the difference. This hammer wasn't made in the normal span of time. It comes from out here."

"So what was it doing in eighteen-sixteen?"

"That's why I was so interested in finding it. What was it doing there?"

"Napoleon must have brought it there," said Hasdrubal.

"We can only assume so. But I don't know why."

"Well that's great," Jylling snorted. "What did we almost get shot for, then?"

"If it was Napoleon's," Dhlara replied, "he knew what it was and he wanted to have it there. Now he doesn't have it."

"That is one advantage," Gordon agreed. "In addition, I may not know what this is, but the Ministers of Time might. We can go ask them if they know."

The group went back into the main room of the Ministry of Order and approached the Minister of Order first. Gordon held out the hammer.

"Would you happen to know what this is?" he asked the Minister of Order. The Minister glared at him.

"By God, man, it's a hammer! You hit things with it! Nails! Boards! Small children! Who the blazes are you to ask such damn fool questions at a time like this?!"

"It's more than a simple hammer, I assure you."

"And there's no one more simple than you, I assure you, sir! Get out of my sight and take your quest to find companionship with inert, lifeless, unintelligent tools like yourself with you!" And with that the Minister kicked Gordon in the shin and smacked him across the face.

"Hey!" Dhlara protested.

Gordon turned to her, "I'm fine; it's quite alright."

"He can't do that!"

"I CAN'T DO WHAT?!" the Minister bellowed, pulling his arm back to hit her as well. Gordon's hand shot up and grabbed his wrist.

"That's enough. We just want to know about this hammer."

"There is nothing to know about it! You are doing nothing more than wasting my time!"

"This one doesn't appear odd to you in any way?"

"Of course not! Now GET! OUT!"

Gordon let go of the Minister, who climbed up onto his desk and shouted down at them, his face reddening under his white sideburns.

"OUT! GET OUT, YOU INTOLERABLE MALCONTENTS! GET OUT!"

Jylling scoffed at him. "What time of yours exactly are we wasting here?!"

"GET! OOOOOUUUT!"

"The time you'd spend being utterly incompetent and ineffective?! The time you'd spend abducting random strangers to do your job for you?! OR MAYBE—" Jylling shouted over the Minister's exhortations for them to leave, "—THE TIME YOU'D SPEND CATALOGING YOUR OBSERVATIONS AS THE FOREMOST EXPERT IN INTERNATIONAL CREEPERY!"

"GOD SAVE OUR GRACIOUS QUEEN!" the Minister half yelled, half sung up toward the ceiling. Papers crinkled under his boots as he flailed his arms for emphasis. "LONG LIVE OUR NOBLE QUEEN! GOD SAVE THE QUEEN!"

As the shouting continued, Gordon walked over to the door behind the Minister's desk and opened it, holding his arm out to invite the rest of the group to leave. Dhlara pushed Jylling along in front of her, despite his protests, and they passed Gordon as they went through the doorway. Hasdrubal grinned at Gordon as he followed, looking very amused.

They had entered a wide, circular room with plain, dark wood paneling and floor, and it was bright with daylight coming in through a glass domed ceiling. There were four other doors, each with gold plaques to their right that glinted as they reflected light from above. The plaque beside the door they had just come through read: *THE MINISTRIES OF TIME*, and below that in smaller font, *THE MINISTRY OF ORDER*.

"So, of course talking to him was completely pointless," Jylling declared.

"It was worth a try," Gordon shrugged as he closed the door behind himself. "But yes, I didn't expect much, considering how he is. I don't know why you'd be agitated about it if you didn't either."

"Gordon, he hit you!" said Dhlara.

"It didn't bother me."

"But that's not okay!"

"Of course it isn't. But I'm fine."

"No, look," said Jylling, "nobody talks to me in that way! It's insulting—"

"Oh shut up," Hasdrubal cut him off. "What are you all going to do about it? Go in there and fight him? Huh? Do something about it or not; don't whine about it. We've got more important things to do."

"Where are we, Gordon?" Dhlara asked.

"This is the way to the other Ministries."

"Let's go see Melvin's Ministry," Jylling suggested.

Hasdrubal smirked skeptically. "Do you really expect Melvin to know about this hammer?"

"Hey, you shut up. Melvin's cool. And he's been a lot more helpful than that jackass," Jylling jerked his thumb back at the Ministry of Order door.

"Very well." Gordon led them to the first door to the right. *THE MINISTRY OF MAINTENANCE*, the plaque next to it read. When he pulled the door open, they saw a densely cluttered closet. Mops and brooms were leaning up against the walls; lined up on shelves were rolls of paper towels, many sizes, shapes, and colours of gloves, scrubbers, brushes, rolls of trash bags, soap bottles, bleach bottles, and other cleaning solutions; a vacuum cleaner, a floor buffer, coils of hose, trash bins, dust pans, nets, buoys, and cages made of wire covered the floor. Much of the clutter was piled up and jammed atop or into each other. In front, right by the door, was a mop bucket filled with water and soap bubbles, and in the water was Melvin. He stared up at them over a mound of bubbles, one of his pincers holding a tiny sponge up to his wet hair.

"Oh, hey guys!" he greeted them cheerily.

"Hey, boss," said Gordon.

Jylling squatted down next to the bucket. "Melvin, we need your help."

"Awesome!"

"We found this weird thing that Napoleon had. We don't know what it is; we were wondering if you did."

Gordon held up the hammer.

"That's a hammer!"

"Well, no, it's more than that."

"Oooohh. What's it supposed to be?"

"We don't know."

"Well it looks like a hammer!"

"Gordon says it has to have come from outside of normal time. Do you know where it might have come from or what it might do?"

"Ummm… nope!"

"Alright then—"

"Wait!" There was a splash as Melvin lifted a tiny, bright yellow rubber duck up out of the bubbles and looked at it. "No, sorry, he doesn't know either."

"Okay, thanks Melvin."

"Sure!"

Gordon closed the door. "I think the Ministry of Planning is the most likely to know anything about the purpose of this object," he said.

"Which way is that?" asked Hasdrubal.

Gordon started walking across the room toward another door. Dhlara walked along the wall and came to the door in between the two and read the plaque: THE MINISTRY OF

CHAOS.

"Is Napoleon in there?" she asked.

"I don't think so," Gordon answered. "He hasn't been seen in the Ministries for some time."

"Are there other people in there?"

"I don't know. He kept his branch closed off from the other Ministries."

Dhlara opened the door. A field of grass waving gently in a summer breeze lay out in front of them. Hills carpeted in green bordered the field and rolled up and down into the horizon. At the foot of one of the hills, sitting beneath a clear blue sunny sky, was a stone cottage with a thatched roof. Sheep were grazing around it, their bleating barely audible over the rustling of grass.

"Whoah," went Jylling. "His office is an idyllic countryside?"

"No, it isn't," Gordon frowned. "This is new. He must have changed the door."

Dhlara took off her overcoat, tossed it onto the floor, and stepped out into the grass. She felt the warmth of the midday sun on her skin. Hasdrubal came out onto the field as well, his thumbs tucked into his sash.

"This is awfully suspicious," he said.

"Let's go see what's over there," Dhlara pointed at the cottage.

They all crossed the field, leaving the doorway open in the middle of the grass. Strands of ivy clung to the sides of the cottage and flowers grew in plots of dirt beneath its two front windows. Dhlara knocked on the door. A few moments later, a white-haired old woman opened it. Her hair was short and curled and she wore a tan and brown sweater. Her face crinkled as she smiled up at Dhlara.

"Good morning! Can I help you?" she asked.

"Uh, yes! Hello! I think so, ma'am. We were, well, looking for the Ministry of Chaos."

"You're in the right place, dear! Would you like to come in?"

"Oh, I mean, if it's no trouble."

"Of course not, no! Come in! Come in!"

They filed into her home. Sunlight streamed in onto potted plants clustered around the windows on either side of the front door. On their right, near one window, were several bookcases and a round table with chairs. A beige wool couch with its back to them was on their left, sitting on top of a brown shag carpet. Pointed at the couch was a little black and white television set with knobs and dials; from atop its stand, it flickered images of people in suits talking to each other with grave expressions on their faces. A few feet away, a bright yellow bird slept in a cage with its feathers puffed up. The woman went into the small kitchen in the center of the cottage, passing under a handmade length of fabric with the words *The Ministry of Chaos* stitched in red letters surrounded by white.

"Would you care for some tea?" she asked.

"That would be wonderful, thank you," Dhlara answered

"I've put the kettle on!" the woman informed them as she came bustling back. "Sit, sit!"

They bunched up onto the couch. She walked over to a rocking chair by the window and plants and turned it to face the couch.

"So what brings you to the Ministry of Chaos?" she asked as she sat down.

"Well, my name is Dhlara, and this is Jylling, Hasdrubal, and Gordon, and we have been investigating some trouble that is believed to have been caused by the Ministry of Chaos."

"Hmmm. I don't know what that could be. Sometimes Sir Chirpington doesn't like to get back into his cage, the naughty boy. Are you sure the trouble started here?"

"Is that Sir Chirpington?" Dhlara looked at the bird.

"Sir Reginald Taswell Chirpington," she nodded. "He's all tired out from a bit of a squawk this morning."

"We're sure the trouble didn't start here, exactly, ma'am," said Hasdrubal.

"You can just call me Eglantine. And that's good to hear. Is there something I can help with?"

"Who is the Minister of Chaos?" Dhlara inquired.

"I am."

"Really? When did you become Minister?"

"Oh, a few weeks ago. A nice gentleman in a dashing uniform came and asked me if I would like to be the Minister of the new Ministry of Chaos the government created. I told him I didn't have any experience with being in government, or chaos, or administration, but he said I was perfect for the job! Just the sort of person they were looking for, he said."

"Is that so…" said Jylling.

"What do you do as Minister?" asked Gordon.

"Not too much, honestly dear. What I do isn't very different from what I was doing before I was Minister. There don't seem to be any official duties for me to perform. I'm what you call a figurehead, I suppose. But that's alright with me."

"Where did the man who made you Minister go?"

"I don't rightly know."

"Did he say where he was going? Or where he would be?"

"No, he didn't say anything like that, but we had a nice chat over tea. We talked about the country and about how he always wanted to own some land here. And he knows French! That's such a lovely language."

"Would you happen to know if there is anything special to this?" Gordon pulled the hammer out of his vest and showed it to her.

"No, I'm afraid I don't. Looks normal to me, but then I guess I don't know tools very well anyway. I can use a spade and that's about it!"

"Well, it sounds like you're doing a good job, Eglantine," said Dhlara. "We'll continue our investigation elsewhere."

They stayed another ten minutes, drinking tea and discussing sheep, the weather, and famous people named Reginald, until finally Jylling stood up and said it was time to leave. The group said their goodbyes to Eglantine as they left and filed back into the open doorway sitting out in the middle of the field.

"Napoleon has abdicated his Ministry, it seems," Gordon said as he shut the door behind him.

"So that door didn't always lead to her house?" Jylling

asked him.

"No, the real Ministry of Chaos is much more similar to the Ministry of Order, and it's still physically there on the other side of this door, but this door has been altered so that it doesn't lead there."

"We were going to the Ministry of Planning," Hasdrubal reminded them. "That sounds like a more informative Ministry."

"Yes we were. Over here." Gordon went to the next door over; this time the second line of the gold plate read *THE MINISTRY OF PLANNING*. He tried to open the door, but the handle stayed in place when he tried to turn it. He pulled a ring crammed with jangling keys out of his vest and flipped through them one by one until he selected one in particular and opened the door with it.

White fluorescent light poured out from a warehouse-size room filled with men and women in white lab-coats, crammed shoulder-to-shoulder facing a wall of black chalkboards. Drawings in chalk on the boards depicted a circle with mushroom shapes rising off of it, a stick figure person with a warhammer fighting a serpent in water, a crowd of stick figures with their arms held out in front of them chasing other stick figures, a circle projecting a line into the shattered parts of another circle, a circle with squat oval shapes topped with domes hovering above it, and a stick figure with the head of a lion stood on top of a pile of stick figures with X's for eyes. On desks along the sides of the room were beakers, bubbling cauldrons, glass containers that held various swarms of insects that scurried and buzzed about within, small rockets, and glass-domed vacuum chambers with intensely bright orbs levitating inside.

In unison, the entire gathering of lab-coated people turned around and stared at the group standing in the doorway. A sea of magnified eyes looked at them through thick horn-rimmed glasses momentarily, then the room erupted into a frenzy of motion as the men and women hastily pulled covers down over the chalkboards, took their lab-coats off and threw them over the objects on the desks, and lined up standing in front of the desks and boards to block them from view. After everything in the room was obscured, they all stared at the group in the doorway.

"Sorry," said Gordon. "We're only trying to find some information."

A short woman with brown hair pulled back into a ponytail pushed her way through the crowd to the front.

"Well, what is it?!" she pressed. "We're terribly busy; we're working on a very big project right now and this sort of thing just can't be late!"

"We found this in the nineteenth century and we think Napoleon brought it there. I can tell it doesn't come from normal time because it looks like things that come from the Ministries. Do you know anything about what this is or what it might do?"

Hasdrubal leaned his head out from behind Gordon's shoulder.

"We know it looks like a hammer," he said.

She reached out and took it from Gordon and adjusted her glasses as she examined it. She went over to a table nearby and flipped a lab-coat over, uncovering a microscope. Several of her colleagues gathered around her as she slid the hammer under the lens and looked down the eyepiece. They conferred with each other for a minute and then she returned it to Gordon.

"We don't know about this individual item specifically. It has abnormal properties, and it is made of material from outside of the normal realm of time, but we don't know what its intended function or purpose is."

"It isn't one of your prototypes, or involved in any planned sequences?" Gordon asked.

"No, it isn't. Now, we have quite a lot to do, so good day, Mr. Haften!" And she closed the door in his face.

"What *are* they working on in there?" Dhlara asked Gordon.

"I'm not sure. Some big, important project. It's the same one they've been working on for a while now."

"But what do they do in there? What kind of project is it?"

"They plan the sequence of events throughout time."

"Whoah, hey guys!" Jylling interrupted. He had wandered over to the last door. "This goes to the Ministry of Action! Why didn't we start here? Sounds like these people will know what to do!"

"And what is that, exactly?" asked Hasdrubal.

"Do stuff! Take charge! Not sit behind a desk or in a laboratory and delegate! Come on, it's time we talked to somebody who actually knows what to do." He flung open the door, and the sound of gunfire roared out. He dived onto the floor behind the wall of the lobby. Everyone else dropped into a prone position. Through the doorway was a lush and humid jungle, sunlight filtering down to the ground through a dense canopy of vegetation high above. Large trees with vines hanging from their branches and dense clusters of plants with huge leaves obscured the source of the noise from view, but the cacophony of continuous and unbroken gunfire thundered out from the jungle.

After a minute or two of this, the deafening sound cut off, followed by the cracking of wood and thumps and thuds of heavy things hitting the ground. Gordon and Hasdrubal stood up and put their backs to the wall on either side of the doorway. Gordon craned his head out and peered into the jungle, then looked back and waved for the rest of them to follow him. He led them through the overgrowth until they came to a clearing of fallen trees and torn up vegetation.

A hulking, shirtless man with shoulder-length black hair and a pink feather boa wrapped around his neck stood in the center of the clearing with his broad back to them. On his back was a metal box with a chain of bullets protruding from it. His oiled skin was tanned brown and shined in the sunlight, and his thickly muscled arms gripped the handles of a minigun, which was connected to the other end of the chain of bullets. He turned and faced them, his square-jawed face impassive behind a pair of aviator sunglasses. Gordon and everyone behind him dropped to the ground again as the minigun swung around with its wielder.

A bright orange muzzle flash burst from the topmost of its

six barrels and the roar of gunfire continued, bullets ripping through the air above their heads. Everyone on the ground clapped their hands over their ears. Explosions of splinters, dust and bits of greenery filled the air as the bullets impacted furiously behind them. He slowly turned the gun back and forth, ceaselessly pouring bullets into the jungle for several minutes.

The firing abruptly stopped again and the man set the gun down. Her ears ringing, Dhlara looked behind her; the part of the jungle they had just walked through was flat and clear. The trunks of the trees had fallen and the rest of the vegetation had been shredded into a mulch of plant material that now blanketed the ground. She stayed down with her hands clasped over her head until she began to hear again.

"EXCUSE ME SIR!" Jylling bellowed at the man as he took off his metal backpack. "ARE YOU THE MINISTER OF ACTION?"

The man ignored him.

"ARE YOU THE MINISTER OF ACTION? WE ARE LOOKING FOR SOMEONE WHO KNOWS ABOUT SOMETHING WE FOUND."

The man gazed blankly into Jylling's face, then held up his hand and snapped his fingers. Suddenly, the jungle was gone, and Dhlara found herself lying on a paved street. Rows of houses lined the street, and the stranger was now wearing a black leather trenchcoat.

"HOLY CRAP!" Jylling yelled.

The man raised his hand and snapped again, but this time at the end of the snap his forefinger pointed at one of the houses. The building exploded into a billowing fireball and chunks of brick and wood rocketed out in all directions. Snap. Another explosion.

At once, they all ran back towards the door they had come in through. Houses exploded one by one next to them as they ran. As they reached the doorway standing out in the middle of the street, Gordon dashed behind the door and held it, ready to slam it shut behind them. Hasdrubal and Dhlara ran into the lobby, and Dhlara turned back to see Jylling lifted off his feet by a fiery explosion behind him. The force of it threw him into the air and through the doorway with his arms outstretched in front of him and a shocked expression on his face. Gordon slammed the door shut as Jylling hit the floor.

"Jylling! Are you okay?!" Dhlara rushed over to him. He popped up onto his feet, unhurt.

"Uh, holy crap. I think I'm okay. My elbows hurt," he said, folding his arms and looking at his elbows. "What the hell just happened?"

"That's the Minister of Action," said Gordon.

"That guy's insane!"

Gordon shrugged. "Maybe. But I think that's what he does."

"All the time?!"

"As far as I can tell."

"Well why didn't you think to warn us there was a psychotic lunatic expending ammunition in every direction in there?!"

"The single time I tried to talk to him he was in a standoff with two other guys. There wasn't as much shooting then."

"So that's it, then?" said Dhlara. "That's all the Ministries?"

"Indeed," Gordon answered.

"God*dammit*," Jylling muttered. "So nobody in this stupid place knows anything about even Napoleon's useless crap that he leaves lying around. Nothing but one unhelpful jerk after another. This is just incredible."

"Is there anyone else who might know more than these Ministers?" Dhlara asked Gordon.

"No one I know of, other than Napoleon."

"If we want to figure all of this out, we're going to have to do it for ourselves," said Hasdrubal. "We ought to return to the Ministry of Order, since it seems we are making camp there, and figure out what we should do next."

They nodded in agreement and headed for the door labeled *THE MINISTRY OF ORDER.*

VII

Somewhere Far Beyond

Hasdrubal leaned back in his chair in the Ministry of Order and propped his feet up on the end of the table, satisfied and full after eating another meal Gordon had prepared. His fez lay on the table next to his cleared plate. Dhlara and Jylling, cleared plates also in front of them, sat on the benches on either side of the table, while Gordon stood off to the side near an aisle of bookshelves. Near the other end of the extremely long table, the Minister of Order sat at his desk drinking tea from a small ceramic cup, holding the accompanying saucer in his other hand. His head tilted back as he finished the contents of the cup. When he was done, he dashed the cup and saucer on the ground and they burst into pieces.

"TEA!" he bellowed.

When another cup and saucer was brought to him by one of the soldiers in red uniforms, he drank the tea, smashed them both on the floor, and repeated his shouted demand. This had been going on for some time, and ceramic shards were littered all around his desk.

"Well, what do we do now?" Jylling sighed, exasperated.

"What can we do?" wondered Dhlara. "If nobody here knows anything about whatever that thing is, where do we even begin figuring out what it's for?"

"Hey, I remind you all that we didn't travel to Elba to find a hammer of mystery," Hasdrubal pointed out. "If we can't find out what it is, then let's put it to the side for now."

"Oh yeah," said Jylling. "So you are now sufficiently convinced that Napoleon has changed history?"

Hasdrubal folded his hands over his chest and grinned at

Jylling. "I am indeed! What we saw on that beach gave a pretty clear notion that Napoleon has traversed time and changed the future."

"Well, the past," Jylling corrected him.

"It's the future to me. But the question still remains, why did you two not know of the things he had changed in your own time? If those things really changed, why were you not aware of them in the further future? How could your past really be changed if it doesn't appear to be any different?"

"Is that why you were in Elba in the first place?" Gordon asked.

"Yes, it was."

"If I'd known that, I could have helped sooner. I think I know why they would not have known about what Napoleon did. And there is something else all of you would probably want to see, too."

"Then why is it?"

"I'll have to show you. We'll have to go back to the Ministry of Maintenance."

"You know, that sounds a lot less lofty now that I know it's just a broom closet Melvin lives in," Jylling remarked.

"That's where we have to go all the same."

The group of four got up and headed past the Minister of Order's pile of destroyed drinkware and into the brightly lit lobby. They came to the door to the Ministry of Maintenance. Gordon opened it. This time the mop bucket was empty, but a muffled growling noise came from within the pile of cleaning devices and various debris behind it. Gordon went in and, carefully stepping through and around a floor scrubber machine, a collection of trash bins, what looked like a nest of lightly used sponges, and a pile of coiled hose, he picked up a vacuum cleaner with a bag attached to it. Something thrashed around inside the bag and continued to growl. He rapped his knuckles on the front of the vacuum cleaner. The commotion inside the bag stopped, and a little pincer burst out, then ripped a line down the bag. It retracted, and Melvin's dusty head popped out through the hole.

"Hello!" His mouth hung open in an excited smile.

"I'm going to show them outside," Gordon told him.

"Cool! Can I come?"

"Sure."

"Alright!"

Melvin hopped out of the bag onto the floor and scurried away through the mess. Gordon led the group after him, until they came to a door at the back of the room. Cut out of it at the bottom was another, much smaller door with its own little handle. He pushed open the bigger one. On the other side was a long wooden pier jutting out into an endless expanse of calm, deep-blue ocean water under a clear sky. Melvin stood smiling at them from the flat top of one of the pier's wooden pylons. Far off in the distance, there was a single shape on the otherwise unbroken horizon.

"Wow..." Jylling said under his breath as they stepped out.

Dhlara turned around. The pier they were standing on was connected to an oddly shaped building of light wood. She could see the exterior of the room they had just left, a small little one-story high box with its door still open. Behind that was the three-story high cylindrical center of the building, which had a glass dome for a roof. It occurred to her that the lobby of the Ministries of Time was exactly the same. Two slightly shorter wings were attached to the right and left of it, and both were very long. The entire building sat in the ocean with no foundation, the sea water lapping at its sides.

"I cannot find the sun anywhere," Hasdrubal remarked as he looked up at the sky.

Dhlara looked up. Though everywhere around her was bright as day, she could not see the sun, or any sun.

"Of course you don't," Gordon replied. "This is not the Earth. We are at the edge of time. All of that out there," he waved his arm at the ocean, "is time."

"You mean," said Jylling, "everything that's ever happened is a bunch of sloshy water?"

"In a way."

"But how is there no sun?" asked Hasdrubal. "Where is all the light coming from?"

"Well, that I don't really know. But you can see that there

is no sun, and there is light."

"What is this building?" Dhlara asked.

"That is the Ministries of Time," Gordon answered.

"Oh. You mean we haven't gone somewhere completely different by going through that door?"

"No, we didn't. Many of the doors in the Ministries are portals to places in time, such as in the hallway of the Ministry of Order, or the doors to the Ministry of Chaos and the Ministry of Action. But the one we just went through is just a plain door. This little room in front is the Ministry of Maintenance," he said as he walked over and closed the door. "Behind it is the hub of the Ministries of Time; that," he pointed to the wing on the left, "is the Ministry of Order, and that," he pointed to the other wing, "is the Ministry of Chaos."

"I thought the Ministry of Chaos was an open countryside," Jylling scrunched his face in confusion. "What's in there?"

"The door to the Ministry of Chaos took us somewhere in time. Through it, we traveled through time, like any door in the hallway you've been in. In this case, to Wales in the nineteen-eighties, I believe. The Ministry of Chaos has its own offices, just like the Ministry of Order, but the doorway to it has apparently been diverted, as you have seen. Speaking of the hallway, if you look over there," he pointed to the horizon near the wing on the left; a small, much shorter part of the building extended from the Ministry of Order out into the horizon as far as Dhlara could see, "that's it." At regular intervals, where each of the doors would be on the inside, waterfalls were pouring out from the side of the wall.

"That's the hallway in the Ministry of Order?" she asked. Gordon nodded.

She looked on the other side of the building and saw that the Ministry of Chaos had its own shorter section that spanned far out into the distance. "Does the Ministry of Chaos have its own hallway?"

"Yes."

"So this is what you wanted us to see?"

"A part of it, yes. If you'll come with me, I'd like to show you something." He walked to the end of the pier where a rowboat bobbed up and down in the water. Melvin jumped off the pylon, ran past Gordon, and lept into the boat. He plonked himself down onto the front of it, stretching his legs out to either side and curling them around the sides of the craft to keep himself in place. As he grinned at them, Dhlara and Jylling climbed in and sat down at the other end of the boat, and Hasdrubal took the seat near Melvin. After untying the boat from the pier and retrieving a set of oars from under the seats, Gordon sat in the middle facing Dhlara and Jylling and began to row.

"First, I want to warn you that you should take care not to fall into this water," said Gordon as he pulled on the oars. "This is time itself, and when you go into it, you could end up anywhere at any time."

Melvin turned all the way around to face them with his legs still clamped onto the boat. His eyes grew wide and he raised his eyebrows. "You could be lost forever!"

"Though, since you all have your watches, you would likely be able to return to the Ministries, but it is still dangerous, and it would be far more dangerous if you had no way of coming back. Once you go in, there is no way for anyone else to know where or when you went."

"All of a sudden I feel a lot less okay with being in this dinky boat, Gordon!" Jylling declared. "Why are we in here if it's that bad?!"

"He just said we're fine," said Dhlara. "Just keep your watch on."

"Yes, you are most likely fine; I am only trying to inform you about what it means to be where you are. Now, here is what I wanted to show you," said Gordon, pulling his oars back into the boat. "Look at the ripples in the water that this boat makes. Think of this boat being here as a change in time. Before, there was no boat. Now there is. The ripples from this boat being here in the water don't hit the pier until later, after they travel there. You can drop something into the water here, and it will be here in fact, but the water over by the pier will not know it until the ripples reach it.

"This is how a change can exist in a time in the past, and yet not be known yet to those in the event's future. Change in time is not instantaneous; it has to cascade outward."

"So, you're saying we're changing time with this boat?" Jylling surmised. He leaned over the side and looked at the boat. "Is there the bottom half of a rowboat somewhere in time?"

"I think he's saying Napoleon's a rowboat," said Hasdrubal.

"Guys," Melvin turned around again. "I'd like to be a rowboat."

"I wasn't saying any of that," Gordon replied.

"I understand what you're saying, Gordon," said Dhlara. "Napoleon could have changed the Battle of Waterloo before we came to the Ministry of Order, but we may not have known about it in our own time because the effect of the change had not reached our time yet."

"That is what I was trying to say."

"How long would that take?"

"I don't know precisely. It is a difficult thing to measure, and length depends on distance. But it happens very quickly relative to the Ministries."

"That solves the conundrum for me well enough," said Hasdrubal.

"What's that out there?" Jylling asked Gordon, pointing to the growing lump on the horizon.

"That is the other thing I wanted to show you; it is Napoleon's fortress."

"His *fortress*?!"

Gordon nodded and dropped the ends of his oars back into the water. Dhlara gazed out across the glistening ocean at the grey mass in the distance.

"Why didn't you mention that he had a fortress before?!" Hasdrubal glared at the back of Gordon's head. "Why didn't anyone mention that?!"

"The Minister of Order yells about everything, and there's nothing he likes to yell about more than Napoleon. I guessed he would have told you about it. He knows about it," Gordon answered as he rowed toward it.

"What's a fortress doing out there that Napoleon can just *have*?!" Jylling questioned.

"There wasn't. Napoleon built it."

"There's land over there?" asked Hasdrubal.

"No, at least there wasn't. He made a kind of floating island and built his fortress on top of it."

"How'd he just build a fortress? One man can't build a such a structure."

"Oh, yes, his soldiers did the work itself."

"French soldiers?"

"Indeed."

"Wait, so Napoleon's out here with a fort and an army," Jylling summarized, "and Wellington's in there with, as far as I can tell, a handful of soldiers whose primary function seems to be handing him teacups to smash. History is screwed."

"Maybe there's more to Wellington than it seems," Dhlara suggested.

"No, he's just a crackpot who thinks he runs the world. Napoleon wants to fill the world with squids and *then* run it. Everything's just a power grab around here. Melvin, do you have any secret plans for world domination?"

"Yep!" Melvin answered, facing Jylling with an excited expression.

"Uh... you do?"

"Yep!"

"...What are your secret plans for world domination?"

"I will be crowned Chief Friendship Emperor Supreme of All the Places and everybody will bring me tasty snacks!"

"Melvin, that sounds like a truly well considered plan," Hasdrubal told him.

"Yup yup!"

"Well, what can we do about this fort?" Dhlara wondered aloud.

"In all honesty, I didn't mention it sooner in part because it doesn't seem that there is much you can do," said Gordon. "I'm taking you closer to it to have a better look at it, if you'd like. Maybe seeing it will give you some ideas."

The shape grew larger as Gordon's oars pulled the little boat along the surface of the water. Soon enough Dhlara could clearly see the grey stone walls of the fortress, and that they were laid out in the shape of a star. A circular stone tower stood in the center of the fortress. A set of two massive wood and iron doors barred the only entrance through the walls. Little silhouettes of soldiers moved back and forth on the ramparts.

Hasdrubal whistled. "That is an impressive fortification."

Melvin spun around and stared up at him, his eyes wide. "What was that?"

"The fort..." Hasdrubal pointed, "it looks strong..."

"No, what was that noise?"

"I whistled."

"...What?"

"I did this:" Hasdrubal pursed his lips and whistled.

Melvin brought his lips together and blew, his cheeks puffing up, but only created the sound of air being expelled from his mouth. He tried again, harder, his face reddening, but accomplished nothing better.

"Hasdrubal," Dhlara said over the sound of Melvin blowing air, "if history really was changed by Napoleon, then shouldn't your plan in eight-ten actually work?"

"Yes, I think it should indeed. Perhaps I ought to get back there," he replied.

"What plan was that?" Gordon asked.

"I went back to the year eight-ten to help a king of the Vikings defeat the founder of the Frankish empire. No more French people, no more Napoleon. If I go back and finish that up, this fort should just go away."

"Not quite."

"What does that mean?"

"Anything that is brought through the time machines at the Ministries, such as the one the Minister of Order brought you here by, effectively creates an independent version of what has been transported. Anything that travels by that device is separated from its dependence upon its prior experience within time."

"I don't think I understand any of that," said Jylling.

"In basic terms, if you go back and kill Napoleon at Elba, or Waterloo, or wherever, he will have died there, but the person who was the Minister of Chaos and who built that fort will still be alive."

"So when we go through the time machine," said Dhlara, "we become new people?"

"In a way, yes."

"Well that sounds like a lot of crap," Jylling scoffed. "I'm me."

Gordon stopped rowing and held up his hand. He pointed to a spot in the water behind Jylling and Dhlara, about a hundred feet off to their left. "There's something down there," he warned.

At that moment, a large wooden frigate burst out of the water, its prow pointed at the sky. Shocked, they watched as the nearly vertical warship shot up from the depths of the ocean into the air. The stern reached several dozen yards above the surface as the ship flew forward, water dripping from its keel, before its prow started to descend, leading it into a fall. The vessel was level again by the time its hull crashed back down into the ocean alongside their boat. Foamy waves rolled out from the impact, forcing the occupants of the little rowboat to brace themselves as it was tossed up and down.

When the water calmed, everyone in the boat looked up in stunned silence as men bustled about on the newly arrived vessel, climbing rigging, shouting commands, and unfurling the sails high above them.

"WHHHFFFFFFFF!" Melvin's cheeks puffed up as he blew air at the ship.

Gordon gripped his oars and used them to turn the boat away.

"Ho there!" a voice cried at them from the deck behind them. "Stay where you are or we'll shoot!"

Dhlara turned around and watched as the figure waved other men over, who then lowered the barrels of several muskets over the gunwale pointed straight at them. The boat under her jerked away from the ship as Gordon pulled on the oars.

"Fire!" the voice yelled. Fire and sparks flashed and smoke billowed from the barrels of the guns. Bullets whizzed around them and plunked into the water near the boat, sending up little columns of water from the impacts.

Gordon lifted his oars out of the water.

"That's right! Now you'll stay there and wait for President Olinger!"

"What are you doing?!" Jylling protested to Gordon. "Keep going! Let's get out of here!"

"I agree; I don't think we should sit here and surrender," Hasdrubal said over his shoulder.

"We're well within range of those guns. One of us could get killed. I don't want to risk it," Gordon answered calmly.

But it didn't calm Jylling. "I have no idea who they are or what they'll do if we stay here! Let's take our chances!"

"Gordon's right, you know," said another voice from the warship. Sunlight glinted off of President Olinger's large rectangular spectacles as he leaned on the gunwale with his elbow. Over his elbows were tan patches on his dark yellow tweed jacket. His red tie hung out over the side of the ship as he looked down at them. "If you go any further and these muskets fail to hit you, I'll have the men down below practice their gunnery on your dinky little boat and everybody in it." He reached down and slapped the side of the ship, drawing their eyes to the closed gun ports below.

"We mean no harm and we haven't committed any act against you. I see no reason to threaten us," Dhlara called out.

"Guys," Jylling whispered out of the corner of his mouth, "use your watches."

"I don't care what you don't see," the man said. "You can see that I've got a frigate full of six-pounder cannon and you have not."

"NOW!" Jylling shouted, and he disappeared.

"Oh yes, I should have mentioned. Your watches? They can't get you out of here anymore. I have a device onboard that has changed their coordinates."

"Crap!" Jylling's voice drifted down to them from behind

the captain.

"And before the rest of you want to try anything, I'll let you know that if you jump into that water to go somewhere in time, the only place your watch can bring you back to is this ship, as your friend has just discovered. Very helpful of him. I'm sure you all will be more cooperative now that I have a hostage."

"What do you want?" Dhlara asked.

"Row yourselves over here," the president ordered, "you're coming aboard."

Gordon rowed over to the side of the frigate and stood to grab onto a set of horizontal blocks of wood several inches thick and a few feet across sticking out of the flank of the ship, each spaced out from the next to form a kind of ladder from the waterline up to the top deck.

"Ah-ah, no you don't, Gordon." President Olinger drew a flintlock pistol and pointed it at Hasdrubal and Dhlara. "I'm not having you come up here and go into some whirlwind of beating everyone on this ship senseless. You're going to sit there and wait until I have all of your friends, and *then* you'll come up. And if you try anything, I swear to you I'll kill 'em all. Got it?"

Gordon nodded.

"Alright good. Now pretty girl and surly cohort: get the hell up here," he waved his gun at them and the deck.

Dhlara put a foot onto the lowest block and scaled the side of the ship. Reaching the top, she swung her legs over the gunwale and landed on the wooden deck. She was surrounded by the crew, all white men, and many of them were pointing muskets and pistols at her. They wore a variety of plain clothing; she saw breeches with knee-high socks, breeches with bare legs below, long pants, a lot of loose white long-sleeve shirts, some white t-shirts, and a few bare torsos. Several of them near the mast to her left held Jylling by the shoulders and were pinning his arms behind his back. One of his eyebrows was raised and the other lowered so that he glowered at his predicament with indignant anger.

"Mister Kutter, check the little sea tart for weapons," the

president ordered.

Now that she was a few feet away from him, she could see he had a very square face, pale blue eyes, and a wide, protruding, dimpled chin. His brown hair was parted at the right side of his head and gelled to stay pushed to either side so that his forehead was bare. So much of his hair was parted to the left that it looked like a kind of cap on top of his head. He ran his fingers through his moustache as he watched one of the crew step forward and pat Dhlara down.

"Nothin' 'ere, president," the sailor called.

"Splendid."

Hasdrubal's head appeared as he reached the top of the ladder. He climbed up over the side of the ship and his boots thumped against the wood as he dropped onto the deck. President Olinger walked over to him and grabbed the pair of pistols tucked into his sash.

"I don't know who you are or what you'll do, so I see no reason for you to be armed. This will all be a lot easier if I have all the weaponry, you see," he said as he handed the pistols off to the crewman behind him. "Take them and put your guns to the back of their heads," he told his crew. The men closed in around Hasdrubal and Dhlara. She took several steps back, recoiling, but several pairs of hands grabbed her roughly and held her arms behind her back and gripped her shoulders. Hasdrubal's face was contorted in restrained rage; the side of his lip curled up into an angry sneer as the same was done to him. They were guided in the form of shoves to stand next to Jylling. Dhlara felt the barrel of a gun press against the back of her head. Olinger leaned over the gunwale and called down, "Alright Gordon, you can come on up."

Gordon ascended and lightly stepped down onto the deck. He stood rigidly upright with an impassive expression as he glanced over at the three restrained figures, then stared at Olinger.

"Now then, Gordon, I think we can reach a perfectly reasonable accord here. I have your useless chums, or passengers, or whoever they are, and you are a blubberingly moral sentimentalist who would rather I didn't kill them. So! I won't kill them, and you won't go on a rampage of punching everybody on this ship in their kidneys. You can trust that I won't kill them because I value the structural integrity of my internal organs, and I can trust that you won't cause any harm to me or my crew or our aims, because I will kill any of your worthless pals in an instant. In fact, since there are three of them, I could kill one just to prove it." He paused and cocked his head to the side, as if he was suddenly considering what he had just said.

"That won't be necessary," Gordon replied, interrupting Olinger's pondering.

"Ah, wonderful! See?" He grinned as he held out his arms and looked at Gordon, then at his hostages. "We trust each other already!"

"Who are you, and why are you so keen on shooting us?" Dhlara asked.

"He is Egmond Olinger—" Gordon started.

"*President* Egmond Olinger—" Olinger interjected over him.

"—an accountant from Luxembourg."

"—dictator for life of the World Government of Luxembourg!"

"*Luxembourg*?!" Jylling reacted, incredulous.

"Is that a country or something?" Hasdrubal asked.

Olinger laughed as he came face to face with Jylling. "This is why I want to shoot all of you!" he said as he tapped the barrel of his gun against Jylling's temple. "Nobody is allowed to denigrate my homeland any longer! Forever it's been German Reichs and French emperors and Belgian whatever. Even the people running this place are an arrogant British moron and the one French asshole nobody ever seems to get tired of! It's all absolutely insufferable. But not anymore! This time is for Luxembourg!"

"For the 'World Government of Luxembourg'?" Dhlara inquired.

"Yes! Precisely. Aren't you a clever girl. Since we can't live in our own little place and be left alone, since all of history is just a big litany of one autocratic monarch after another absorbing everything less powerful than themselves, fine! Prepare to be absorbed, rest of the world, because Luxembourg ain't gonna take it anymore!"

"That's insane," JyLing cut in. "Your country is tiny and almost nobody lives there. You guys can't do anything."

"If you're not going to use your brain to comprehend anything anyone is saying, what's the point of me not shooting it? Okay? That is how everything has been determined in the past: how many citizens, how many soldiers, how much money, on and on. But now, out here, we can manipulate time itself! Who needs a million soldiers, when you can have one guy with a gun to shoot at something a million times in the same moment? Anyone can do everything with infinite time, and all of time is right here! And what is stopping me from taking all of it for Luxembourg, huh? You? A doddering old English buffoon? A disinterested, unambitious, glorified tracker? Listen, for all the things this guy can do," he reached up and put his hand on Gordon's shoulder, "he spends his time sifting through dragon crap to find out where the stupid beast went so he can bring it home safe and sound. This place is just a power vacuum; one man can take it all for Luxembourg and make all the countries of Europe pay in kind."

"You forgot about me!" a voice announced cheerily. Melvin had climbed up from the rowboat and stood perched on the gunwale. "I'd like to be a hostage!"

"Melvin! Get down!" Dhlara urged him, jerking her head back out toward the water.

"Okay!" And he hopped down onto the deck. Dhlara groaned. He looked around in wonder as his little metal legs carried him over to Olinger. "This is a pretty cool ship," he said, looking up at Olinger. "So are you guys, like, time pirates or something?"

Olinger bent down and gripped Melvin's hair. He lifted the animated head up to his face as he stood up; Melvin dangled in front of him, his mouth hanging open in a big smile. "Melvin, you are an idiot and a nuisance. Goodbye." With that, he dropped the Minister of Maintenance and swiftly punted him out to sea.

"BYYEEEEEEE!" Melvin's voice drifted back to them as he soared through the air. He fell in an arc until he hit the water with a *kersploosh*. He didn't reappear.

"HEY!" Dhlara pushed forward against the hands restraining her.

"What the hell, man?!" Jylling cried as he craned his neck to look for Melvin in the ocean.

Olinger clutched his stomach as laughed. "Ha ha! Now he has to go annoy someone else somewhere in time forever! Well then, this has been a tremendously productive day, hasn't it? Got rid of the miniature irritant, neutralized Gordon, and captured a gaggle of inept time-travelers. And there's still quite a lot left to do! I've wasted more than enough time with you lot. You don't do anything I wouldn't like, and I won't kill you, okay? That's all you really need to know. Take their watches," he instructed his crew. "And whatever weird crap Gordon's got! Search all of his pockets and everything; I don't want them to have any traveling devices. Mister Muller! Bring us alongside the Ministries!" he barked at the quarterdeck.

"Aye sir!" replied a squat, thick-necked man wearing the tattered overcoat of a red naval uniform standing beside the helm.

As the sails billowed and pulled the vessel forward, one of the men holding Dhlara unfastened her watch and removed it from her arm, then did the same to Jylling and Hasdrubal and handed the watches to Olinger. A wide, burly crewman started putting his hands into Gordon's pockets and patting his clothes. He put his hand into Gordon's vest and pulled out the hammer.

"Well, what have we got here," Olinger wondered aloud. He took it from the crewman and examined it. "Sure just looks like an ordinary hammer."

"It is," said Gordon.

"Ah, no, I don't think so. If you've got it, it must be some fashion of secret time hammer. What does it do?" he asked as he studied it with narrowed eyes.

"Nothing. That's the truth."

104

"No, I don't suppose you would tell me. Ah well." Olinger tapped Gordon's head with the hammer several times. "At least if I have it, you don't, whatever it does. Keep searching him."

Things continued to be extracted from his vest and pockets, including rope, a knife, a lighter, a pipe, a pocket watch, and a pile of token-shaped objects like the one he had used to transport the dragon.

"Is that it, then?" Olinger asked.

"Yes sir."

"Very well. When we're done here, take this one," he put his thumb out and jammed it into Gordon's chest, "chain him up as much as you can, and have him stay on the upper deck. The other three, tie their hands behind their backs and put them in the brig and keep a guard posted. If he does anything at all, if you hear any trouble whatsoever, shoot one of them. If any of them try to get clever and argue or negotiate with you, pistol whip 'em."

"Yes sir."

"What do you mean to do with us?" Hasdrubal demanded.

"Whatever I like, really," Olinger answered.

Dhlara felt her hands being tied together behind her back with rope while the warship came to a stop alongside the pier on the right. She could see the infinite row of doorways spanning out in front of the ship and the cylindrical, domed lobby of the Ministries slightly off to the right. Several of the sailors brought lengths of metal chain over their shoulders and started wrapping them around Gordon. A couple dozen more crewmen passed by carrying metal hooks with four curved prongs attached to coils of rope. They headed to the gunwale and one by one climbed down the side of the frigate onto the pier.

"You have the command, Mister Muller!" Olinger called back to the quarterdeck. "Take our guests to our place of business and give them a very private piece of real estate!"

The stumpy man laughed. "Aye aye, sir!"

"Well, chaps," Olinger grinned at his prisoners, "good riddance to all of you."

He went over the gunwale as well and descended onto the pier. The ship lurched forward and slowly turned to the left. Olinger joined the crewmen already gathered in front of the door to the Ministry of Maintenance, who swung their metal hooks at their sides with the rope and tossed them up in the air. They flew above the glass dome of the lobby of the Ministries of Time and then fell, crashing through the panes of glass. Each man pulled on his rope until it was taught, securing his hook in place before he gripped the rope with both hands and vertically walked their way up over the Ministry of Maintenance and up side of the lobby. Dhlara lost sight of them as they reached the top, the ship having turned enough so that the rear of it now blocked Dhlara's view of the building.

She looked back at the prow; their course had straightened out, sailing obliquely away from the hallway on their right. She heard creaking above her and, gazing upward, she saw the sails stretched to their limit. The ship picked up speed.

"Wuh-oh. This isn't natural..." Hasdrubal muttered.

The whole vessel creaked and groaned as it continued to gain momentum. Faster. Faster. Suddenly, the bow pitched down, causing the deck under her feet to slant downward in one huge lurch and water to pour in over the prow. Continuing at full speed, the warship drove itself into the ocean. She watched in wide-eyed disbelief as the masts, crewmen, decking, everything in front of her disappeared beneath the waves, until finally she smacked into the surface of the water and felt herself being carried away.

VIII

Journey Through the Dark

Egmond Olinger kicked open the door to the Ministry of Order. The shattered glass of the broken dome lay scattered about on the floor of the lobby behind him. Pieces crunched under his crewmen's shoes as they gathered by the door. The ropes of their grappling hooks hung from the dome's metal frame and dangled a few inches off the floor. In front of him, inside the Ministry of Order, the Minister of Order was sitting at his desk studying a map of the world, despite the fact that it was thoroughly wrinkled and covered in boot marks. Both of the stairways near his desk had a soldier in red uniform standing guard near the top. He spun the seat of his chair around and glared at the newcomer.

"You there! I say, have you defeated Bonaparte yet?!"

"Not yet, no. But his time will come," Olinger answered as he casually walked over to the desk. His men poured into the room. Five of them stayed near Olinger while the rest tramped down the stairs and fanned out, disappearing behind the rows and rows of books.

"What purpose is served by coming here, then?! Old Boney's out there, and it is your duty to put an end to the ruddy little corporal and his dastardly plans!"

"I am not overly concerned about him. More importantly, you're a goddamn lunatic who has no idea what you or anyone else who has ever existed is actually doing."

The Minister was so scandalized his whole body jerked in rage. "WRRUH! HOW DARE YOU SIR!"

"Now now, there's no use in shouting. I am well aware that your yelling is only limited by the capacity of your lungs, but all it does is annoy me. It, like everything else you do, is useless and ineffectual."

"I WILL HAVE YOU HANGED!"

"No, you won't. I'm taking control of your pathetic operation," Olinger announced in a loud voice. At this, gunshots blasted from behind the bookshelves. The sailors behind Olinger drew pistols and fired at both of the guards nearby. They dropped their muskets, clutched at their wounds, and groaned as they fell over. The room was filled with the din of angry shouts mixed with the resounding discharges of small arms.

The Minister lept to his feet. "THIS IS TREASON! RANK TREACHERY!"

"Of course it is, you blithering old sot. And before you have any more uselessly obvious things to say, I have been waiting a very long time to do this." He lifted the side of his tweed jacket, grabbed the handle of the pistol tucked into his pants, and pointed it at the Minister's gut. He pulled the trigger, causing the hammer to snap down onto the metal plate, and sparks and smoke spat out from the end of the barrel. Traces of smoke wafted up from the barrel as he grinned smugly at the Minister, whose uniform had a hole where the bullet had passed through.

"BY GOD, YOU SHOT ME, YOU MISERABLE COWARD!" The Minister ripped the pistol out of Olinger's hands and tossed it to the ground. He pulled his arm back and slammed his fist into his would-be murderer's face. Olinger's head whipped backwards and he fell onto the floor. As the men behind him approached to help him up, he scrambled back onto his feet, holding his face with one hand.

"Alright old man, I did not see that coming," Olinger admitted. "No matter, all of your men will be dead soon enough, and I am sure I have enough men to hold you down."

"A THOUSAND SPINELESS DOGS AREN'T WORTH AN ENGLISHMAN'S SPIT!"

"I was really looking forward to that killing you," Olinger sighed. "Restrain him."

His crewman stepped toward the Minister, who put his fists up in front of him, ready to strike. One of the larger men moved to grab him, but the Minister gripped one of his arms and punched him in his sternum. The man staggered backward, clutching his chest and gasping before he collapsed. The other four rushed forward and tackled the Minister to the ground.

"TRAITORS TO THE CROWN! USURPERS AND PRETENDERS!" he roared while he kicked and punched at the men piled on top of him.

"Mister Schmitt!" Olinger yelled.

After a few moments, a member of his crew ran out from behind a bookshelf carrying a musket he had taken from one of the soldiers. His shirt was soaked with blood and sweat and had been ripped in several places. "Yes sir?!" he answered.

"Get more men to come hold this idiot down!"

"Yes sir!" The officer called several names and three more crewmen joined him. They ascended the stairs and joined the fight on the floor. The Minister continued to bellow as he resisted, occasionally eliciting yelps of pain from his assailants when his fist or boot connected with someone's organs or somebody's cranium. Olinger, after he had reloaded his pistol, stood nearby and kicked at the Minister whenever he was exposed. Eventually, the sailors managed to pin him down with his back against the floor. Two men were putting all their weight on each of his limbs. Blood had soaked into his uniform around the bullet hole in his stomach, but he still yelled and thrashed.

"SNIVELING VILLAINS! UNHAND ME AT ONCE AND DIE!"

"Gag him, Schmitt," Olinger commanded. The officer, who had been helping to restrain an arm, took off his shirt, stuffed it into the Minister's mouth, and tied the sleeves together behind his head.

"RRGGRRHHGGG!"

"That's much better. Now, let's try this again." Olinger leveled his pistol at the Minister's chest and fired a second time. Though the bullet had cut another hole in his red uniform, Olinger's captive barely seemed to notice as he continued to struggle unabated.

At that moment, a headless body sprinted into the room

through the door to the lobby. Most of its pale skin was exposed, only covered by some underwear and a pair of socks, and a top hat where its neck should be. The body attempted to stop, but its sock-clad feet slid across the smooth wood floor, and it toppled over, its chest thumping against the floor. Olinger turned with a confused expression as he watched the body get up on all fours and crawl down the stairs.

"Stop that… body!" he called down to the rest of the room. Several men emerged from behind the bookshelves and fired pistol shots at it. It jumped back up onto its feet and sprinted for the far side of the room, toward the hall of doors. It passed corpses of the Minister of Order's soldiers lying on the table, up against shelves of books, and on the ground, until it finally came to the doorway to the hall. Two dead soldiers were slumped against the wall on either side.

The body kept running. It slammed into one of the doors at full speed and fell over. One of Olinger's sailors stepped in front of the door as the body sprang back up onto its feet. The crewman put his hand out against the body's chest to stop it while he studied it with a very confused face. The body put out its hands blindly and touched him. The hands followed their touch, feeling up the man's side up until they gripped his shoulders. The sailor reached out with his other hand to pick up the hat, but the body kicked him in the groin and shoved him aside. It ran its hands over the door, feeling for the handle.

Once it found and turned the handle, it ran into the hallway and held out its arm, running a hand along the surface of the wall and doors on the right. Sailors chasing it burst through the doors into the hall and shot at it with pistols and muskets. Suddenly, as bullets whizzed by, it stopped at a particular door, gripping the side of the doorframe to not slip and fall again. It tore open the door and dashed through the opening, flinging the door shut behind itself as it ran.

IX

Lost Souls in Endless Time

Water rushed around Dhlara; everything she could feel or hear was little more than a swirling, muffled roar. Her eyes were closed, still stinging from the saltwater. She had completely lost her orientation; she couldn't tell how deep she was, where she was going, or what direction the surface was. All that she knew was that she was being swept away in the current with her hands tied behind her.

But then her feet pressed against something solid, and she felt it lifting her up. The muffled roar was broken by the clear sound of wood creaking as cool air blew on her skin. She opened her eyes: she was on the deck of the frigate again, this time under a clear morning sky. Squinting, she had just enough time to see the sun hanging above the front of the ship, before the prow began to lower away from it, and she realized the ship had flown out of the ocean, just like she had seen before. Her stomach rose; she felt her body enter a freefall as the ship beneath her dropped. The ship splashed back into the water and she collapsed heavily onto the deck.

"Get up, you weakling," said a voice behind her. One of the sailors grabbed her arm and pulled her upright. Hasdrubal and Jylling had similarly fallen over, but Gordon had not, even with chains around him. Their handlers shoved all of them except Gordon, who was kept standing where he was, toward a square hole in the deck and down the set of stairs in it.

At first, Dhlara couldn't see anything as her eyes adjusted to the darkness. Instinctively, she walked with caution into the darkness, but this prompted harder shoves. After a few moments of this, the hinges of a door groaned as it was opened and she was made to sit on what felt like a stool. Her back was

111

pressed up against someone else's and rope wrapped around both of them. The hinges squealed again and several pairs of boots tramped away from the door and back up the stairs, leaving the prisoners to sit in creaking darkness.

"Welp, this is officially *super awesome*," came Jylling's voice through clenched teeth behind her.

"It would appear that we are rather pickled," Hasdrubal's voice remarked from off to her left. He sounded almost amused.

"Still messing up your idioms," Dhlara advised him. "Jylling, is that you back there?"

The person she was tied to poked at her with his finger. "*Yes*," he answered with continued displeasure.

"So, we're trapped in a ship we didn't know existed half an hour ago," Dhlara recounted.

"*Yes.*"

"And we seem to have gone somewhere else, but we don't know where."

"*Yes.*"

"This calls for a daring escape plan."

"My hitherto fully prepared escape plans all called for the liberal use of gunfire," said Hasdrubal. "This situation is now somewhat altered."

"*Super. Awesome.*"

"That's not very helpful, Jylling," Dhlara rejoined.

"Hey, you know what the plan was?! *Not* get ambushed by some sort of magic ship that swims! You know what the backup plan was?! The guy who brought us out here *does not, in fact,* hand us over to random morons manning a swimming ship! What is his problem?!"

"I don't take him for a coward or a collaborator," said Hasdrubal. "I think he really didn't want us to get hurt. You saw him fight that enormous fire lizard. That's not what I would have done, of course. I'd risk you or me getting shot any day rather than surrender."

"You know what? I actually appreciate that."

"Yeah well, that's not what happened," Dhlara reminded them. "We're here now, and we need to not be."

"We're tied up inside a big dumb boat!" Jylling exclaimed. "How do we get out of this?! And hang on, how do we keep coming across boatfuls of murderous goons anyway?!"

"What are you talking about? The Vikings were perfectly fine."

"Oh yeah, I'm sorry, you're right: it turns out the Vikings don't kill *everybody all the time*. What nice guys! I'm sure they were very kind to the place they were invading."

"I think Jylling's correct, in a way" said Hasdrubal. "I don't see very many opportunities for us to get ourselves out of this predicament." Then he added in a low voice, "And that aside, even if there was, talking about it would inform the guard standing outside."

"Is there someone out there? Can they hear us?" Dhlara whispered.

"There is; I can hear somebody out there shifting their feet, and it stands to reason that they can hear us. This is not a favourable situation. I think we will have to wait and see what they do."

*

They spent the rest of the day in darkness. Around dusk, someone opened the door, and lantern light and the cacophony of many men conversing nearby rushed into the room. When her eyes adjusted to the light, Dhlara saw that the lower deck was full of crewmen having a meal. The man at the door set two buckets onto the floor of their small room, one filled with water and the other with hard tack, and he untied them so that they could eat and drink. After he closed the door behind him, they ruefully took up the hard tack and consumed it. The water tasted strange and had bits of gunk floating in it, but it wasn't saltwater, at least. Once fifteen minutes had passed, the seaman returned, he removed the buckets and what was left in them, and tied the prisoners up again.

"So Romans destroyed your home, huh?" said Jylling during the second day, after a long stretch of bored silence in the dark. There was a pause before anyone else spoke.

"Yes, they did," Hasdrubal answered slowly.

"That must have stunk."

"It does."

"Fighting the Romans didn't go very well, did it?"

"No, it evidently did not. Not by the end of it, anyway. What is the point of this?"

"I don't know. Nothing really going on. Gotta talk about something."

"And that something is the destruction of my people?"

"I mean, unless you have something else to talk about." Another pause.

"Not so much," Hasdrubal admitted.

"Why did they destroy Carthage?" Dhlara asked.

"I think it might have had something to do with my family." She could almost hear a smile in his voice.

"Were they famous or something?" asked Jylling.

"Yes, we are. We are still famous even in your time, but all things degrade with time. For example, two thousand years later, my brother's name is used as the title of a movie where a weird English guy pretends to eat people! And yet barely any movies about my family. The people of the future are very strange."

"Well, did your brother eat people?"

"No! Of course not!"

"Maybe that's why you don't have a city anymore. The Romans got sick of your brother eating all the people."

"Jylling, you are spectacularly unaware of history, aren't you?"

"Maybe so. But I don't need to know very much. You can get along just fine making up stuff as you go."

Hasdrubal laughed. "That may be, but one conversation with someone who actually knows something and you look like an idiot."

"Yeah, well, at least I still have my country."

"There is a time where it doesn't exist either."

"So what did your family do that Rome didn't like?" Dhlara cut in.

"There are many reasons, but I would wager the most

important is that my brother brought an undefeated army right up to the gates of Rome itself."

"That would do it," said Jylling.

"What about yourselves?" Hasdrubal inquired. "What are you two anyway? Are you together?"

"Oh, no, not at all," Dhlara answered quickly as Jylling shook his head.

"Is that so? Why?"

"What do you mean 'why'?" Dhlara asked.

"He's a man, you're a woman, you like each other. Have you tried it?"

"No."

"Well, kind of. A little," Jylling added.

"Ah, I see. So who called it off? She did, didn't she?"

Jylling cast a sideways look at Dhlara and nodded. Hasdrubal laughed.

And then several days passed this way, with someone coming in with a pair of buckets at the beginning and end of every day, until one morning, after they had eaten, the sailor ordered them to follow him to the upper deck. They tramped past the guns and up the stairs, squinting as they came out into the gray, yet still brighter than where they had just been, light of an overcast day. Dhlara looked around, but couldn't see Gordon on deck. On her left was a vast emptiness of mildly choppy ocean. The frigate had anchored near an island off the starboard side, however. A little ways inland of the beach, palm trees hung their waving leaves over little tufts of grass poking up through the sand. Beyond that was an untamed jungle of lush trees mixed with a tangle of leafy shrubs that covered the ground.

The squat, dough-faced Mr. Muller stood on the shore of the island, directing a party of sailors he had taken with him in cutting down a couple palm trees. More of the crew further down unloaded wooden barrels from beached boats and stood them up in neat rows atop a set of large, horizontal wooden doors near the jungle covering some sort of underground passageway or room, while others were using buckets and shovels to fill the barrels with sand.

The man in the lead ushered them into a boat hanging by ropes off the side of the ship and climbed in himself along with three other crewmen. The boat was then lowered and the men rowed them across the clear blue-green water to the shore and motioned for them to get out.

"Ah, there they are!" Muller cried when he spotted the three of them as they stepped out. "Good morning, lady and gentlemen," he greeted them, taking each of them by the hand and shaking it as he looked up into their faces. "I want to explain to you exactly what is going on here, so that you may fully understand your situation and how pointless it is to try to deviate from it. For me personally, I do not think crude threats and bravado are very convincing. I know you will not submit unless you are actually convinced it is a fait accompli, and I respect that. But you will find we are very thorough indeed, and I hope you will find yourselves persuaded in the end. I do not wish to hurt any of you, but if you require me to, I shall, I do assure you. Now then, do you see these sort of cellar doors over there?"

None of them spoke or nodded, but they looked back at him in recognition. Nine barrels had been placed on top of the doors and were all being filled with sand.

"Your friend," he continued, "is in there as we speak. It is obviously not very safe to keep him on board the Eruewerer, as one oversight on our part could enable him to free you or wreak havoc on my crew, and that won't do. So we will leave him in there, weigh down the doors, and keep you all confined to the quarters we have provided you. I have explained to him this arrangement, so he knows if he attempts to leave this area in any way, one or all of you will come to harm. And I will know if he does, because I am leaving a few of my men on this island with the watches you provided us, and if anything at all is out of order, they will use the watches to instantly transport themselves back to our ship to report to me.

"The three of you, of course, cannot accomplish anything. If you refuse to comply with sitting peaceably in the brig and instead try some futile escape attempt, all of you would very likely die or be pointlessly maimed. And even if you could free yourselves, where would you go? We are in a time quite foreign to you, and very far from either your homes or the Ministries. The only way back to anything you know is by my benevolence. Otherwise, you are as good as dead.

"Beyond that, even if you could get away, Gordon is here, and you don't know where here is. He will not know you are outside of our control, and you will not be able to come find him, so he will remain here believing he is safeguarding your lives, and those barrels can be filled with dynamite just as easily as with sand. But do not worry, this is not a permanent state of affairs, either; once the president has achieved his aims, then we will not need to continue holding you as our prisoners, so it is in your best interests to cooperate. Is this all perfectly clear?"

"How do we know we're somewhere else in time?" Jylling pressed skeptically. "I haven't seen anything yet to tell me that. There's just been a whole lot of ocean, ocean, and more ocean. For all I know we're still on the surface of time and not very far from where we started."

"While I am eager to prove the fact of the year we are to you, Mister..." Muller replied searchingly. He let his words hang for a moment, and then he continued, "Well, you have noticed, sir, that we have specifically chosen a remote island with little traffic, and as such little evidence of the current time is at hand. Unfortunately, we have pressing business to attend to, and I cannot take you to such proof straightaway. The convenient thing about facts, however, is that they're true whether you believe them or not. Should you find yourself somewhere else than with my men or this ship, you would discover the truth soon enough."

"You imagine you have fashioned quite the plan, don't you?" said Hasdrubal.

Muller smiled. "I do indeed. I know it is difficult to accept such a scenario so far out of your control, but I think you will find things will be much easier on your mind if you do. Do any of you have any questions about this arrangement?"

"You've made yourself understood well enough."

"Very good. Then it is time for you to go back onto the ship."

At this, Hasdrubal turned to Dhlara and Jylling in turn, directly making eye contact with them with an important look, like he was trying to indicate something to them, and then he bolted for the jungle. After a moment of realization, they lurched forward themselves and ran after him. Dhlara felt the hands of the crewmen who had rowed them over trying to grab her arm and shoulder, but she twisted herself out of their grasp and sprinted over the grassy sand.

"What is the point of this?!" Muller called after them. "There is nothing around for miles! You won't be able to go anywhere!"

Ahead of her, Hasdrubal, heedless of their captor, leaped over the trunk of a fallen tree and plunged into the overgrowth. Jylling crashed through the bushes and vines after him. "Don't shoot at them! Just go in there and get them!" Dhlara heard behind her. Branches whipped back across her face and snagged in her hair as they fled deep into the jungle. She followed Hasdrubal's path through the vegetation, changing direction suddenly when he gripped the trunk of a tree and swung around it to dart off in a different direction. He repeated that several times, sometimes going right and sometimes left, and led them around or over boulders and impassable knots of plant life, until finally he slowed down and trotted to a halt. Jylling stopped behind him and bent over with his hands on his knees.

"Okay... so what... is the plan here?" he asked, panting.

"No idea whatsoever," Hasdrubal answered with a strained voice while he looked around at their surroundings.

"What?... Are you... serious?"

"I very much am. Why do you have some expectation that I'm going to get you out of this? I'm trying to get myself out. You're free to come up with something clever instead of following me."

"He's right, Jylling," Dhlara said between deep breaths, trying to assuage the burning sensation in her lungs. "You saw what it's like on that ship. If we go back there's no way we can find a way out of there."

"Yeah, no kidding... but we're on some remote island... and

we don't even know *when* we're on it... with dozens of armed men probably coming here right now looking for us. And if we don't have some sort of cunning plan… we're gonna end up right back on that stupid boat, except now the whole crew is going to be mad at us and way more vigilant."

"Good," said Hasdrubal. "If they're going to try to keep me as a prisoner, then they won't have an easy time of it."

"That's not good enough," said Dhlara. "We need to get out of here. I don't care about annoying them."

They heard a commotion behind them; many raised voices and pairs of running feet were quickly coming closer to their position.

"See?" Jylling hissed. "They're coming to get us!"

Hasdrubal dropped down onto his hands and knees, crawled under a bush at the foot of a tree and started picking up dirt and leaves and anything that was on the ground and throwing it on top of himself.

"*What the hell are you doing?!*" Jylling's voice rose to a higher pitch.

"Hiding," came the response from underneath the foliage. "If you're going to stand there and uselessly run your mouth then at least stop doing it in my direction."

Dhlara followed suit and found a similar piece of leafy cover. Jylling stood alone, listening to the approaching pursuers, and then he ran over to a fallen tree trunk and burrowed into the pile of decaying organic material that had gathered around it. Taking handfuls of the stuff, he patted it down all over the exposed parts of himself until he, with a very displeased expression, dropped a fistful onto his face and buried his arm by his side.

After they had silently lain in their makeshift camouflage for a few minutes, the group of sailors came tramping past them and headed on further into the jungle. And they continued to lay there, even after the sailors had left. Hours passed, and several more groups passed by, sometimes in different directions. Finally, after the orange light of dusk was beginning to show through the trees and it had been quite a while since they had heard any unusual noise, Hasdrubal got up onto his feet and stepped out into the open.

"Are we done with this, then?" the pile of debris queried.

"For now," Hasdrubal answered.

Jylling stood up with dirt, sticks, and chunks of rotting something cascading off of him. Bits of brown goop stuck to his clothes. Dhlara emerged from her bush as he brushed himself off.

"So, I'm incredibly hungry," he announced as he cleaned off his pant leg.

"Yes, that happens. We need to find out if they're still searching the island before we go looking for something to kill."

"Kill?"

"I don't think there is much in the way of food here except whatever animals live here," said Dhlara.

"That is my thought exactly," Hasdrubal nodded. "And in addition, there are a good number of things that grow that can be very bad to eat. Things in the ocean, too. A lot of poisonous things grow or swim, and I don't know what all of them are. I don't think I've been in this area of the world before. But in general, if something's running around on land and you wring its neck, it'll be perfectly fine to eat."

"That's lovely." Jylling looked a little disgusted.

"If you wanted to eat well you should have stayed home and never gone about on some venture like this."

"Funnily enough, that's what I was trying to do before I got time traveled."

Hasdrubal laughed. "Oh well, then. Now let's go see if there's anybody to disturb us if we hunt some critters."

The three of them spread out, but stayed close enough to see each other, and searched for signs of their erstwhile captors. Dhlara gazed intently around her as they made their way through the jungle, looking for movement or colours that were out of place. She listened to the rustle of the wind through the trees, trying to discern if there were any faint sounds of human origin hidden underneath the dominating natural sounds. She couldn't see anything other than the normal brown of dirt and trees and the green of leaves, and she couldn't make out any hidden sounds.

After walking for some time, she saw a large, sloped boulder nearby. She scaled its incline, keeping herself low in case anyone she was unaware of was looking in her direction, and peered over the top. Through the branches of a cluster of trees she saw a beach with a sixteen-foot-long boat like the one they had been rowed ashore in that had been pulled up into the sand. She waved at Jylling and Hasdrubal until they noticed her and came over. She pointed at the beach and they climbed up the rock as well to take a look.

"Well, isn't that a jolly boat," Hasdrubal remarked.

"Whoever brought it here is sure to be around," said Dhlara.

"I think we ought to take our chances and seize it for ourselves."

"Yeah, but what would we do with it?" said Jylling. "Where would we go?"

"I don't know. That's the way of life, isn't it? Come on, let's hurry up before they come back."

The trio jumped down from the rock and cautiously made their way toward the boat. Hiding themselves behind the trunks of trees, they came to the edge of the beach. They looked up and down the shore, but saw no one. Hasdrubal rushed forward, sprays of sand kicking up behind him from his boots as he sprinted to the landed craft. He gripped the ridge of the hull and waved for Dhlara and Jylling to come up and help him. They swiftly crossed the open beach and took hold of the boat as well, their feet digging into the sand as they all pushed it toward the small ocean waves.

"Hey! Stop right there!" a distant voice to their left cried out. A party of ten men were running at them from the treeline further down the beach.

"Come on!" Hasdrubal urged Dhlara and Jylling. "Push! We're almost free!"

Dhlara's shoes became soaked and filled with sand as the three of them splashed into the tide. Jets of water popped up around her as she heard the claps and cracks of pistol shots. Once they felt the boat begin to float on its own, Dhlara stepped into it and took up one of the oars laid out loose on the seats. When Jylling in turn got into the boat and sat down, Hasdrubal gave out a guttural noise of surprise and tripped, falling bodily into the foamy water.

Dhlara dropped her oar and jumped out, landing near Hasdrubal as he attempted to stand back up. He lifted himself up with his right leg, but when he tried to put his weight on his left, it gave out and he fell down face first. Dhlara took his hand to help him into a kneeling position, then put his left arm over her shoulders and wrapped her right arm around his side to support him as he hobbled toward the boat. Looking at his feet, she saw the current around his left foot carrying away streamers of blood.

"I… I think they shot me…" Hasdrubal muttered.

"You'll be fine, I've got you," she reassured him.

Jylling braced his arms against either side of the boat and kept it steady as Hasdrubal tumbled into it.

"Let's go!" Dhlara shouted as she hopped into the back end.

Facing her, Jylling picked up his oar, dipped it into the water, and rowed vigorously, pulling on it with all his strength. As she grabbed her own oar and whirled around in her seat, the ten crewmen came running, and splashing, after them. The one in front had his arm outstretched, reaching out for the boat. Dhlara set her oar into its groove on the side of the hull he was approaching, then pulled back on it as hard as she could. She felt the wood in her hands vibrate as the end of the oar slammed into the man's skull. His body went limp and floated away. The other nine continued to wade in against the current, but as Dhlara and Jylling rowed the boat into deeper waters, they struggled to keep up.

Soon, the sailors gave up the chase, dragging the body of their incapacitated crewmate with them as they returned to the beach.

"Now what?" Jylling said as they pulled further away from shore.

"I think we might actually have to go back. He's hurt pretty bad, and if they want to keep us alive, maybe they'll—"

"No," Hasdrubal's strained voice came up from the bottom of the boat.

"We don't have any way of taking care of that injury, Hasdrubal."

"And we don't have any food or anything to drink, either," added Jylling.

"No. We risked getting shot so that we... could escape," Hasdrubal responded between breaths. "There's no point in going back."

"You'll die," Dhlara argued. "And we may, too. We don't have anything we need to stay alive."

"The only reason we're not already dead... is because they're afraid of Gordon. This is the best chance... we have of living. If there's an island here... there may be others... around."

Jylling groaned. "Alright, let's hope something's out there."

"Give me your shirt," Dhlara said to him.

"What? Why? You've got one."

"I'm going to try to bandage his leg up and stop the bleeding."

Jylling pulled his arms into his sleeves, lifted his shirt over his head, and tossed it to her. Hasdrubal grimaced with his jaw clenched as she wrapped it tightly around his leg just above his ankle.

"Well, what direction do you want to go?" Jylling asked.

Dhlara pointed a little off to the right. "I guess that way."

And then the two of them took up their oars and rowed out into the open ocean.

X

Wolves of the Sea

"Hey! Hey, wake up!"

Dhlara drifted into consciousness and opened her eyes. She had slumped over onto the side of the boat to get some sleep as best she could after they had rowed all night and into the morning, and now the glaring sun of a hot midday beat down on her. The arm she was resting her head on felt alternately numb and full of sharp, tingling pain, while her head itself was wracked with an intense headache. Almost all of her body was sore, at least so it seemed to her, her empty stomach churned and growled with displeasure, and she was immensely thirsty. And, on top of everything, she was still exhausted, but Jylling, however, continued to try to rouse her.

"Hey! Dhlara!"

"What is it?" she groaned, lifting her head up and looking around. Then she noticed they were not surrounded by endless ocean anymore: beyond Jylling and the front of the boat, there was not just an island, but an entire white sand coastline spanning out as far as she could see on either side. Somehow, they had managed to find land.

"Look!" he exclaimed, but instead of calling her attention to the land, he pointed off to the left, at four approaching ships in the distance. Their billowing square-rigged sails wavered in the haze of heat. "Somebody's coming, and they're going to see us."

"I think we might need them to," she said.

"What? How is that? We have no idea who those people are."

"Neither of us can treat a gunshot wound. We need to find someone who can, and quickly." She looked down at

124

Hasdrubal, who was still lying down in the center of the boat: his face was pale and covered with sweat, and his chest rose and fell with each breath he took as he lay unconscious.

"There's that coastline, and if there's ships around here, there must be some sort of civilization over there. Maybe they'll have a doctor."

"That could be miles inland, though," she said through a yawn, stretching her arms out in front of her. "And if those are military ships, I'll bet they've got someone aboard who's treated a lot of injuries like this."

"If they are of some country's navy, we could find ourselves in an awful lot of trouble. What if they know or work for Olinger? That'd be even worse."

"He's hurt and we have to try to help him."

"Alright, fair enough."

They rowed their little boat toward the sails on the horizon, which steadily grew larger with every passing minute. Soon enough, the ships were more clearly visible, and Dhlara saw that one of them was a triple-masted frigate, much like Olinger's vessel, while the other three were smaller, single-masted sloops. The frigate led the fleet, foam collecting at the waterline of its bow as it cut through the glistening sea. As it came closer, however, Dhlara could more clearly see it was not so similar after all, having a rounder shape, shorter length, and higher poop deck. It appeared to slow down as it came near the tiny boat. A man in a yellow wig leaned over the side of the ship and grinned at them.

"Oh, hello there!" he said, raising a hand and waggling his fingers in greeting.

Dhlara cupped her hands around her mouth and called up to him, "We have someone with us who is very badly hurt and needs medical attention!"

"Oh dear! That's not good! We have three of the finest French surgeons, so you can come onboard and I'll make sure they take care of him!" He threw some netting over the side. "Put him in that and we'll bring him aboard!"

Dhlara and Jylling rowed up alongside the frigate, picked Hasdrubal up by his hands and feet, and placed him into the net. The man called to the crew behind him, "Alright, pull him up, you chaps!" and Hasdrubal's limp form was hoisted upward until several arms reached over the gunwale and brought him onto the deck. Then a rope ladder was lowered for the two of them to climb up.

As Dhlara stepped onto the top deck, the man's round face smiled broadly at her; his light blue eyes on either side of his hawk nose shone with excitement. He wore a dark blue dressing gown with an intricate, monochromatic floral pattern, and its shoulders had smudges of yellow powder from his wig. His legs stuck out from the bottom of the gown, entirely clad in long white socks without any sort of footwear, and he held a book in his left hand.

"Hello again!" he said cheerily. "Welcome aboard the Queen Anne's Revenge! I'm a pirate now! I'm Captain Edwards!"

Dhlara heard Jylling groan behind her as he ascended the rope ladder. "Pirates! Of course…" he muttered.

"His wound is very serious," she nodded at Hasdrubal, who was being picked up by a pair of sailors, "he was shot almost a day ago."

"I told the surgeons that they must do everything they can! One of them was on a warship, you know. I think your friend will be all right!"

"Thank you. We really appreciate this," she said as she followed the men carrying Hasdrubal down a set of stairs into the gundeck, then down another set into the lower deck. He lifted his head to look around as they pushed aside a canvas curtain and laid him out on a table. A thin man wearing a smock and small round spectacles unrolled a leather pouch of metal instruments next to Hasdrubal. He tied his shoulder-length gray hair behind his head and carefully started to undo the shirt tied around Hasdrubal's ankle.

"Oh," Captain Edwards said from behind her, "we should go somewhere else. This could be gross."

"I want to make sure he's okay."

"I will do everything I can for him, madam," the bespectacled doctor assured her with a thick French accent, pausing to look at her assuringly. "I know what it is like to be at the mercy of these men; I will take good care of him."

Hasdrubal slowly lifted his head up off the table and cleared his throat. "I am about as well as I can be."

"Okay. I'll be back," she told him.

He nodded.

She turned around and followed Edwards back up to the top deck. They walked over to Jylling, who stood shielding his eyes from the sun with his hand, watching the three sloops as they sailed through the wake of the flagship.

"This is your ship, I take it?" she asked Edwards, gazing around at the black and white men of the crew working on deck. Some of them, especially the black men, wore plain, tattered clothes, but here and there were fresh shoes, a colourful jacket, or a clean pair of pants. Unlike the last ship they'd been on, the top deck was crowded with cannon on each side.

"No, it isn't." He jabbed with the book in his hand at a vastly smaller sloop sailing nearby, off the starboard side and a little further behind. "That's my ship."

"You're the captain of *that* ship? Not this one?" Jylling inquired over his shoulder.

"That's right! Paid for it with my own money!" the captain said, grinning.

"Why are you over here, then?"

"Captain Teach is a good friend, and he wants me to rest and recuperate aboard his ship!"

"Rest from what?" Dhlara asked.

"Captain Teach and the crew thought I deserved a rest, after being an exceptionally daring pirate!"

"Could I ask you what year it is, Captain?"

"Yes!"

She waited for an answer, but he just smiled placidly at her. "...What year is it?" she reiterated.

"Seventeen eighteen!"

"Well then. That's good to know."

"Where are we?" Jylling asked.

Edwards looked up at the sky, thinking. "Off the coast of

Florida, I guess. I don't really know. I'm not much of a mariner. I've gotten sea sick a few times, actually. Sometimes the deck is too wobbly for me. I'm sure Captain Teach could tell you exactly where we are. Would you like to meet him?"

"Sure," said Dhlara.

He led them to the cabin door on the quarterdeck and rapped his knuckles on a window pane. "Enter!" a voice called from within. He opened the door and led them inside. A man across the room was hunched over a writing desk; his long, braided black beard hung over a loose white shirt, the sleeves of which were pushed up to his elbows. The feather quill in his hand wobbled as he scratched words onto the pages of a book, one of many laid out on the desk among the sheaves of paper, rolled up parchment, and several mostly full glass decanters. Rays of sunlight streamed in from windows behind him, through which Dhlara could see the other ships of the fleet cutting their own wedges of wake in the glittering ocean water. Jylling followed Dhlara into the cabin and gasped.

"Captain!" Edwards addressed the man.

"What is it, Edwards?" Teach replied without looking up. Dhlara heard a Scottish accent in his voice. His black hair was tied up in a knot behind his head, revealing a forehead shining with sweat.

"These guys were adrift and we saved them! They are curious about our whereabouts."

Teach looked up and glared at Dhlara and Jylling with deep blue eyes. "We're full up, so you better not have come here wanting to sign on, boy," he said to Jylling.

"No, sir," Jylling quickly answered, and earnestly. Dhlara looked over at him with a puzzled expression; he seemed overly apprehensive.

"What about you?" the captain asked Dhlara. "Precisely what business do you have here? She yours?" he asked Jylling.

"We honestly only came in search of help," Dhlara explained. "Our friend was shot last night and he needs serious medical care."

"You had the doctors see to him?" Teach asked Edwards.

"Yes, I did."

"How'd he get shot?"

"We were prisoners aboard a ship much like this one," said Dhlara.

The captain sat back in his chair and put his quill down. "Like this one, you say? What kind of ship was it? Whose was it?"

"I'm not sure. It had a lot of cannons on it, so some kind of military ship, I guess."

"Bloody hell!" Teach's chair scraped against the wood floor as he stood up. He was thin yet muscular, and well over six feet tall, and his face now took on a look of consternation. "What colours did it fly?! Was it a king's ship?!"

"I didn't notice any flag."

"Who manned it?! English?! Spanish?!"

"I think they're on their own. I don't think they're a part of any navy."

"Impossible. There's not a pirate sailing these waters with a frigate, other than myself."

"I think that's a ship we ought to stay clear of," said Edwards.

"Definitely." Teach stroked his beard. "They'd taken you prisoner, had they?"

"Yes," Dhlara answered.

"What for? How many of you was there?"

"Just four of us. The two of us and our wounded friend managed to escape."

"Four? Why were you being held?"

"I suppose you could say we were sort of political prisoners. Collateral."

Teach grunted. "You'll stay with us, then. Captain Edwards, let my quartermaster know that accommodations are to be made for the three of them, if you please." He took the top off one of the decanters, poured some of its contents out into a metal cup, then threw his head back and drank it.

"Where are we right now, Captain?" Edwards asked.

Teach rubbed his temple with his fingers and grimaced. "What's that?"

"Where are we?"

"A couple days south of Charles Town. Now, if you'll excuse me, I have the matters of the company to attend to." He pulled his chair in as he sat back down and clanked the cup onto the desk. He picked up his feather quill, dipped the tip into an inkwell on the desk, and resumed scratching ink onto the page. Captain Edwards escorted them out of the cabin and back onto the sun-baked open deck.

"Now that's a captain!" he marveled. "Isn't this smashing? Both of you are very lucky. There's no better a pirate to sail with than Blackbeard!"

"Hang on, that's Blackbeard in there?" Dhlara said incredulously.

"*Of course it is!*" Jylling hissed. "How many pirates with a fleet of ships have a great big black beard?! Don't you think a name *means something*?! They called him Blackbeard because he had a *black. Beard.*"

"Yeah, well, I don't see how it matters. He's letting his doctors heal Hasdrubal and he's letting us stay on his ship. That's about as much as we could expect from anyone."

"He's a bloodthirsty villain! He'll cut your throat for the glint of gold!"

"I don't know about that." Edwards smiled blankly.

Dhlara stepped closer to Jylling and whispered near his ear, "I think a person with sense would know not to disparage a pirate captain within earshot of his crew."

Jylling cleared his throat. "Actually, he's quite a nice guy, now that I've met him," he announced loudly.

"So where are we meant to be, if we're staying here?" Dhlara asked Edwards.

"Oh yes! This way!" The captain spun around on his heel, his whole body wavering back and forth as he came around. After pausing to first steady his footing, he strode across the deck to a muscular, bald man shouting up at some crewmen climbing the web of rigging.

"Trim the head yards by the main, you lot! Get on it!"

"Mr. Davies!" The wigged captain addressed him cheerfully.

"What? Oh, 'allo. What do you need, Edwards?"

"*Captain* Edwards! I'm a captain, don't you know," he corrected the quartermaster, yet while sounding completely unperturbed. "I saved these excellent people and they're going to stay with us, so we need to give them a room."

"Do the captain know about this? You know ladies ain't allowed on board, sir." He gave Dhlara a beady glare.

"Captain Teach said you're to give them quarters."

"I don't rightly know what to do about that. She's... she's a she, you know, and that's liable to be a problem. No offense, ma'am."

"He said you're to give them quarters."

"Wull, I suppose they can take the doctors' lodgings..."

"Great!" And Edwards spun around again, but this time he pitched too far to his right, causing him to stumble awkwardly as he headed back for the stairs. Dhlara and Jylling followed, and he led them down through the gundeck to the lower deck, past the drawn curtain in front of the surgeons' area, and through a short and narrow hallway into a tiny room with three beds crammed into it.

"You'll sleep here, and whatever else you've gotta do," he told them while he plopped himself down on one of the beds. Dhlara thanked him, and he nodded. And kept sitting and smiling. She patted the sides of her legs nervously, then sat down on the opposite bed.

"So, how long have you been doing this?" she asked.

"Sailing or being a pirate?" the captain replied.

"Either one."

"I was on a frigate once when I was much smaller," he said, swinging his knees side to side. "But I've only been sailing properly for a few months. Started being a pirate then, too! I think I'm pretty good at it."

"Oh really? Why'd you decide to be a pirate?"

"Being rich got boring and pirates are dashing!"

"Oh. Okay. Right on."

Edwards looked around at the ceiling, still smiling.

"Listen," said Jylling from the doorway, "we've had a rough couple of days. Would it be alright if we had a few moments to rest?"

"Yes! Of course! I'll see you later, then!" Edwards hopped up and Jylling stepped back to let him leave, then sat down on the recently vacated bed.

"That is a pretty weird pirate," he whispered, leaning in toward Dhlara and jerking his thumb back toward the direction Edwards had gone.

"He certainly is not what I would have expected," she said, shaking her head.

"He's kind of an idiot, but there's still something likeable about him."

Dhlara chuckled. "Sounds like you like him a lot more than Blackbeard."

"Well, there aren't stories still told three hundred years from now about the vicious cruelty and greed of the dread pirate *Edwards.*"

"That's true," Dhlara replied as she laid down in the bed. Her head pounded with a headache from how little she'd slept, and she was still tired from the day before. She closed her eyes and they sat in silence for a minute.

"We're really screwed here, aren't we?" said Jylling.

Dhlara opened one eye and watched him as he sat on the bed, picking at his fingernails. "What do you mean?"

"We're stuck here. In seventeen-eighteen. There isn't a way back."

"There is. Olinger goes back and forth with that ship of his somehow."

"All that means is he can and we can't."

"Right now, anyway. That's the only way back, so we'll have to figure something out."

"He could just leave. Go somewhere else in his stupid ship and then we'd be here forever."

"Well, then we'll go find Gordon and maybe he'll have some way to get us back to the Ministries."

"I guess." Jylling yawned.

Dhlara's mind wandered, and she was soon asleep.

*

When she woke up, she sat upright and stretched as she looked around. The bed Jylling had been in was empty, but Hasdrubal lay sleeping soundly in the third bed, which was pushed up against the wall between and perpendicular to the other two. She looked down toward his wounded leg, but, after a moment of confusion, she realized everything below halfway down his shin was gone, and the stump of what remained had been wrapped in bandages.

She got up and walked over to the surgical area. The curtain was pulled back and the table, since it had no legs and hung from the wall by ropes, had been folded up against the wall.

"Good evening, madam," said a voice behind her, which she recognized as the doctor she had spoken with before. She turned around; he was coming down the stairs. "I trust you slept well?"

"Uh… yeah… so, my friend seems to be, well, missing his foot."

"Ah yes, I had to remove it to save the limb, and perhaps his life."

"That, uh… is he okay now?"

"Excuse me, I don't think I understand."

"Will he heal all right? Is he going to be fine?"

"I cannot say, I am afraid. We will have to see what is the plan of God."

"Okay… well, thanks."

"Of course, madam." He nodded his head and stepped aside to allow her to pass. She nodded in return and went up the stairs.

The sun was setting when she came back up to the top deck; it bathed the port side in an orange glow and cast a long shadow of the ship out onto the surface of the water to starboard. She paused to feel the wind rush through her hair and listen to the hum it made as it passed through the rigging. There were fewer men on deck than there had been midday, but a number pirates were still busy tending to the ropes and sheets. A voice drifted down from above, up amidst the sails:

"There once were a man, hey-oh
Who sailed with us an' far ay-way
As little a fellow as there ever were
Laughed off o' the shore by all he know

So he sailed three score or more
Loved every woman in every port
Drank every drink that could be drunk
And he laughed every day and sang out loud,"

For the next verse, most of the sailors on deck joined in:

" 'Oh, life with you, my old shipmates
As grand a livin' as I could have asked
And there's a place of endless dance and fun
Waitin' just for us at the end of time. "

Smiling as she listened, she spotted Captain Edwards laying down on the gunwale, his legs dangling down on either side and his face buried in a book he held only inches away. While she walked over, the lone voice continued:

"Said farewell to many a man too young
Saw his pals all die and his beard grow long
Saw the rum dry up and many a captain go
Still he sang out loud from his high old nest

Standing near him, she tried to read the title on the cover of the book, but she realized it was upside down. She took it from him and turned it rightside up before handing it back.

"Oh, thanks!" he said happily, and he buried his face in it again.

"It was upside down."

"Huh?"

The crew on deck had taken up their part again:

" 'Oh, life with you, my old shipmates
As grand a livin' as I could have asked

134

And there's a place of endless dance and fun
Waitin' just for us at the end of time."

"It was upside down!" she said louder, leaning in.
"Yes it was!" he replied from within the pages.
"So anybody who can read can see that's wrong."
"Oh, none of them can read anyway."
"Can you?"
"Of course I can! But I like the smell the most. Reminds me of home. I've got a whole library back in my cabin on the Revenge."

Then one mornin' a ball shot him through
Brought him low and the devil took his life
We sewed him up in his hammock tight
But his body were singin' as it fell to the sea,

'Oh, don't you worry, my old shipmates
I got to take a trip down far below
But we'll all meet again someday, so I'll wait,
I'll wait for you at the end of time."

Meanwhile, Jylling sat alone on the portside railing of the poop deck, watching the sea roll away as the ship passed over it. Over the singing, he heard somebody's boots clomping up the stairs and, looking behind him, he saw the ship's captain. Teach's piercing blue eyes stared at Jylling from beneath a tricorne hat. He had put on a somewhat tattered and faded black overcoat, and a cutlass now hung at his side. In his hands were the same decanter and metal cup, though the former's contents had apparently been significantly diminished by the past few hours.

"Care to irrigate?" Teach called to Jylling.
"Uh… I don't know what you mean."
The captain walked over as he poured from the decanter, then he held the cup out for Jylling to take. "Have a drink, laddie."
Jylling looked at it nervously, but took it and tentatively

drank a bit. He scrunched up an eye in a slightly displeased face.

"Hah!" Teach laughed. "Now there you go. Not many things better than some brandy and an ol' sea breeze, aye?"

"Aye," Jylling obligingly agreed.

Teach left him with the cup, drinking a swig straight out of the decanter, and went over to the man at the wheel. While they conversed, Jylling noticed that Teach's face was sweatier than the weather warranted, and his face was flushed. The pirate captain bent his head down to listen to the other man, and squinted his eyes as if he were trying to concentrate. After a minute or so, he descended the stairs again, leaving the other man to man the helm. Jylling turned around and watched the light decline behind the land to the west as he finished his drink.

XI

Under Jolly Roger

Dhlara woke up the next morning in one of the three beds in the little room. She sat up and rubbed her eyes. Jylling slept soundly in the bed across from her, but Hasdrubal lay facing her in the middle bed, his upper back and head propped up by a stack of pillows. Blankets covered his lower half, but she unconsciously glanced at his left leg and saw the blankets lying flat where his foot should have been. She caught herself and looked back up into Hasdrubal's eyes.

"How're you feeling?" she asked.

He didn't respond. He gazed in her direction, but his eyes were unfocused, as if he wasn't actually taking in what he was seeing. A muscle at the side of his jaw bulged as he clenched his teeth and clutched a metal cup that was sitting on his stomach.

"Hasdrubal? How're you feeling?"

He jerked and looked her in the eye. "Bad," he answered, and drank from the cup.

"They gave you a ration of booze, I take it?"

He grunted and stared off again.

She swung her legs off the bed and stood up to yawn and stretch, after which she walked out of the room, gently squeezing Hasdrubal's shoulder as she passed him. Opposite her was an open doorway to another room full of barrels and crates. As she went up the stairs, she heard a rustling noise. To the right, morning sunlight streamed down into the gundeck from the stairway that led up to the top deck. A motley red-feathered chicken dropped down into view, its wings fluttering, and it landed on one of the stairs. The bird cocked its head sideways, looking at Dhlara, then hopped onto the floor and

137

took off running.

A pair of boots clomped down the stairs, and the young man they were attached to swung his head left and right as he scanned the floor, causing his mess of brown hair to toss back and forth.

"How do you lose a bloody chicken?" a second person asked, his bare feet now descending the stairs as well. A tattered pair of breeches revealed themselves above the feet, then a pale and pudgy shirtless torso, with hands on either side clutching several eggs.

"The latch was loose," the man preoccupied with the poultry hunt answered.

"*You* left the latch loose, you mean, you careless bonehead," the other countered, grinning at him with a crowded and crooked set of teeth. A frazzle of orange hair stuck up from the top of his head.

"I'll wring his stupid chicken neck when I find him…"

"You'd better not, unless you're going to start laying eggs. Ah, no, nevermind that; I wouldn't want to eat your eggs anyway." As he spoke, he spotted Dhlara. He stared at her in surprise for a moment, then nodded to her, putting one of his egg-filled hands up to his forehead, and turned away.

The sound of clucking and rustling feathers came from further down the ship. The brown-haired pursuer took off after it.

"Put it in its cage properly this time!" the shirtless man reminded him as he followed.

Dhlara watched the two of them run between the cannon lining both sides of the ship, chasing a little red blur at their feet, then she climbed up to the top deck. She felt the warmth on her skin as she walked into the sunlight. A breeze blew across the deck and whipped her hair around until she held it back with one hand. Captain Edwards stood nearby on the starboard side of the deck; his back was to her as he gazed out over the water.

"Good morning," she said as she came up alongside him.

He jerked and turned toward her, causing the sides of his yellow wig hanging down around his face to wobble. "Oh, good morning!" He smiled.

"So what's going on?" she asked.

"Going on?" he repeated.

"What're we up to?"

Edwards frowned in confusion. "Whatever you want to be up to."

"*What business is the crew of this vessel currently engaged in?*" Dhlara reiterated, stressing the point with deliberate enunciation.

"Ah, yes! Piracy!" He waggled his eyebrows and appeared to be very pleased with himself.

"Here?"

"Yes!" He pointed upstream, away from the fleet spread out in the mouth of the ocean inlet. "Now, out that way is Charles Town. A fine city, full of merchants and treasure. And well-guarded! There are walls and redoubts and even a full battery of guns! It'd be a very foolish bunch of pirates to try to sail anywhere near it." He gave her a knowing nod and a grin and waited for her response.

"...Do you happen to be a foolish bunch of pirates?" she asked cautiously.

"No! We are not!" He stuck his forefinger up into the air. "As you can see, the city lies a few miles inside an inlet, which means anybody coming in or out of the harbour has to come through here." He held out his arms and motioned to banks on either side of him, before he pointed at the *Revenge*, a hundred yards away; a cutter was lashed to its side. "Ah, and right there, you can see the pilot boat that we seized. There are many shallow spots between here and the harbour, so they employ pilots who know the safe paths to guide vessels in and out of the bar."

"And now they're prisoners aboard a pirate ship," said Dhlara.

"And now they're prisoners aboard a pirate ship!" Edwards repeated with evident glee.

"Looks like there's another one coming."

A sail was visible on the horizon. Edwards took a spyglass out of a pocket in his morning gown, extended it, and held it up to his eye. "By Jove, there is!" he exclaimed. And with that, he collapsed the spyglass and shoved it back into his pocket as he ran below deck.

"Where are you going?" Dhlara called after him.

"I need to be ready for battle!" he answered as he stomped down the stairs and out of sight.

A few minutes later, with the approaching ship now appearing larger than before, Edwards hurried back up the stairs to Dhlara. He had exchanged his flowery gown for a gold-embroidered deep blue dress coat with white lace sticking out from under its wide cuffs. Beneath his coat he wore a purple waistcoat with a ruffled white jabot at his neck. A rapier without a holster hung at his hip, the blade running alongside the purple breeches and white stockings that met at his knees. Buckled black shoes with slightly raised heels clacked on the deck as he walked. What hadn't changed was the yellow powdered wig on the top of his head.

"Much better," he grinned, holding up two pistols.

"Look alive you lot! Clear the decks for action! Set the sails!" a voice called. Mr. Davies stood between the mainmast and the foremast barking orders at a now frenetic crew. Men hurried across the deck and dashed up the rigging or down the stairways to the decks below. Captain Teach watched the commotion as he stood on the bridge.

"Yes, that's right!" Edwards said sternly to the sailors passing by him. "Get to work right quick, now!"

Soon enough, the *Queen Anne's Revenge* was underway, turning its prow so that its bowsprit pointed the way to the oncoming vessel. As it drew closer, Dhlara could see that it had two masts and its size was somewhat larger than the single-masted sloops in Teach's fleet, but still much smaller than the frigate. When the two ships were a mile distant, Teach walked to the fo'c'sle and raised a spyglass to examine his quarry. He whipped back around and bellowed, "Let fly the black flag! Give them a shot across their bow!" Davies shouted down through the closest stairwell for the bow gunners to fire, and the booming crash of a cannon shot roared in response, accompanied by a cloud of smoke that billowed out in front of the frigate. Leaning out over the gunwale to get a better view, Dhlara looked up, while squinting and shielding her eyes from the sun with her hand, at the flag being raised by one of the pirates at the top of the mainmast. It caught the wind and unfurled, revealing a white skeleton holding a spear pointed at a red heart.

The smaller vessel remained on course for a minute or two, then started to turn hard to starboard. "Another shot!" Teach shouted. The other bow gun fired, sending a second ball whizzing away. The ship sailed through the smoke emitted by the cannons, sending it wafting around Teach as lifted his spyglass again. After a few minutes, he collapsed it between his hands and announced, "White flag! Take her in and secure them!"

Edwards, crestfallen, jammed his pistols back into their slings underneath his coat. "Surrender again. Nobody's tried to fight us since Captain Teach took this ship."

"Isn't that a good thing?" asked Dhlara.

"Yes, for the crew. But I came here to do some pirating."

"Isn't this what pirating is?"

"Of course not! It's about dashing sword fights and volleys of cannon fire! What's the fun in stealing if you can't have a fair fight for it?"

"I think the point of stealing is to end up with more than you have already. I don't know if it's about the fun of it."

"Before I met Captain Teach, I did more than accept surrendered goods. Teach is a gentleman and a fine captain, but when I am well enough to take command of the Revenge again, there's going to be a fight!"

"What happened that you aren't well enough to command?"

"A vicious battle with a Spanish man o' war! It was bigger than the Revenge, and more guns, too, but I gave him a mauling he won't forget! In that fight, however, I sustained a few injuries. Captain Teach was kind enough to take command while I heal."

"Hey, Dhlara." She turned around; Jylling had come up on deck. "What's going on?" he asked. "What's the racket about?"

Men rushed past him to the starboard side brandishing pistols and musketoons.

"We've gone a pirating!" Edwards eagerly explained as he led the three of them toward the middle of the deck, after being jostled a few times. "First, that ship! Then, a city!"

Jylling spun around on his heel. "Nevermind, then. I'll be below."

"I thought you'd have more of a stomach for adventure than that!"

Jylling waved his hand in the air as he walked away. "Not today, I don't. Maybe tomorrow."

"Tomorrow it is!" Edwards clutched the front edges of his coat in his hands as he called after Jylling. "He seems like a fine fellow," he added, after Jylling had left.

"He is," said Dhlara. "So what's going to happen here, to them?"

Edwards looked back at the ship flying a white flag; it loomed large in front of them now. The wind had been let out of the sails and it floated stationary as the *Queen Anne's Revenge* approached. "In a moment, we'll board her take everyone aboard as prisoners and send a crew over to man her. Anything that they've got in the hold, or on their persons, or anywhere in general that we'd like to have, we'll take."

"You aren't going to kill any of them, right?"

"Of course not! They surrendered! We're just here to rob them."

As the ships came alongside one another, the crew of the *Queen Anne's Revenge* tossed grappling hooks onto the deck of the smaller vessel, then pulled on the ropes, bringing them closer together. The sailors on the other side held their hands in the air while planks were placed across the gap between the gunwales. The pirates crossed the planks with their small arms pointed at the surrendering mariners. No resistance was attempted, so a squad of boarders continued on to below decks. Soon, the passengers and the rest of the crew were ushered at gunpoint up to the top deck. There, they were instructed to cross over to the *Queen Anne's Revenge*, and their boots and shoes clomped on the wooden planks as they complied.

The new arrivals onboard made it necessary for Captain Edwards and Dhlara to relocate to the port side of the deck, standing just outside the huddled mass of captured people, who were surrounded by pirates brandishing pistols, swords, and knives. From this place, Dhlara could still see Captain Teach as he stood atop the starboard side stairway to the quarterdeck and watched his hostages come on board his flagship. His broad cutlass hung at his side and he had two braces of pistols slung over his coat. With narrowed eyes and a furrowed brow, he silently studied the men and women below him. One of these men came to the front, pushed forward by one of Teach's scruffy men behind him.

"This 'ere's the captain," the pirate called up to him.

"Captain Robert Clark, of the Crowley," said the tall, fat, brown haired prisoner.

"Well Captain Clark," said Teach, "I thank you for choosing to avoid an unnecessary effusion of blood. I am Captain Teach, and I think you know the sort of business my men and I are engaged in here."

"Aye, I do. You're pirates," Clark answered.

"Every man aboard. And what business were you engaged in here, with the Crowley?" Teach asked.

"Taking passengers to London."

"I expect you to keep your men and passengers in peaceable good order while your cargo is unloaded. We don't mean to kill anyone today, but whoever gets in our way will be run through and their corpse will be dumped overboard."

"There won't be any need for that; we won't cause any trouble."

"Ensure that is understood by everyone here."

"I will do so."

"Captain!" a voice among the passengers called. A middle-aged man in a white wig pushed his way through the crowd and stepped up next to Clark. A little boy had followed him, silently crying, and he held onto the back of the man's coat as he hid behind it.

"What is it?" Teach snapped.

143

"My name is Samuel Wragg," he said, putting his hand on top of the boy's head. "I am on the Council of the Province of Carolina, and I can assure you that any of your demands will be complied with, so long as these people are not harmed."

Teach's dark beard parted and revealed a yellow-toothed grin. "The Provincial Council? Well, it seems we've caught ourselves a mighty big fish!" There was a low rumble as his men chuckled at this.

As the *Crowley* was searched and its valuables brought over to the *Queen Anne's Revenge*, Captain Teach barraged Clark and Wragg with questions, such as how many ships lay at harbour in Charles Town and how well armed they were, until he announced to them, "The lot of you will now return to your ship and wait peaceably in the hold while a decision is made as to what to do with you." And then, after they had accordingly escorted their prisoners back over to the *Crowley*, the pirates gathered on the top deck of Teach's ship, looking up at him on the bridge. To Dhlara, there looked to be about a couple hundred of them in total.

Edwards groaned. "This is going to be boring," he said, turning around to lean on the side of the ship and look out over the water.

"Why's that?" Dhlara asked.

"Captain Teach is going to give a course of action to the men and ask for their approval, and anyone who has other ideas can say so. It's ghastly tedious."

"That sounds incredibly democratic, actually."

Edwards snorted. "What's the point of being the captain of a ship if you can't tell people what to do?"

*

A few hours later, the discussion had finished and Teach's sailors had unanimously voiced their assent to his plan. The people in the *Crowley*'s hold once again found themselves crossing over to the frigate at the behest of armed men and looking up at the pirate captain, awaiting an indication of their fate. This time, however, they came without as much fine clothing and jewelry as they had before; they had been relieved of them by the pirates.

"It has been decided," Teach announced. "Two of my men will go ashore with a list of valuable items to be delivered to us as a ransom for your lives. Until the entire ransom is received, every one of you will be held as prisoners aboard this ship. If either man is harmed in any way, you will all be killed, and your heads will be cut off and sent to the governor."

The prisoners looked stricken and whispered amongst each other nervously, until Samuel Wragg at the front spoke up again. "If it please you, Captain, I would offer some ideas on how to better secure the delivery of this ransom, as we are all anxious to make it entirely unnecessary for you to harm anyone here."

"Go on," Teach nodded.

"Well, one of your hostages might go ashore with the two men of your buccaneer embassy to the governor, so as to be able to personally represent the danger and peril so many eminent men of Charles Town are in, and beseech the governor to save the lives of so many of the King's subjects by surrendering to your demands. The common people of Charles Town, as well, may be panicked or enraged by such demands, and their conduct toward your men is not something anyone here nor the governor can answer for, but it would be calming to them to have a hostage pleading with them to respect your representatives."

"Yes, I think this is a reasonable proposal. Who of you would go ashore?"

"If you approved, I could accompany them. My position would induce them to listen and cooperate, and I would leave my son, William, here with you as a sign of my good faith."

Teach smiled wryly at him. "No, you being held aboard my ship is inducement enough. It will have to be someone else. Who among you would go?" he asked all of them, looking over Wragg.

"I would," a voice came from the crowd.

"Step forward!"

A spindly man came to the front. "I am Benjamin Marks,

and I should like to give my assistance to this mission."

"You're from Charles Town?"

"Yes; I'm a pewter smith and I keep a shop here."

"Were you bringing anyone with you on this passage to London?"

"My wife," he said, looking back over his shoulder.

"Very good! She'll stay with us until you bring us the ransom. Now say goodbye to her; you'll be heading out soon," Teach informed him, then turned to talk with one of his officers.

Meanwhile, Jylling had come back up on deck and walked over to Dhlara. "It is impossible to sleep with this racket going on."

"The racket is they're going to extort the town," Dhlara summarized. "Apparently they captured some valuable people."

"Well at least they're not firing their cannons anymore. Where's Captain Edwards?"

"I'm not sure. He's wandered off somewhere."

"For saying he's a captain, he doesn't seem to do much."

"Aye, and you'd better hope it stays that way," a passing deckhand remarked.

"What?" said Jylling.

"That man Edwards is as poor a captain as I've seen," he explained, shaking his head with disgust. "Orders his crew to fire on every ship he sees, even a Spanish man of war, and there's never a fight he's won. All he's good at is eating his nails. We voted him removed from command of the Revenge after he attacked a ship double our size and guns."

"Wow. He's that bad?"

"He's as bad as they come. You'd do well to steer clear of any service under him, lad."

"Thanks. I'll keep that in mind."

The mariner nodded and went back to his work.

As predicted, Marks was summoned to join two of Teach's crew who were preparing to board a longboat that was about be lowered down into the water. Addressing Marks as he got in, Teach warned him, "You will have exactly two days to return here with everything written on that list and my men, Reeds and Starley here. If this mission of peace is met with betrayal by the people of Charles Town, we will come over the bar to burn every ship at anchor before the town and beat it about its ears!"

Beneath gray clouds that had gathered since morning, the prisoners from the *Crowley*, the pirates of Teach's fleet, and Dhlara watched as the three messengers rowed away toward Charles Town.

*

Five days later, Dhlara, Jylling, and Captain Edwards stood under a midday sun, looking up at Captain Teach as he thundered down at his hostages from the quarterdeck of the *Queen Anne's Revenge.* "Another two days have passed, and your Mister Marks has failed to do as he swore to do!" he roared and pointed at them accusingly. "I have been nothing but patient and lenient with you and your accursed town, and how have you rewarded me?! How has your governor rewarded me?! With treachery! Deceit! What can I do, as a man of my word, but kill all of you?!"

"Perhaps there have only been more difficulties in procuring what you requested, as before," Samuel Wragg offered hopefully.

"No, Mister Wragg! I gave your man an entire extra day simply because of your pleading, not even counting these last two, and what has come of it?! For all I know, your governor has had my sailors arrested, or worse! Why does that blasted Marks not return?! What reason can there be, but that he has left you to die?!"

"He sent Mister Hallett over to try to explain to you the obstacles he has had to overcome, and no one could expect him or Governor Johnson to have control over the weather."

"That was two days ago, Mister Wragg! I was understanding and forgiving then, and now what?! Lies and betrayal!" Teach slammed his fist down on the railing of the quarterdeck.

"Lies and betrayal!" a man from the *Crowley* shouted. "Damn Mister Marks to hell!"

"I know the bar, Captain!" another shouted. "I can guide your ship safely through the bar, and if the people of Charles Town don't send you your ransom, I will help you burn it to the ground!" At this, many other men yelled their agreement, particularly the crew of the *Crowley*.

"You would man these guns and fire upon that wretched place?!" Teach shouted. A cry went up from the hostages that they would. "Weigh anchor, then! Set sail for Charles Town harbour! Send the women and children and cowards below, and we will see if you are true to your word!" The deck came alive with pirates rushing to get the ship underway.

"Is looting cities a thing you've done a lot of?" Jylling asked Edwards.

"No! This is easily our finest adventure!" the captain answered happily. "Now, you'll have to excuse me, I need to be ready for battle!" He hopped off the cannon he had been sitting on and pushed his way through the bustle and crowd of hostages to the stairway to the lower deck.

Soon, the *Queen Anne's Revenge* was sailing further into the inlet, being guided through the maze of underwater sandbars by one of the *Crowley*'s crew. Teach's fleet, which was made up of not only the original four ships, but also an additional eight ships they had captured over the past five days, including the *Crowley* itself, followed the flagship upstream. They sailed past several tiny islands, past the mouth of a river a few miles off the port side, until the inlet narrowed as they headed north and Charles Town could be seen on the western bank. The water of the inlet lapped at a brick wall that ran north to south along the waterfront of the town. The wall was largely straight, except for a few triangular protrusions and one large half-circular bulge, all of which bristled with the barrels of cannon sticking out of square holes. Rectangular bastions on either end of the wall held more guns, and large Union Jacks waved in the breeze above these works. Clearly visible behind the wall were the buildings of the town itself, a flat expanse of two or three story structures, aside from the occasional higher reach of a church steeple. Several ships lay at anchor alongside the wall with their sails furled. The *Queen Anne's Revenge* positioned itself opposite the half-circular battery, and the rest of Teach's ships arranged themselves in a line above and below the frigate.

"Make ready to fire!" Teach shouted.

"Please, Captain, just another hour!" Wragg called up to him. "Whatever the delay is, perhaps now having so many of your guns pointed at them, they will be inclined to more readily accept your demands!"

"No more delays, Mister Wragg! Charles Town will burn for its insolence! Run out the guns!"

"Here, hold these," Captain Edwards told Dhlara, shoving his pistols at her while they stood on the port side of the ship.

"Are they loaded?"

"Not yet!"

She took them, and he pulled a spyglass from an interior pocket of his coat. Extending it, he put it up to his eye as he faced the town. "This is going to be good!"

"What are you looking for?" Jylling asked.

"Cannonballs are about to start crashing into those buildings! It's going to be a great show, if I can see it through the smoke."

"There's people in those buildings, Captain," Jylling reproached him.

"They oughtta get out of them, then. Cannonballs probably hurt. Where do you think they'll hit first?" Dhlara and Jylling just frowned and gave no response. Edwards didn't seem to notice. "I wonder if all their cannons will shoot at us! Then we'd *really* have a fight! That building... what? Aw, come on!"

"What?" Jylling asked, looking at Edwards as he peered through the spyglass.

"There's a little boat with a guy waving at us. Probably Mister Marks. Let's hope Captain Teach doesn't notice him."

"What?! Are the pirates with him?!"

"Yeah, looks like it."

Jylling bolted for the bridge, shouting, "Captain Teach! Captain Teach!" as he ran.

"What is it, boy?!" Teach called down as Jylling rushed past pirates ready to fire their cannon.

"Mister Marks is down there! There's a boat with Mister Marks and your men in it!"

Teach brought his own spyglass up to his eye and scanned the harbour. After a few moments, he said, "So it appears. Stand down, men! Let's see what develops!" The gunners relaxed, though still stood at their posts, and the hostages nervously tittered at this sudden relief of tension.

The whole fleet waited as three men in a tiny boat rowed up alongside the frigate, where the boat was then hoisted up by ropes. When it was level with the top deck, everyone aboard could clearly see Marks, Reeds, and Starley, including Captain Teach, having come down to meet them. The two pirates exited the boat and lifted a chest out of it, which they carried over to their captain and placed at his feet. They handed him a small key, which he used to unlock the chest, and pirates and hostages alike gathered around for a look. Jylling, Dhlara, and Captain Edwards had already been standing nearby, and were now pressed closer in by the curious mass of people. Teach opened the top of the chest, revealing a collection of labeled bottles and various metal instruments. The hostages and Marks stared at Teach, waiting for his reaction. He kneeled down and picked up one of the bottles, read the label, and swished a silver liquid around inside.

"This is indeed everything on the list. What the devil took you so long?!" Teach glared at Marks.

"Well, sir," Marks hesitantly answered, "after we were rescued by the fishermen, I brought your demands immediately to the governor and the council, all of whom immediately ordered the ransom be collected and delivered to you, fearing for the many lives of the King's subjects being held aboard your ship. However, once the chest was ready, and I wanted to return here, I could not find either of your representatives. I alerted Governor Johnson, who gave out for there to be a city wide search for these men, so that they may be returned to you unmolested as soon as possible. I am sorry to say that no one could find them until this morning, when it was discovered that they were asleep in a tavern, having consumed a tremendous amount of drink. I regret that it was only in the last few hours that I were able to sufficiently rouse these men and convince them to join me in bringing you the ransom."

Teach laughed and slapped one of his messengers on the back. The man's face was a sickly pallor and his grimace became even worse at his captain's roar of amusement. "Had a bit of fun, did you?" Teach asked him. The pirate grunted. "Well, you've been true to your word, Mister Marks," Teach loudly announced, so that the rest of the prisoners could hear. "You and everyone else from the *Crowley* will be put back aboard her and we'll leave you and all the other captured ships here in the harbour, true to my word. We'll be keeping your goods, and your finer things, of course, but you'll be safe and sound in Charles Town by the end of the day. It has been a pleasure doing business with you," and then he took Marks's hand and shook it.

Marks, startled, unconsciously left his hand limp in Teach's grasp and hurriedly cleared his throat to say, "Thank you, Captain!" as the pirate turned away and headed for the bridge.

Captain Edwards, who by now had retrieved his pistols, pushed past several of the crew of the *Queen Anne's Revenge* and bent over to inspect the contents of the chest himself. He brought one of the bottles close to his face and said in a puzzled voice, "Mercury?!" He set it down, held up an instrument which looked like it was used to inject some sort of substance through a narrow hole, and looked at it in confusion. Putting it back as well, he rifled through the chest, pushing vials aside to investigate what was further down. "No jewels, no gold doubloons, no bullion, no specie, nothing!" he exclaimed, exasperated. "Where's all the bloody treasure?!"

"It's right here," one of the pirates told him. "That's medicine."

"Medicine?! Nobody ever heard of a horde of *medicine*!"

"There's many a man on this ship suffering from ailments a chest of Spanish coin can't cure. That's why the cap'n's the cap'n."

Edwards stood up and stared at the sailor, giving him a look as if he thought he was insane, then walked back over to

Dhlara and Jylling. "These are some rubbish pirates," he said.

XII

Burning Bridges

After the hostages and captured ships, but not the cargo and valuables they had carried, had been returned to Charles Town as promised, the fleet sailed north along the coast for a few days. On the last of these, Dhlara and Jylling stood on the top deck of the *Queen Anne's Revenge* under a midday sun. Hasdrubal sat on a chest that had been brought up on deck for him; a pair of crude wooden crutches rested against the gunwale. What remained of the lower part of his left leg was still bandaged, but his health had noticeably improved. He was turning over a simple, wooden prosthetic foot that the ship's carpenter had made for him. The carpenter had called it a foot, but only because that is what it was meant to replace; in reality it was just a slightly cone shaped narrow block of wood. Leather straps for attaching it to his legs flopped around as he rotated it.

"Well, Hasdrubal, at least you'll make a pretty good pirate now," Jylling joked.

"No he wouldn't," said one of the crew as he passed them.

"What?" asked Dhlara.

The mariner turned around to face them. "He wouldn't make a very good pirate. How's a man supposed to run out a gun or board a ship missing a foot? There's no need for such a fellow when there are so many able-bodied men who can go on the account."

"But pirates have peglegs!" Jylling protested.

"Not here, they don't. Sorry, mate," he nodded to Hasdrubal and left.

"He's right," said Hasdrubal. "I'm not much of a fighter anymore."

"Ah, fighting's overrated anyway," said Jylling. "You might—"

"Have somebody shoot you?" Hasdrubal grinned ruefully. "I am one who knows it. I have no desire to be one of these pirates anyway."

"Well, neither do I, but this is where we are, and who knows how long their hospitality will last," Dhlara said in a quieter voice.

"Do we know where we're headed, anyway?" Jylling asked.

"A place called Topsail Inlet, if I remember right," she said.

"What's there that they're going to plunder?"

"What Captain Edwards told me is they're actually going to rest there for a few days and then sail to a place called Bath to get a pardon from the governor there."

"A pardon?! After besieging a whole city?!"

"That's what he said."

"Well, what do we want to do? Like you said, we can't stay on a pirate ship forever."

"I don't know. I don't know where there is to go."

"Even if they'd let us stay here," said Hasdrubal, "we should not want to. A ship full of men engaged in crime is bound to have hardships. We ought to find a place to live and provide for ourselves as best we can."

"I do *not* want to live in the seventeen hundreds," said Jylling.

"No, we don't," Hasdrubal agreed, "and neither does Gordon, I assume. But here we are. We ought at least make our current situation better, if we don't know how to get out of it."

"I can ask Captain Edwards what Bath is like," Dhlara suggested. "Maybe we can live there."

Hasdrubal nodded. "Yes, and if that isn't a suitable place, he might know one that is."

"I'll go find him, then. Do you need anything?" she asked Hasdrubal. He leaned his head back against the gunwale and waved his hand.

"No, thank you."

"I'll go with you," said Jylling.

154

They walked toward the stern of the frigate. As they came to one of the stairways leading down to the lower deck, they heard a voice ranting. "No! No! I don't know what they do in France, but I don't do that!" The same red haired sailor Dhlara had seen in pursuit of a chicken came up the stairs. He saw Jylling, who had an eyebrow raised at him. "Don't let that doctor try to cure you of anything!" he told Jylling. "No, that ain't a doctor at all, that's a man who wants to shove great big things up another man's John Thomas, that's who he is!"

"...What are you on about?" Jylling said slowly.

"We went through all this trouble with this wretched Charles Town to get that medicine out of the blasted governor, and now this doctor tells me the medicine comes in a huge thing that's gotta be shoved up where I don't want it! No, sir! That's how I got this ailment in the first, by putting things where they don't belong!"

The man who had operated on Hasdrubal came up the stairs as well. "I am not a doctor," he said.

"Ah HA!" the red-haired pirate exclaimed.

"I am a surgeon, which is not a physician, and if you would not like to be cured that is of no consequence to me. It is up to you."

At that moment, the ship beneath their feet jolted and lurched, pitching them forward. They were all thrown down onto the deck amid the noise of groaning and cracking timbers. As they lay flat, they felt the deck tilt hard to starboard beneath them. The ship, though its sails were still full, came to a sudden stop.

"What was that?!" the surgeon cried.

Captain Edwards, wearing his morning gown and a pair of slippers with his brace of pistols in his hands, came running up the stairs, pushing past the surgeon. "Is there a fight?! Shall I repel boarders?!" he yelled excitedly.

"No, there's not a fight!" the red-haired man answered with disdain as he got back to his feet. "I'd say we just ran aground!"

"The ground attacked us?! The traitor! Whoah!" Edwards lost his footing on the now slanted deck and fell down. The surgeon came up onto the deck as the rest of the crew below started to rush up the stairs to find out what had happened. Dozens of crewmen crowded the portside gunwale, all looking over the edge and pointing. Dhlara got up and went back to Hasdrubal, who was now sitting on the railing and gripping the rigging. His chest and crutches had slid down across the deck and now lay against the starboard gunwale.

"Are you alright?" she asked him.

"Yes, I am! That was quite a tumble! We appear to have hit a sandbar, however," he said, leaning back and looking over his shoulder at the water beneath him. Dhlara held onto the railing and looked down as well. She saw the top of a pile of sand that lurked just below the surface of the ocean. Even this close she could barely see it through the reflections of light, but the blue-green water was clear enough.

As the pirates gazed at the cause of their new misfortune, one of the sloops, the *Adventure*, pulled alongside the *Queen Anne's Revenge*'s starboard side and its crew threw ropes across to the stricken vessel. They were fastened to the railing by the men of the flagship and tugged taught by the *Adventure* in an effort to pull the frigate free, but it stayed still, completely unmoved. After a while of this without any greater success, it was given up, and the *Adventure* was pulled in closer to the frigate and the crews began transferring cargo to the sloop.

"Captain Edwards!" Captain Teach called from the quarterdeck. Edwards, now wearing his full dressing gown ensemble, came up to the bridge and the two captains conversed. Several men were sent below decks, then, after a few minutes, they came up again and reported back to the captains. When the conversation was over, Bonnet descended from the quarterdeck and walked over to Dhlara, Jylling, and Hasdrubal.

"The ship's ruined!" he said airily.

"That's it? It's done?" said Hasdrubal.

"Yes! The keel is broken. They'll be taking the men and provisions onto the other ships. Meanwhile, however, I'm going to go ahead to Bath and get a royal pardon. You all should come with me!"

"What about everything here?" Dhlara asked.

"Captain Teach will take care of everything, and he'll join us in Bath with the rest of the fleet in a couple days."

"We actually were thinking about staying ashore in a city or town we come to. Is Bath a good place to settle?"

"I don't know," Edwards shrugged. "But we can find out if you like it when we get there!"

"That sounds okay."

"Brilliant! Come on, they're readying a longboat for us," and he turned around and walked off toward the portside. Dhlara looked down at the listing deck of the *Queen Anne's Revenge*.

"I'm guessing your crutches won't do very well with the ship like this," she said to Hasdrubal.

"No indeed."

Dhlara and Jylling took each of his arms over their shoulders, and slowly the three of them walked across the deck, following where Edwards had gone. When they came to the portside gunwale, they looked over the side and saw a longboat in the water lashed to the frigate. A rope ladder hung down to the boat. Edwards sat on top of one of several barrels that had been loaded into the boat; behind his head was the canvas of a triangular sail attached the boat's small mast. Two other pirates sat in the front; one of them had a scraggly brown beard with shaved cheeks and upper lip, and the other was clean-shaven with shoulder-length black hair, but both were young and fit.

"Come on, then! Climb aboard!" Edwards called.

"You guys go on, I'll go get your crutches," said Jylling.

Dhlara put a knee on the railing and swung her other leg over the side to the ladder. She climbed down to the boat and then stood at the bottom, waiting to help Hasdrubal. He came down much more slowly, gripping the rope with both hands before moving his one foot, but easily accomplished his descent on his own. Jylling came back and handed the crutches down, then joined them in the boat. Hasdrubal sat next to one of the barrels while Dhlara and Jylling took their spots in the back. Several sailors aboard the flagship untied the ropes attached to the railing and tossed them down into the longboat.

"Alright you fellows: east!" said Edwards.

The pirates in the front put out oars and dipped them into the water, pulling the boat away from the damaged hulk of the *Queen Anne's Revenge* until the canvas caught wind and sped them on. Captain Teach stood on the poop deck watching them sail away. "I'll see you in Bath, and we'll toast the Act of Grace!" Edwards called, waving at him.

"Farewell, Captain Edwards," Teach shouted back.

*

They had sailed for a day, camped on shore, and sailed again for the rest of the next day when they arrived at Bath at dusk. They had passed islands of sand dunes, then long stretches of flat land covered in tall trees that came right up to the tranquil coastline, until they passed the mouth of a river and came to a clearing in the trees right by the water, which contained a small town of no more than twenty buildings. Edwards directed the boat be put ashore, which was done.

"Very good!" he exclaimed as he hopped out of the boat. "Now, let's go find this governor." He strode off toward the closest building and knocked on the door. "Hello!" Dhlara and Jylling heard him say as they followed after him. The two pirates were close behind. Dhlara and Jylling had learned from the past few days that the one with the beard was named Jack Allen, and the other was Stephen Dillon. "Where is Governor Eden?" Edwards continued. A low, annoyed voice answered, to which Edwards gave a "Thank you!" and spun around on his heel and marched off toward another building. Coming to another wooden house not much different than the first, he again rapped his knuckles against the door. After a few moments, a plainly dressed man in his forties opened the door. He seemed surprised by Captain Edwards's appearance, looking up at the yellow wig, down at the blue dressing gown, and down again at the buckled shoes.

"Good evening," the man said.

"Hello! Are you the governor Charles Eden?" Edwards

inquired.

"Yes, that's right. Who are you?"

"I am Major Stede Bonnet, also known as the pirate Captain Edwards. I have come to surrender myself to you and receive the King's Pardon."

"Are you now? Are you not the same Edwards as sails with the pirate Teach? You took two ships this year that I recall, and now there are rumours that you blockaded Charles Town. The pardon was for crimes committed before January fifth. I will have all of you as prisoners and you'll face the proper justice!"

"I understand the limit of the pardon, but I did not hear of it but very late, and in hopes of making up this difference I have also brought four barrels of molasses and sugar to be surrendered as well."

"Four barrels? I will have a look at them and then we will see what can be done."

Captain Edwards, or Major Bonnet, or whoever he was, led the governor to the longboat resting on the shoreline, in which Hasdrubal was still sitting. Eden stepped into the boat and lifted the lid off one of the barrels. He poked at the dark liquid inside, licked his finger, then opened another barrel, this one white inside with sugar. He picked up a cone-shaped chunk of it and knocked it against the rim of the barrel, creating a thunking sound.

"Do you repent all of your sins, Major Bonnet?" said Eden as he picked at the cone.

"Oh yes, I do!"

"Will you go a pirating any longer?"

"No, never "

"How about the rest of you? Do you repent your sins and your crimes against the crown?" Eden looked around at everyone else who had accompanied Bonnet.

"We do indeed, sir," Dillon answered, with Allen nodding his agreement. Jylling and Dhlara awkwardly nodded their heads as well.

"I'm sure you learned a lesson, didn't you?" the governor leered at Hasdrubal, after glancing down at his missing foot.

"I did," he replied.

"It can be supposed that a man who repents after the fifth of January is not so different from a man who repents before then. Bring all of these barrels over to my house and I will issue your pardons."

"I should also like to sail to Saint Thomas and get a Letter of Marque to fight the Spanish," said Bonnet.

"I can endorse such a voyage. Let's go set everything in order," said Eden, and he and Bonnet walked back to the governor's house. Dhlara and Jylling helped Dillon and Allen unload the barrels from the longboat and carry them over to Eden's home, whereupon Bonnet came out carrying a stack of papers.

"We are all now officially retired pirates!" he announced happily.

"I never was a pirate," said Jylling.

"No matter, you've now retired from it anyway. Let's go sail south again and see if we can't meet Captain Teach on his way up here and give him the good news."

"Hang on," said Dhlara, "what's this about 'Major Stede Bonnet'?"

"That's my name," said Edwards.

"You gave your name to us as Edwards," she replied.

"Of course I did. If I'm going to go be a pirate, I should have a pirate name."

"But Stede Bonnet is your real name?"

"Yes, it is," he said, and walked back toward the longboat.

Dhlara motioned for Jylling to stay behind. She leaned in close and whispered, "This place really doesn't look like a good place to live."

"Yeah, this place looks terrible," Jylling agreed. "Barely anybody lives here, and that's gotta be for a reason. Might be easier to keep living with pirates. I'm sure they'll come into a port better than this at some point."

With that, they returned to the longboat and pushed it back out to sea.

*

They did not see Captain Teach or any of the ships of the fleet at any point between Bath and Topsail Inlet. Stede Bonnet, Allen, and Dillon had talked it over during the next day and night of sailing, and decided it must have taken Teach longer than he expected to unload all of the cargo and equipment from the *Queen Anne's Revenge*. Or perhaps he had even managed to free the frigate from the sandbar, discovered the damage was not as dire as was first thought, and even now the ship was undergoing repairs.

Upon returning to Topsail Inlet in the morning, however, and rounding an island of sand dunes, they saw the *Queen Anne's Revenge*, still motionless and broken, but now abandoned. The *Revenge* lay at anchor nearby, but, strangely, it appeared just as lifeless. No one walked its deck; no one was up in the rigging; they could not see anyone onboard at all. And, looking around, they saw no sign of the *Adventure*, or any other ship. They sailed up alongside the *Revenge* and climbed aboard, which was considerably easier to do on the sloop compared with the frigate. Dhlara and Jylling helped Hasdrubal up while the pirates quickly searched the ship.

"It's all gone," Allen reported as he came up from the lower deck. "Everything in the hold is missing, except for a few barrels of meat."

"And there's certainly no one onboard," Dillon added.

"This is outrageous! Blasted pirates stole from me!" Bonnet exclaimed, absent-mindedly taking out his pistols and brandishing them. He ran up to the quarterdeck and looked out at the ocean around him. "We'll have to hunt down the traitor Teach and give him a battle!"

"There's only three of us and a cripple, sir," Allen reminded him in a tired tone.

"The rest have deserted us! We have to sail with what we have!"

"Teach can't have taken hundreds of men with him on just the Adventure. And if he had, we still can't bring a fight to anyone with a crew like this."

"Where am I to get a crew, Jack?!"

"Fish Town isn't far from here. We can put in there and

see if we can find anyone to join us, and ask if there is any word about Teach and everyone else."

"Fish Town! You there!" Bonnet shook his gun at the four of them. "We sail for Fish Town! And then, *revenge!*"

The skeleton crew set about getting the ship underway, with Jylling and Dhlara helping where they could based on instruction from Dillon and Allen. Soon enough, after the anchor was raised, the sails set, and the longboat taken up, Allen was at the wheel and the *Revenge* was sailing north into Topsail Inlet, passing islands of sand with wafting dune grass off the portside, and they soon arrived at Fish Town, which appeared to be was sandier than Bath, with fewer trees, and, if anything, even fewer buildings. They docked at a runty wooden wharf amid a handful of fishing boats, and even as they were tying the ship down it became clear the town was awash with pirates. Far more men, and they were all men, milled about the houses than could possibly live there. And, more than that, the sound of drunken singing carried over to the *Revenge*.

"I believe we have found our shipmates!" Bonnet declared.

"Captain Edwards!" someone said. "I knew it was the Revenge when I saw it on the horizon," they said. The red haired crewman they had last seen aboard the *Queen Anne's Revenge* strode up carrying a clay cup.

"What happened? Where's Captain Teach?" Bonnet pressed.

"Same day as you left, he and at least a hundred hands turned their swords on the rest of us and took everything we had. He must have designed to run his ship aground, because those that turned needed no convincing; they acted as if they already knew his plan."

"He meant to wreck such a powerful ship?" asked Bonnet.

"Seems that way."

"Why would he do that?"

"I don't know; perhaps he got sick of splitting shares with the likes of us."

"Where did he go?"

"I couldn't say. He just left us here after taking what we had that he wanted and sailed away."

"Come aboard, Pell, and we'll track him down!"

"Aye, I might go with you," Pell replied into his cup as he went to swig the last of what was inside.

"Fantastic! Now we just need a few more men and we'll go get the rascals."

"I don't know how many here will join. There's a number of them disposed to retire from this life, and there's others talking about starting their own company."

"Who can retire at a time when there's thieves to catch?!"

"I thought we just retired?" Jylling interjected.

"Before *I* got pirated! Now things are different!" Bonnet explained. "I meant to retire with all the plunder I'd taken!"

"Teach kept a couple dozen — souls we'd taken with the Adventure, in the main — aboard with him," Pell informed them. "I think he meant to set them on a maroon island. If we could find them, they'd be in a position to accept an offer to sail with us."

"Splendid idea!" Bonnet exclaimed. "Set a course for Maroon Island!"

The *Revenge* was loosed from its moorings and sailed back out of the inlet. After it was explained to Bonnet that any island could be used to maroon people, and Pell did not know exactly which one Teach had intended to use, the wigged captain took his spyglass out and surveyed any islands they passed. They had not traveled very far when he announced a sighting, "Oh, hello! There's people over there. Do you suppose they're ours?" Everyone aboard looked toward where his spyglass was pointed: at a strip of sand that barely came up above the water. It was only sand — no trees, no grass, no brush — and a group of waggling blobs whose motions were recognizable as those of people.

"They do appear to be marooned," Pell remarked. "Even if they aren't our men, they might be willing to become so, for a rescue."

"Bring us over to them! But don't get too close," Bonnet ordered.

Allen piloted the *Revenge* toward the island until it was a hundred yards off the starboard side. A jolly boat, which was smaller than the longboat, was hauled up by ropes and brought level with the gunwale.

"Come along, Dhlara, Jylling!" said Bonnet as he stepped into the boat. "Let's go get some pirates!"

"Do you really need us?" said Jylling.

"Of course I do! Those two can manage the ship, and Hasdrubal should rest."

Jylling followed Dhlara into the boat and it was lowered down to the water. They sat in the front and took up oars, but Bonnet laid himself out, putting his hands behind his head and his buckled black shoes up onto the side of the boat. He smiled contentedly as he watched them row. When the hull bumped into the edge of the island, Bonnet jumped out of the boat and splashed through the shallow surf up to the dry sand. Turning around, Dhlara and Jylling saw that the people on the island, and there were indeed about two dozen of them, had gathered closeby, having watched their approach.

"Captain Edwards!" some of the men cried.

"Hello, boys! Are you tired of being here?"

"Yes!"

"Well, I have just been pardoned by the governor of North Carolina, and I have a commission to bring the Revenge to Saint Thomas to privateer for the Danish king against the Spanish. Any of you that want to can come with me, and perhaps we can find that rascal Teach and teach him a lesson along the way. Or, you could stay here, and do whatever it is you're doing here."

A roar went up as the starving men competed with each other to voice their desire to leave the island with him.

"I'll go a privateering with you, sir!"

"Three cheers for our good captain!"

"To Saint Thomas!"

Bonnet looked over his shoulder at the occupants of the boat and grinned. He ordered three of the maroonees into the boat and to take up the two other oars, and they all rowed back over to the *Revenge*. Everyone but the two oarsmen transferred from the boat to the sloop, and then the boat was rowed back to the island. Over several trips back and forth, the jolly boat ferried the twenty-five newly re-recruited pirates onto Bonnet's ship. As this transpired, however, another boat sailed over to the *Revenge.*

"Ship ahoy!" a voice called up.

Bonnet leaned over the portside railing. "Ahoy! What is it?"

"Am I speaking with the captain of this vessel?" a man standing up in the back of the boat asked. He was very thin and held a wide-brimmed fisherman's hat in his hands. The rest of his boat only held another two men, who were seated.

"Yes! Who are you?"

"My name's Bates, sir. Can I interest you or your men in some fresh cider or apples?"

"I think so. Bring up what you have and I'll look at it."

Several crates of apples and jugs of cider were brought on board, accompanied by the crew of the boat. Bonnet and the apple merchant agreed to a price, which Bonnet paid in coins he produced from a pouch inside his dressing gown.

"Thank you, sir! And take care if you mean to sail north! For my part, I am sailing to Charles Town," Bates advised Bonnet as he stepped toward the railing to return to his boat

"Why is that?" Bonnet asked.

"Pirates, sir. Why, only two days ago, when we was at Ocracoke Inlet, we saw a pirate sloop at anchor. They were carousing about something; celebrating robbing some poor souls, I wager."

"Did you see their captain?" asked Pell, who had come over after overhearing the conversation.

"Tall man. Big black beard. Do you know of him?"

"We do," said Bonnet.

"Don't tell me he robbed you?"

"Yes, and marooned my crew."

"Well, then, I would stay clear of Ocracoke, if I was you. Now if you'll pardon me," said the boatsman, putting his hat on his head, "I'll be on my way, captain."

As Bates climbed back down to his boat, Dhlara leaned over to Jylling and Hasdrubal and said in a low voice, "Bonnet seems really intent on fighting something; I think he's going to go straight after Blackbeard now. We're going to need to get out of here soon if we want to avoid combat. Maybe we should see if we can get a ride from this guy. I haven't seen anywhere yet that looked like a better place to live in this area than Charles Town."

"I agree," Jylling whispered. "If Bonnet's as bad a captain as they all seem to think, this might not end well."

"Will he have a problem with us wanting to leave?" Hasdrubal wondered.

"I don't think so; he seems to like us well enough," said Dhlara. She approached Bonnet. "Captain, we appreciate all the help you've given us, and we thank you for saving Hasdrubal's life, but we are not the fighting sort, so we would like to inquire if we could go with that boat to Charles Town and live a calmer life."

"What, you don't want to do battle with Captain Teach?" Bonnet asked.

"If it's all the same to you, we'd prefer to be on our way."

"That is entirely acceptable to me." He went to the railing and called down, "Ahoy, Bates! I'll give you twice as much to take three fine people with you to Charles Town!"

"I would be glad to, sir!" Bates replied.

Bonnet threw down a pouch of coins to the boat, then took out another and handed it to Dhlara. "Take this with you, to aid you on your way," he told her.

"Oh," she blurted out, surprised. "I, well— thank you, Captain!"

"Now go on, then! We have a damnable pirate to chase!"

"Okay! Thank you!" she repeated, and rushed to climb down to the boat. The unloading of most of their wares to the *Revenge* had created more space, but the boat was still crowded by the time all three of them were aboard. Ropes were thrown down from the sloop, and the little sail pulled them away south. As the distance grew, Stede Bonnet walked to the stern of his ship and waved goodbye.

XIII

Another Stranger Me

Bates brought Dhlara, Jylling, and Hasdrubal to Charles Town without incident. They used the money Bonnet had given them, which they discovered was quite considerable, to obtain room and board at an inn near the docks called *The Three Harmonious Fish.* After a few weeks, Hasdrubal became a tutor to the children of several wealthy merchant families, educating them in many areas such as ancient history, math, and navigation, for which he was paid well. Dhlara and Jylling, however, had less knowledge and skills to impart or apply, so Jylling found work as a dockhand, while Dhlara became a servant at the inn.

This lasted for several months, through the summer and into the fall, with the three of them sharing a single room as they learned about their new job and surroundings and talked over what had happened to them, and what they could do to get back to the Ministries. They came to the conclusion that Stede Bonnet must not be a very good pirate to give away so much money, and Teach must have intended to wreck the *Queen Anne's Revenge* in order to steal from Bonnet and the rest of the pirates. They decided, too, that all they could do was save the money they earned and one day charter a ship to search the area where Bonnet had found them for the island Gordon was on, if he was still there.

Pirates, for much of this time, remained the center of Charles Town's attention. Ships were regularly taken by pirates lurking at the bar between Charles Town and the ocean, and not long after the time travelers arrived, another pirate crew copied Teach's example and forced the city to pay a ransom. But in early October, Stede Bonnet became the one most talked about, when he and his entire crew were brought into port as prisoners by Colonel William Rhett, who had been sent out of the city the month before to hunt pirates. Despite Bonnet's previous encounter with the city and the continuing attacks on ships that left their harbour, the people of Charles Town seemed to like him. While he was held prisoner in the provost marshal's house, he was regarded as a brave, honourable gentleman whose primary enemy had been aristocrats and immense fortunes. The idea of such a person had a way of appealing to those who were not aristocrats or fantastically rich, which happened to be almost everyone.

In late October, however, news spread fast across the city: Stede Bonnet had escaped. Governor Johnson ordered a search across all of South Carolina to recapture him, and offered a reward of seven hundred pounds. Within a couple weeks, it was announced that Colonel Rhett had taken Bonnet prisoner yet again, and this time he was locked up in a wooden building atop the strongest point in the harbour's defensive wall, known as Half Moon Battery, which Dhlara recognized as the half-circular bulge of brick bristling with cannon she had seen from the deck of the *Queen Anne's Revenge*.

Meanwhile, another pirate captain, Christopher Moody, had become an increasing concern to Charles Town. Governor Johnson announced that he would bring Moody to justice himself, and put together a fleet of four ships, which included Bonnet's sloop, and a crew of three hundred volunteers. A few days after Bonnet's recapture, a pair of vessels were seen lurking in the bar, prompting a rumour to spread that the ships were Moody's, and that the governor would sail his fleet out to challenge them. A crowd gathered on the wall looking out over the harbour, eager to see a battle. Dhlara, Jylling, and Hasdrubal were in their midst, curious as to what would transpire.

Soon enough, Johnson's four ships left their docks, but with their gunports closed, so as to appear to be merchantmen. At the sight of this, one of the two suspicious vessels set sail and approached the departing fleet just as they were leaving the harbour. The crowd laughed when they saw it raise a black flag to the top of its mast, and watched with anticipation as the governor's fleet made no hostile action in response, allowing the pirate to sail unmolested between two of their ships. As it came alongside them, however, Johnson's ships threw open the hatches to their gunports, ran out their cannon, and fired all of them at once. Dozens of iron balls crashed into the pirate ship from both sides, breaking through the wooden hull and blasting showers of splinters at the surprised crew. The crowd cheered at the sudden roar of cannon and jets of fire and smoke. After that, both of the pirate ships turned and attempted to sail away, but the governor's fleet gave chase, and for several hours there was a ferocious battle. In the end, the pirates surrendered, and they were brought into port as prisoners aboard their own ships.

A few days later came November 10th, which had been announced as the day Stede Bonnet would be tried for piracy. The rest of his crew had already been tried and hung, except for a handful who everyone agreed were forced by threats to join. Dhlara, Jylling, and Hasdrubal had decided they wanted to be present at the trial, not only to learn Bonnet's fate, but they also felt they owed a debt to the eccentric captain, so they could at least show him they had not forgotten about him, even if they couldn't do much to help. Hasdrubal happened to be a tutor to the son of a merchant named John Guerard, who was friends with the owner, Garrett Vanvelsin, of the house that the trial would be conducted in. After a few inquiries and exchanges of coin, Hasdrubal had arranged for the three of them to be allowed to be present at the trial.

That morning, they walked down the brick sidewalk of Tradd Street, heading toward Vanvelsin's house. They each had an overcoat or cloak on, which they now hid their hands inside for warmth. Beneath his overcoat, Hasdrubal wore a bright red eighteenth century suit with black knee-high boots; he had had a proper prosthetic foot made for him, which looked and functioned much more like a foot and could be fit inside normal footwear. He still walked with a noticeable limp, however, and it hurt to wear for a long period of time, so he had readily adopted the popular custom of walking with a cane.

Jylling had put on a plain brown suit and brown shoes with his legs clad in white stockings, and Dhlara wore a white petticoat and light blue woolen short gown. Both Jylling and Hasdrubal had on tricorne hats, whereas Dhlara's head was covered by a simple shawl. Jylling had grown his hair out from his old buzzcut, and now tufts of black hair poked out from under his hat.

Accompanied by the clack of Hasdrubal's cane, they walked until they came to a large house at a street corner on their right, in front of which a crowd had gathered. After the trio made their way through the throng, Hasdrubal knocked on the door. A man in black and white clothes opened it.

"Good morning! Please come in, sir," he greeted Hasdrubal. They all stepped inside and the servant closed the door behind them. "You were expected, sir. May I take your coats?"

Once he had all three over his arm, he led them down a hallway, past a line of soldiers, to a large, wood-paneled parlour filled with people. Against the far wall, behind a long table on a raised platform, sat eleven men wearing long black robes and full bottom white wigs. To the left, seated in chairs in front of a set of windows, were twelve men of more average appearance. Two smaller tables were in the middle of the room; two men in normal suits and white wigs sat at the one on the left facing the judges, and behind the one on the right sat Stede Bonnet, in plainer clothes than his usual and without his own accustomed wig, or any wig. Soldiers in red uniforms stood guard near him.

Closest to the three of them, however, was a set of four pew style benches, which were mostly filled with spectators. Hasdrubal led them to one on the right and they shuffled into their seats as the clerk of the court, standing at his desk in front of and slightly beneath the judges' platform, read aloud from a sheet of paper.

"The jurors for our sovereign lord the king, do on their oath present that Stede Bonnet, alias Edwards, alias Thomas, late of the island of Barbadoes, mariner; David Heriot, late of the island of Jamaica, mariner; Edward Robinson, late of

170

Newcastle upon Tyne, mariner," and so it went on in laborious detail. After more names and details, he came to what sounded like a description of the crime, "did piratically and feloniously set upon, break, board, and enter a certain merchant-sloop, called the Francis, Peter Manwareing, commander, then being a sloop of certain persons — to the jurors aforesaid unknown — and then and there piratically and feloniously did make an assault, in and upon the said Peter Manwareing, and other his mariners, whose names to the jurors aforesaid are unknown, in the same sloop, against the peace of God, and of our said now sovereign lord the king." and so on for several more minutes as he read a description of all the things taken from the sloop and their monetary value.

Once the clerk finished and sat down, the centermost judge, whom Dhlara, Jylling, and Hasdrubal knew from his prominence in South Carolina to be a man named Nicholas Trott, looked at Bonnet and asked, "How do you plead?"

Bonnet stood up and answered, "Not guilty."

"You are to come upon your trial this day upon the first Indictment, and you have pleaded not guilty, so that what evidence you have must be ready," said the judge, an older man with a stern face.

"My pleading not guilty is because I may have something to offer in my defense, and therefore I hope none of the bench will take it amiss."

The clerk announced that the trial for the first indictment, for piratically taking the sloop *Francis*, would proceed. Then the twelve men by the windows were told to rise, take a Bible in their hands, and repeat after the clerk, saying, "I swear by Almighty God that I will faithfully try the defendant and give a true verdict according to the evidence." Once they had all finished swearing the oath, they were asked to sit down again.

"You may begin," said Trott to the two men of the prosecution at the left table.

One of them, the assistant attorney general Thomas Hepworth, stood to address the court, "May it please your honours, and you gentlemen of the Jury; the prisoner who now stands arraigned at the bar has been guilty of many piracies, committed many robberies, ruined many families, and been the occasion of many most cruel and inhuman murders, and all that within a very short time past. Should I here descend into all the particulars, I shall take up too much of your time.

"You know, all of ye, I believe, after what manner he lately fled from justice. Nay, he was not satisfied with his own escape, but he must tamper with the king's evidence, to avoid others being prosecuted, and prevailed with the Master Heriot to run away with him, who has been since killed. And I believe the prisoner at the bar cannot, upon reflection, but think himself answerable for that man's death. Nay, some people took particular notice of the prisoner's behaviour at the time when Teach having got the command from him, he began to reflect upon his past course of life, and was then filled with such horror, that he was perfectly confounded with shame at the many detestable crimes he had been guilty of, and said, lie would gladly leave off that way of living, being fully tired, and having got considerably by it, but he should be ashamed ever to see the face of an Englishman: therefore if he could not get to Spain or Portugal, where he might be undiscovered, he would live and die in the same course of life, viz in piracy and robbery.

"The trial of this man ought to be the more considerable, as he was the great ringleader of them, who has seduced many poor, ignorant men to follow his course of living, and ruined many poor wretches, some of whom lately suffered, who with their last breath expressed a great satisfaction at the prisoner's being apprehended, and charged the ruin of themselves and loss of their lives entirely upon him.

"We shall now proceed to call our evidences."

One of the guards brought over the red-haired Pell, who was made to stand in front of a chair to the right of the judges' bench. The clerk held out a Bible, told Pell to put his hand on it and raise his other hand, and say, "I swear by Almighty God that the evidence I shall give shall be the truth, the whole truth and nothing but the truth." When he finished, he was instructed to sit in the chair.

"Pell, begin with the first Indictment, and when you was

first acquainted with Major Bonnet," said Hepworth.

"It was at the bay of Honduras," Pell told him, "but Captain Teach was commander in chief."

The second prosecutor, the attorney general Richard Allen, stood and asked the witness, "This, I observe, was before they went to Topsail Inlet at North Carolina."

"Yes, sir, for when we came to Topsail Inlet, Robert Tucker was chose quartermaster and we went out to go to Saint Thomas's for a commission to go a privateering against the Spaniards, but the first vessel we saw we took."

"What did you take out of her?" asked Hepworth.

"We took some provisions."

"Had you no provisions on board the Revenge?" Allen inquired.

"Yes, sir, some beef, pork, and flour."

"What was the next vessel you took?" Hepworth asked.

"A sloop belonging to Bermudas. After we had discharged her, we took another in which were eight negroes. We took out two and left three men and two women, and sent three bands more which made eight, and the next day we gave chase to two ships belonging to Glasgow in Scotland, and in the evening we came up with them, and the other turned tail, and we never saw them more after that. And after we had taken some tobacco and other goods, we discharged them. We took, as I remember, two vessels belonging to Bristol, when Captain Read was taken."

"What do you know of Captain Manwareing?" the attorney general asked.

"We were at an anchor near Cape James alias Cape Inlopen, and a little before night we saw a sloop come to an anchor at the month of the river, and we sent off the dory with five bands, and in a little time they returned with Captain Manwareing. And the next day we hauled the sloop long-side the schooner which we had taken before, and hoisted out several hogsheads of molasses and rum, and put them on board the canoe, and put some pitch and tar on board the sloop."

"Who gave you orders for the doing of that?"

"I cannot tell, sir."

"Did you see Major Bonnet on board Manwareing's sloop?"

"I cannot say he was, neither do I know certainly that he was not."

Judge Trott broke in, "Was he not your commander?"

Pell nodded, "He was called our captain, to be sure."

"That is all," the attorney general said as he and Hepworth sat back down.

"Have you any questions to ask the king's evidence?" the clerk asked Bonnet.

"I do," he answered, and rose to his feet. "Do not you believe in your conscience," he asked Pell, "that when we left Topsail Inlet, it was to go to Saint Thomas's? And there were near forty hands, and they concluded to a marooning?"

"I did believe it was so till after we were out."

Trott glared at Bonnet and said, "That was what they accused you for on their trials: that you deceived them, under a pretense of going to Saint Thomas's."

Bonnet smiled and shrugged at the judge, saying, "I am sorry that they should take the opportunity of my absence to accuse me of that which I was free from."

One of the judges sitting beside Judge Trott spoke up, "If there were forty hands on board, it cannot be thought that he had power to command them."

"But he was commander in chief among them," Trott countered, "and that after they went a pirating; was it not so, boatswain?"

"He went by that name; but the quartermaster had more power than he," Pell answered.

"What do you mean by your evasions? Was he commander in chief, or was he not?"

"He was."

"Then who had the greatest power?" the judge pressed the witness. Pell shifted in his seat, uncomfortable with the question, but remained quiet.

Allen continued his questioning: "Do you know if he received his share of Captain Manwareing's goods? Or did any receive it for him?"

"Sir, it was the quartermaster took care of that."

Judge Trott cut in again to ask Pell, "He was commander in chief, and therefore I suppose he had a double share?"

"I did never enquire whether he had or not."

"Boatswain, tell the truth!" the judge demanded, pointing his finger at the sailor. "Had he his share, or had he not?!"

"He had it."

Stede Bonnet interjected, "Boatswain, did you ever hear me force any man to go?"

"No, Major, I cannot say I did," Pell answered.

"Do you not remember, that when we left Topsail Inlet, and they began to quarrel about provision, that I said I would leave the sloop?"

"I do remember you said so."

"But if you did take some for provision," Trott questioned Bonnet, "would no less than thirteen vessels satisfy you?"

"It was contrary to my inclination," Bonnet answered, causing Trott to raise an indignant eyebrow.

"We proceed to call another evidence," said Hepworth.

Pell stood up and was ushered away from the witness chair by the guards. A young man in a dark green suit and a brown wig stepped up and was sworn in by the clerk before he took his seat.

"Captain Manwareing, look upon the prisoner at the bar; do you know him?" Hepworth asked.

"I know him very well," the witness answered.

"Give the Court an account of your being taken by him."

"I arrived at Cape James, alias Cape Inlopen, the thirty-first of July, and after being at an anchor some time, we saw a dory coming, as I said before. So I was ordered on board the Revenge."

"And before whom was you brought?" Trott asked him.

"Before the man at the bar, Captain Thomas he was called then, and so I gave him my papers; and it being night, he said but little more that night. Next morning, they hauled the sloop longside the schooner, and hoisted out the rum and molasses out of the sloop, and put on board the schooner, and the first of August we sailed in company to Cape Fear. But indeed the gentleman was very civil to me."

The attorney general stood to ask, "Did you ever hear him give orders to take out any goods?"

"He was on board the sloop himself when it was done."

"Do you remember any particular goods taken out?" asked Hepworth.

"Yes, sir."

Hepworth nodded to the clerk and resumed his seat. The clerk said to Bonnet, "Will you ask the king's evidence any questions?"

Bonnet stood, asking, "I beg leave to ask whether you ever saw me share among the rest?"

"You was in the round-house, and a bundle and some pieces was brought and I saw you take it, and give it the negro boy, to put into the chest."

"There were several that I kept their shares for, but it was not mine."

"It was put away by your order."

"Did you ever hear me order anything out of the sloop?"

"Major Bonnet, I am sorry you should ask me that question, for you know you did, which was my all that I had in the world. So that I do not know but my wife and children are now perishing for want of bread in New England. Had it been only myself, I had not mattered it so much, but my poor family grieves me."

Bonnet put his hand on his chin and opened his mouth to speak, but then only waggled his jaw and looked up at the ceiling.

"Will you ask any more questions?" the clerk asked him.

"No, sir," the pirate captain said happily and returned to his seat.

"We will call another evidence," said Hepworth.

A tan, fit, handsome man answered the call for a James Killing, and was sworn in and replaced Captain Manwareing in the witness chair. Upon being asked, he gave the same information as Manwareing had about Bonnet's capture of the Francis, until Hepworth asked about the goods onboard.

"Were the twenty-one hogsheads of molasses, and the rum taken out?"

"Yes, sir," Killing affirmed.

Allen pointed to the pirate, asking, "And all by Major Bonnet's order?"

"Major Bonnet gave orders for it to be done."

Judge Trott pressed Bonnet, "What need had you of so much molasses?"

"I did not carry it away," Bonnet replied, "and it was contrary to my inclination."

The judge glared at him for a moment, then said slowly, "You gave orders for it to be done, and yet it was contrary to your inclinations."

Bonnet nodded readily.

"Will you ask the king's evidence any questions?" the clerk asked the erstwhile captain.

"No, sir."

"We will call another evidence," said Hepworth.

Another man, a Captain Thomas Read, came and went as a witness, corroborating what had been earlier stated by the rest.

"You now stand on your defense," Trott told Bonnet after Read stepped down. "What have you to say, I shall be ready to hear."

"May it please your honours, there is a young man come from North Carolina, that will say something in my defense."

A teenaged boy named James King was sworn in.

"What do you know of the prisoner at the bar?" the judge asked him.

"When Major Bonnet took out his clearance at North Carolina, the sloop was cleared for Saint Thomas's, for a commission to go against the Spaniards a privateering."

One of the other ten judges spoke up, "Do you certainly know it was so?"

"It was reported to be so by the governor."

"Did you hear the governor declare this?" the attorney general asked.

"No, but Colonel Brice's son told me so."

"Colonel Brice lives fifty miles in the country," Trott said, gesturing in one direction with his hand, "how did he come to inform you of this?"

"He came down out of the country."

Trott gave the boy a quizzical look and turned to Bonnet, "If this be all the evidence you have, I do not see this will be of much use to you, but if you have any thing further to say, I shall be ready to hear you."

"I should be glad to go through both indictments at once," said Bonnet.

Trott shook his head. "We shall go through but one indictment now, therefore you must prepare to speak to that singly."

"May it please your honours," Bonnet addressed the judges with a smile, "and the rest of the gentlemen, though I must confess myself a sinner, and the greatest of sinners, yet I am not guilty of what I am charged with. As for what the boatswain says, relating to several vessels, I am altogether free, for I never gave my consent to any such actions, for I often told them, if they did not leave off committing such robberies, I would leave the sloop, and desired them to put me on shore. And as for taking Captain Manwareing, I assure your honours it was contrary to my inclination. And when I cleared my vessel at North Carolina, it was for Saint Thomas's; and I had no other end or design in view but to go there for a commission. But when we came to sea and saw a vessel, the quartermaster and some of the rest held a consultation to take it; but I opposed it, and told them again I would leave the sloop, and let them go where they pleased. For, as the young man said, Colonel Brice's son can testify that I had clearance for Saint Thomas's."

Trott's voice was measured as he restrained his impatience, "Was colonel Brice's son there when you cleared for Saint Thomas's?"

"Yes, and Colonel Brice's son knew I was designed for Saint Thomas's."

"But, pray, what business had you at Saint Thomas's? Surely after you had contracted so much guilt upon your conscience by your former piracies and robberies, you might have been contented to have lived a retired life in North Carolina, reflected on your former wicked course of living, and repented of the same, and not engaged in new actions."

"I never took a vessel but with Captain Teach."

"Did you not take Captain Manwareing's sloop?" the judge shot back, pointing at the empty witness chair.

"It was contrary to my inclinations, and I told them several times if they would not leave off that course of life, I would leave the sloop, and when Captain Manwareing was taken, I was asleep."

The judge leaned forward in his chair. "How came you to order the dory to be sent off with five hands to take him? And Captain Read swears it was by your order!" Trott stared at the pirate, waiting for his explanation.

"I cannot tell you but that was contrary to my inclinations," Bonnet stated flatly, holding his hands up in a shrug.

"Do not tell any more lies to this court!" Trott glowered at him. "I see through your eyes, and you're bad to the bone! You may go ahead, Mr. Allen."

The attorney general stood up to address the court. "May it please your honours, and the gentlemen of the jury," he said as bowed his head toward them, "the prisoner at the bar hath pleaded 'not guilty' to the indictment, but the boatswain, though he seems to bear a very great affection to him, yet tells you that he was commander in chief among them at the time when Captain Manwareing was taken. Captain Manwareing tells you, when he was brought on board the Revenge, he was brought before him and no other, and that he delivered his papers to him, and he saw his share brought to him in the round-house, and put into the chest.

"Then Captain Manwareing's mate says, Major Bonnet was on board the sloop, and ordered him to show which was the molasses, and which was the rum. And then Captain Read says Major Bonnet was commander in chief, and that he ordered the dory to be sent off with five hands to take Captain Manwareing. Indeed, the prisoner pleads he was under constraint from his men, and that it was contrary to his inclinations, but I think it not common for one that is forced to have such command. And as for what James King says in behalf of the prisoner, that he had his clearance for Saint Thomas's, in what he was accused of before, that he deceived his men with a notion of his going there for a commission."

Judge Trott turned to the twelve men in chairs by the window and began, "Gentlemen of the jury, the prisoner at the bar stands indicted for felony and piracy." He proceeded to recount what each of the witnesses had said about the guilt of Stede Bonnet. He finished with, "So that I think the evidence have proved the fact upon him, but I shall leave this to your consideration."

After this, an officer among the guards was assigned to the jury, and he escorted them out of the room.

Hasdrubal leaned over to his two companions. "He is going to hang," he whispered.

"It really does seem like it," Dhlara agreed.

"Can't we do anything?" Jylling said quietly. "Surely we could defend him better than a kid who knows 'Colonel Brice's son'."

"Are you crazy?" Dhlara hissed. "What could we say? 'Oh yes, he was quite gung ho about being a pirate and actually wanted to fire on your city for the fun of it. Oh, did we mention that? He was also one of those pirates who put your city under siege. And we know because we were on the ship with him, but please don't put us on trial.'"

"And there is also the fact that we are not from this time," Hasdrubal reminded him. "We have gone unnoticed so far, but drawing more attention to ourselves risks our being discovered. I don't know what they would do then."

"It seems a shame that we can't do anything, is all," said Jylling.

"His is a pirate," Hasdrubal countered. "This is the life he chose."

"For sure, he's a thief and an idiot, but does that mean he should be hung?" Jylling countered.

"Many have died without even that much of a reason."

"Yeah, okay? What does that matter?"

"He did appear to be along for the ride more than dictating

events, but I don't know what we can do for him now."

They left it at that and waited for the jury to return with their verdict. After a quarter of an hour, they filed back into the room.

"Foreman, what is your verdict?" Judge Trott asked.

One of the jurors stood and gave an answer: "We find Stede Bonnet, alias Edwards, alias Thomas, guilty."

"Well then, that's settled," said Bonnet. "Good job everyone, that was a splendid trial!" He held his hand out to the guard standing next to him to shake his hand. The soldier didn't move, but Bonnet didn't seem bothered by it. "I believe you'll be taking me back to jail now? Very good!"

∗

Two days later, Stede Bonnet was sentenced to die by hanging. After the date was postponed several times, his execution was scheduled for December 10th. The three time travelers had gone to visit him later in November, and he was still taking it well, in a way.

"That judge lectured me about the Bible and Jesus, so I've written this heartfelt letter of remorse!" the erstwhile pirate captain had informed them cheerfully, holding up a sheet of paper. "I think he'll let me out of here after he reads this."

"I don't think he will, Captain," Hasdrubal said as he leaned against the wall of Bonnet's room.

"Oh don't worry, Jesus is fond of mercy and forgiveness. They'll let me out, and I'll take a new name, and find a new ship."

"A new ship for what, exactly?" Dhlara inquired with narrowed eyes.

Bonnet just smiled.

"It's been nice knowing you, Stede Bonnet," said Jylling.

December 10th came, and the execution was the public event of the day. Many townspeople gathered at the shoreline at White Point Garden to watch Bonnet hang. Later on, the time travelers, not wanting to witness the act, heard from others that the sentence had been fulfilled, Bonnet had died, and the governor had ordered his body to be left hanging in view of the harbour as a testament to the fate of pirates.

That evening, in their room at the inn, Hasdrubal proposed to his compatriots that they should lessen Bonnet's indignity, saying "We ought to bury him properly. A man deserves a burial."

"What? No. Absolutely not," said Jylling.

"Why should we do that?" Dhlara asked. "He was friendly enough, but I really don't like the notion of... dealing with his dead body. That just seems awful."

"It is awful. But the man saved my life. I owe him. I will do what I can to see that he has some measure of peace."

"He is gone, Hasdrubal."

"And yet he has left everything he had of himself behind, and how we treat what is left says everything about us."

"I can understand that, but I don't want to see him dead. I don't want to see anybody dead."

"I am going down there tonight to do what I can."

Dhlara sighed. "I'll help you, I guess."

"What? Seriously?" Jylling blurted.

"Yeah, I'll go," she said.

"This is not what I meant by doing something to help him!"

"This is what we can do for him," said Hasdrubal.

"Aw, man. I'll come with you guys, but I'm not doing anything I don't want to."

"Nobody's asking you to do what you don't want to," said Dhlara.

"Alright then. And if it's too gross, I'm coming back here."

They waited until the middle of the night, then left the inn and walked through the city, down toward White Point Garden. Beyond the buildings, they passed through a flat stretch of land thick with short trees, until they saw a frame of three pieces of wood, two in the ground and one across the top, which made the appearance of a box, inside which hung the body of Stede Bonnet. It faced the water lapping against the sand several yards away. The trio walked around the frame, stepping into the sand of the shoreline, and looked at the deceased pirate. His hands were bound in front of him, yet his face had a peaceful expression.

"Well, this is unpleasant," Jylling whispered in a hoarse voice.

At that moment, the hanging body opened its eyes. Its face split open into a broad grin as it stared at them. Jylling jerked with surprise and shouted, "Waahg!" Hasdrubal's eyes narrowed in confusion and suspicion, and he brought his cane up in his hand, ready to strike. Dhlara's fists clenched reflexively and she took a step backward.

Bonnet's corpse stuck its tongue between its teeth and waggled its head back and forth in the noose with a determined expression, until suddenly the head pitched forward and completely fell off. The rest of Bonnet's body fell heavily along with it, collapsing in a limp heap below the dangling rope that had been intended to take his life. Transfixed, they watched his head roll over so that its face was no longer in the grass, then lift itself upright and rise up a few inches.

"Hey guys!" it exclaimed. The light of the moon glinted on the metal legs coming out of its neck.

"...Melvin?" Dhlara said in disbelief. Hasdrubal abruptly roared with laughter.

"Hi! I spent a while waiting for you," said Melvin. "That rope was all chokey."

"It's been you the whole time?!" Dhlara asked with her eyes wide.

"Yeah! I've been me the whole time!"

"No, you're Stede Bonnet?!"

"Yep!"

"...What?!" Jylling shouted.

"I'm Stede Bonnet!" Melvin repeated.

"But how?!" Dhlara asked.

"That guy kicked me off his boat, and his boat had made me think about pirates, and I ended up here. Well, not here. More southy and fifty years ago."

"Fifty years ago?!"

"Yup!"

"You've been here for fifty years?!" Dhlara held her hands

out in front of her, unconsciously expressing her incredulity.

"Uh, yeah," said Melvin. "That's what I'm saying."

"No. How is that possible? We've only been here a few months," said Jylling.

"You didn't come in with me," Melvin explained. "You probably came in at a different time."

"That ship took us here pretty soon after you fell in," said Dhlara.

"Yeah, but if you've only been here a few months, that means you came in at seventeen eighteen. I came in at sixteen eighty-eight."

"How did that happen?" she asked.

"If you came in on that ship, it decided to take you to seventeen eighteen. I just fell into the water, which is all of time, so you can end up anywhere. I was thinkin' 'bout pirates, so it took me somewhere where there's pirates. It's all pretty simple, really."

"What do you mean you were thinking about it so it took you here?!" Jylling pressed. "How does that work?!"

"I don't know," said Melvin. "That's time, man. Something about thinkin' about stuff makes you go places when you go into time. This kind of thing has happened to me a lot."

"A lot?! What does *that* mean?!" Dhlara exclaimed.

"I've fallen into all sorts of time places. If you don't think about stuff, you can swim around just fine. But you think about something, and bam, then you're there. I'm the best at not thinking about stuff, so they have me go into the water to clean the time barnacles off the bottom of the Ministries."

Jylling put his hands on top of his head. "This is all crazy town nonsense," he declared and walked a short distance away. "Wait," he stopped abruptly and pointed at Melvin, "how do you have a body?!"

"I called it!" the happy head exclaimed.

"Melvin! I don't! Know! What! That! Means!"

"I keep a body in my closet for emergencies. Getting kicked into pirate town is emergency-like, so I told my body to come help. He missed by about twenty years, but that's okay." He patted the shoulder of his body reassuringly with one of his claws.

"You have a body you don't use and keep in your closet?" Jylling reiterated.

"Yup!"

"Is it, like, your *real* body?"

"What?"

"Is it, you know, fleshy?"

"Oh! No. I got levers and stuff in there."

"Melvin, what are you? You're such a *weird* little guy."

"Um, I'm Melvin!" He waved a little pincer at Jylling. "Hi!"

Hasdrubal walked over to Melvin and squatted down to look at him. "I did not recognize you. Why is that?" he asked. "Have you done something? You don't look older."

"Oh, yeah!" Melvin went cross-eyed as he looked down at his own nose. His pincer hands came up to his face and peeled the nose off, revealing his real, sharper nose underneath. He held out the fake nose and grinned, like he'd done a trick.

"How did you get a false nose?" Hasdrubal asked.

"Oh I've got a bunch of them in here." Melvin walked behind his body and reached into the stump of a neck. "Turned up nose," he said, tossing a second fake nose into the air. "Great big fat nose, bumpy nose, gross witchy wart nose," he continued, and more noses flew up.

"What else do you keep in there?" Dhlara asked.

"Collapsible top hat." He took out a roll of black material and shook it, causing it to unfold and pop into the shape of a top hat. "Couple bags of money. You guys can have those if you want. Uh, something called a 'Nixon mask' or whatever."

"Where'd you get the money?" Hasdrubal asked.

"I had a lot more than that. Turns out growing sugar makes a lot of money. Not as fun, though."

"Hang on," Dhlara blurted out, something having just occurred to her, "if it's been you the whole time, why didn't you tell us?!"

"I did! I told you I'm a pirate now! You guys did a really good job of playing along!"

Suddenly, Melvin's body sat up, stood up, and ran straight into the water.

"Melvin, where's your body going?" Jylling asked.

"I don't really know," he answered. "Maybe he's gonna go find Blackbeard. That guy's a jerk, did you know that?"

"Yeah, that's kind of what history says. Or will say, I guess," said Dhlara.

"Welp, it's super fun to be zooming through the universe on this spheroidal spaceship pretending to be pirates with you guys," said Melvin, "but I think I'd like to go home now."

"We don't know how to do that," Dhlara replied. "You don't have a way back?"

"Heck no," he answered.

"If this has happened to you before, how'd you get back to the Ministries those times?" she asked.

"I usually just wait around until somebody finds me. And here you guys are!"

"Yeah, and we can't get back either," said Jylling. "Why don't you just have one of those watches?"

"Wellington won't give me one, and he's all kicky, too. Where's Gordon? Why didn't you guys bring him along? Did he die?"

"No, he didn't die!" Dhlara reassured him hastily. "Olinger's stooge, Muller, he's keeping Gordon prisoner. Or at least that was the last we knew."

"Let's go free him, guys!"

"We don't know where he is, and he's got a time-traveling warship," Hasdrubal pointed out. "He could be long gone."

Melvin walked in front of Hasdrubal and glared up at him. "Are you Gordon's friend?" he asked.

"I've not known him that long, but I suppose I am."

"Well then let's kick butts until they let him go!"

XIV

Bash Out!

At Melvin's direction, the time travelers left White Point Garden and followed a cobblestone street to the docks. A row of two-story buildings stood on their left, and on the other side was a brick wall and the ships moored behind it. They had hastily stashed Melvin inside Dhlara's overcoat, deciding that an odd bulge in her clothes would be less conspicuous than a talking head. Dhlara pulled the collar of her overcoat away from her and looked down into it. "So why have we come here?" she whispered.

"I have a cunning plan!" Melvin's muffled voice answered from inside.

"Ow!" She lightly slapped the side of the lump. "Don't jab so much!"

"Sorry! Putting my nose back on!"

"Why?"

"Because they won't know me without my nose!"

"Melvin," Jylling whispered at Dhlara's coat, "I don't think they'll recognize you without your *body*. And we stuffed you in there so *nobody* sees you, anyway."

"Are we there yet?" asked Melvin.

"Are we *where* yet?" Dhlara countered. "Ack!"

Melvin climbed up her and his face popped out of the overcoat. "There!" he pointed at a two story brick house ahead of them and then climbed back down to her stomach. When they stopped in front of the door, Melvin's metal arm reached out of the buttoned middle of the coat holding a key. "Use this!" he told them. Dhlara took it, unlocked the door, and pushed it open; the room beyond the doorway was barely visible through the darkness.

"Now what?" Dhlara asked.

Melvin dropped out of her coat and ran into the house. The tapping of his legs against the wooden floor sounded loud amidst the total silence of the rest of the building.

"*Where are you going?!*" Dhlara hissed.

"Come on!" Melvin answered. "Ah, this way!"

His three companions stepped into the dark and saw him turned sideways, climbing up a stairway to the left. Up the stairs they followed, to another door slightly ajar at the end of a hallway. Melvin bonked it open with his forehead and entered the room. From the doorway, Dhlara could see that it was someone's bedroom, and that someone was sleeping in his bed in the center. She watched as Melvin scaled the bedding and walked along the man's body until he was standing on his chest. Melvin grabbed the man's nose with one of his pincers and wiggled it back and forth. The owner of the nose sleepily opened his eyes before giving a full-throated yell when he saw Melvin.

"Hello, harbourmaster!" Melvin cheerfully greeted him. When the he yelled again, Melvin clamped his lips together with his pincers. "Ssssshhh ssssshhh ssssshhh. None of that."

The man shut his eyes and mumbled prayer through his pinched lips.

"Hey! Hey!" Melvin tapped him on the forehead. "I'm trying to talk to you!"

"What are you?!"

"I am the previously embodied head of the pirate Stede Bonnet! Since your town recently decided to kill me, and I have nothing better to do, now that I am dead, I will bother you and your descendants forever. Sometimes, I will pinch your nose when you are trying to sleep. Sometimes, I will eat all of your cookies. And I will do other things too, that haven't occurred to me yet, but you will be very annoyed by them, and then you will know that I, Stede Bonnet, am very unhappy about being dead!"

"W-Why me?! I didn't do anything to you!"

"Because I'm a deranged spectre! And because I want to

spend death as I did life riding the waves aboard a ship under my command!"

"What can I do about that?"

"Return my ship to me, so that I can go haunt the high seas, and you will never see me again."

"Yes, of course! You'll have your ship!"

"Well then I'll have nothing better to do than smash all your stuff while you're trying to sleep. Oooh! Or, I could practice being a banshee!"

"But I will give you whatever you want! What more must I do?!"

"What? Oh, right. You did say that. I thought this would be harder. I must be a pretty scary ghost! So, I want you to make my ship ready for me to take command of it tomorrow night, and I want you to load it with provisions for a full crew."

"It will be so, spirit!"

"Good. Now stay right there." Melvin hopped off the bed, climbed up the front of Jylling's coat and took a small sack out of one of his pockets. Returning to the bed, he turned it over and dumped a pile of coins onto the quilt over the harbourmaster's chest. "Take what you need to cover the cost of all that stuff, and then we'll leave."

"Oh! Very well. Thank you!" the man said as he scooped up several coins.

"If my ship is ready tomorrow night, you won't see us again, but if it isn't—"

"It will be! I swear it will be!"

"Good!" And then Melvin jumped off the bed and zipped out of the bedroom.

The group filed back out onto the street, where he stood smiling at them

"So, you got us a ship," said Hasdrubal.

"Yep!" Melvin answered.

"Do you think he'll actually do what you said?"

"Yep! People here are very superstitious."

"What's the next part of your plan?" Dhlara asked him.

"That part is still in development!"

"Well, we still need more than ourselves to sail it, don't

we," Hasdrubal stated rhetorically.

"And I think we need a new captain," said Jylling.

"I can be captain again!" Melvin offered.

"You've done enough of it already."

"No I haven't!"

"What he means," Dhlara explained to Melvin, "is that you've had to be captain for a long time now, and maybe you'd like it if you got a break."

"Yeah, okay. So I can be just a normal pirate, this time!"

"Hang on, that's not what we're doing, right? We're not going back to piracy," said Jylling.

"If we're going to go find Gordon, we can't attack every ship we see," Dhlara told Melvin.

"Alright, I'm a temporarily retired pirate."

"I actually might know where we can find a captain and a crew," said Jylling.

"Where's that?" asked Dhlara.

"I'll show you."

*

Jylling led the group further along the docks, then turned left and followed another street where the buildings were closer together and dilapidated, until they came to an inn with a wooden sign hanging out front that had an engraving of a blackened hand.

As he led them in, they discovered the inn was just as shabby inside as out. The whole place was hazy with smoke, the smell of which was mixed with several other unpleasant bodily odours. Most of the round tables that filled the room sat unused, but a few had men around them. One group of four were drunkenly butchering a song, or perhaps they were each trying to sing four completely different songs, while a pair of women brought metal mugs over to them. A member of the inebriated choir grabbed one of the women by the waist and pulled her into his lap.

When the other woman turned around, she recognized Jylling. "Hi, Jylling!" She waved her hand and smiled as she walked back over to the bar.

Jylling's face turned red. Hasdrubal laughed and slapped him on the back.

"How've you come to know this place, Jylling?" Dhlara asked, eyeing the back of his head suspiciously.

"When you work on the docks, you meet a ton of interesting people."

Hasdrubal laughed again. "I bet you do!"

"Well, I mean, not like that."

"Come on, we've got work to do," Dhlara reminded them. "Why are we here?"

"Over here." Jylling led them into a dark corner where a short, fat, balding man sat slumped over on a table, snoring loudly. The squat, stumpy fingers of his right hand still clutched his mug of beer, and they could see a significant portion of the middle one was missing. Both of his hands were very large for his size.

Melvin climbed up an empty chair, then onto the table, and rapped his claw against the man's head, saying, "Hey wake up, sleepy guy."

The slumbering patron lifted his head and blearily blinked his eyes at Melvin. Once he fully realized what he was looking at, he bolted upright. "What the devil?! What the hell is wrong with you?! You're a goddamned abomination!"

"Hi! I'm—" said Melvin.

"Are you some sort of vision of death, come to take me in my sleep?! Scram, demon, I'm not dying yet." With that, he punched Melvin in the face, sending him flying off the table and landing below with a sickening thud.

Melvin popped back up onto his feet. "I'm on the floor, now!" he announced.

"Whoah, hey, cool it; he's our friend," said Jylling.

"Jylling?" the man blinked at him. "Quit commiseratin' with demons, for God's sake." He tilted his mug to peer inside and inspect its contents, then he held it upside down above his mouth to catch the last few drops. He had a large, dimpled chin, and which was made more prominent by his underbite. Oval and circular scars dotted his face, which was sagging and wrinkled.

"He's not a demon, he's… well, he's a head, but otherwise normal— well, not really normal… the point is he's an okay guy," Jylling explained.

"I don't care," the man grunted.

"Well, anyway, guys, this is Captain Kilik."

"What are you waking me up in the middle of the day for?" Kilik asked.

Jylling frowned. "It's the middle of the night."

"Oh, is it? Well, no matter, you're not supposed to wake me up in the middle of anything, especially sleeping."

"We should have a ship by tomorrow, but we don't have a crew or a captain."

"I'm retired!" Melvin's voice came up from under the table. "Whoah!" he exclaimed as Kilik kicked at him.

"I am too," said Kilik. "There's plenty of gormless idiots who own ships that need captaining. I am nowise wanting of work, boy."

"This isn't normal work, Kilik," said Jylling.

"You mean to go a pirating?"

"No, we've had enough of that."

"War-caperers, then?"

"No."

"What on earth are you bothering me for?!"

"Someone we know is being held prisoner on an island, and we'd like to go free him."

"Someone 'we' know? These two with you?"

"Yeah, they're my friends, Hasdrubal and Dhlara," Jylling jabbed his thumbs in the air back at each of them as he said their names a second time.

"A demon, and now exotic friends. I didn't know you kept such strange company, Jylling."

"Uh, okay."

"Who's holding this person you know?"

"Well… that's complicated."

"Nothing's complicated. You, Curly," Kilik pointed at Hasdrubal, "who's got this prisoner?"

"People from the future," Hasdrubal answered.

"What?"

"They're from centuries from now."

"Jylling, precisely how many morons do you travel with?" the captain asked.

"Hasdrubal is right," said Jylling. "They're from the future."

"That's impossible."

"I'm telling you it isn't; we've seen it, and more things than that that you would never believe. You're staring at people from the future right now. Well, not him," he pointed at Hasdrubal. "He's from the past. But Dhlara and I were born hundreds of years from now."

"Son, I'm a man of the sail. I've heard a thousand fabulous tales of nonsense, and never a one of them has been true. It's easy to put a lie just beyond the edge of the ocean."

Jylling frowned at him for a moment, then picked up Melvin and placed him back on the table. "Hi!" Melvin waved at Kilik.

"How many tales were told to you by someone who went around with a talking head?" Jylling asked.

Kilik gave a wheezy, coughing laugh. "Aye, you've got me there. What's it pay?"

"We can give you this, for starters," Jylling told him as he drew Melvin's sack of coins from his pocket.

Kilik took it and weighed it in his hand. "This might be enough for a small crew. How big's the ship?"

"Just a sloop."

"What kind of work? You need men who can fight?"

"There might be a fight."

"In what way, exactly?"

"The people holding our friend prisoner have a frigate."

Kilik's brow furrowed. "That's quite a fight. You'll pay for injuries and death?"

"We've got more saved up, between the three of us, and we'll pay more if there's danger."

"You'll need to have it ready, if you want men to fight for you. As captain, I'll not send men to die for some damn fool reason if it don't pay. And if it's damn fool enough, I won't do it at all, you got that?"

"We understand. So will you do it? I can guarantee you a trip with us will be more interesting than spending every day in this place."

"I suppose I might. I'll admit, the wind still carries my soul, and perhaps there's something worth seeing, if you came across that unholy monstrosity."

"Good. We'll be at the docks tomorrow night."

"Tomorrow night? That's quite late notice. I can't recruit so many men in a day, especially not if we require the sort of men who won't leave at the sight of your strange acquaintance."

"We've had to wait months already," said Hasdrubal. "We can wait another week."

"A week?!" Jylling turned around in his chair to look up at the Carthaginian.

"That would do far better," said Kilik.

"We can wait a week," Dhlara agreed.

"I'll meet you at the docks in a week, then." Kilik put his arms onto the table and lay his head down into the crook of his elbow.

"Hang on, you're going back to sleep?" Jylling asked in disbelief.

"Apparently it's the middle of the night," the captain responded without lifting his head, his voice muffled as he spoke into the table, "when a man ought to be sleeping."

"Alright, we'll be going, then," said Dhlara.

The four of them stepped out of the inn and wrapped their clothes tighter around them against the cold. As they walked back the way they had come, Dhlara asked Jylling, "So who is that guy, exactly?"

"He used to be a privateer during the War of the Grand Alliance. He has a lot of stories about being a captain, and I kind of like him, and it seems to me we'd have a hard time finding someone around here who knows as much about sailing who wouldn't have a major problem with the sorts of things they might see with us."

"What was the War of the Grand Alliance?" Hasdrubal

asked.

"I don't know," said Jylling. "I've never heard of it, but I don't know anything about this time. He talks about fighting the French during it, though."

"Maybe this won't be so different for him after all, then."

*

As it turned out, the promises made to (or extracted by) the travelers in time were faithfully fulfilled. The harbourmaster had indeed quietly turned the *Revenge*, though it had been renamed the *Royal James* before its capture by the British, over to them with fully stocked with provisions. And, six days after they had taken possession of the ship, its new captain showed up with fifty men. Dhlara, Jylling, and Hasdrubal welcomed them as they boarded the single-masted sloop. They wore coats to insulate them from the mid-morning cold, but the trio could still see that many of them were so tanned their skin resembled leather, and their faces showed the wear of previous voyages. All carried sacks or chests aboard with them. The last person to cross the gangplank was Kilik.

"Glad to have you helping us, Captain," Jylling greeted him.

"Yeah, yeah," Kilik waved dismissively. "Come on, let's go in here," he told them, and led them into the captain's cabin. Inside, the right and left walls were almost entirely covered by bookshelves full of books, except for gaps left for a couple of square windows. A chaotic mess covered the floor; maps, open books, a couple of chairs that had been knocked over, and quills lay scattered about. A skeleton, held upright by its stand, stood facing the stern window, but the skull was missing, and Melvin stood in its place. Pulling on strings attached to the bones, he made the arms and legs wave back and forth a few inches as he went, "Doot doot doot, doot doot doot."

"Hey!" Kilik barked at him.

Melvin stopped, turned around, and stared at him.

"Quit your evil rituals! We've got business to do."

"Okay!" Melvin hopped down off the skeleton.

Kilik walked around the desk in the middle of the room and picked up one of the fallen chairs. He set it behind the desk and asked as he sat down, "So where is it you want to go?"

"We're not really sure," Dhlara admitted.

"How is that?"

"We know it's an island, and we'd recognize it if we saw it, but a lot of stuff was going on at the time…" She unconsciously glanced down at Hasdrubal's wooden foot.

"Ah, I see, so you escaped from this place yourselves. How do you know your friend is still there, if they know you got away? Maybe they moved him."

"We don't know that they didn't. But that island's the only place we know of to look for him."

"But you don't know where it is."

"Not exactly. We rowed for about half a day until we saw the coast, and we got picked up by Captain Teach's pirate fleet, and they sailed north, I think, and came to this city."

"Well, that's something. We ought to be able to find it using that knowledge. I will chart a course and we'll be on our way in a few hours, I expect. In the meantime— where's the little devil?"

Melvin's voice came from under his chair, "You mean me?"

"You're going to help me clean up my cabin," Kilik said as he looked down at Melvin.

"You have a cabin, too?" Melvin asked him.

"Yeah, this one."

"Buuut… this one is mine."

"Not while I'm captain, it isn't."

"I'll stay in the hold, then! There's all sorts of barrels of stuff down there."

"No you won't, either. I'll not have you running about scaring the life out of the crew. I tried to find the best men for unnatural work, but even they won't abide having a chattering head aboard. You'll be staying in here for the rest of the voyage."

"Okay!"

Kilik looked back up at the trio. "Who is it you're trying to rescue, anyway?"

"His name is Gordon," said Hasdrubal, "and we saw him wrestle a dragon out of the sky."

"A conversating head is one thing, but you cannot tell me there are dragons, much less a man who can overpower them!" Kilik exclaimed.

"We've all seen both," Dhlara told him. Hasdrubal and Jylling nodded.

"That strikes me as a falsehood. But supposing what you say is true, what need does he have of your help? If the man can fight a dragon, what is a motley bunch such as this going to do for him? These are the best men I could hire, but they won't fight a dragon, nor any man who can fight a dragon, and so there's no reason to think they would fight against a crew who can restrain such a man."

"Maybe he has already got out on his own," said Hasdrubal. "But the way he was captured in the first place was by the threat of harm to the three of us. He may not know we escaped."

"We will have to find out the state of things when we find the place, by the sounds of it. Let's go on our way, then."

*

The *Royal James* spent several cold days sailing south, eventually arriving at a general search area Kilik had devised from his own knowledge, the timeframe Dhlara, Jylling, and Hasdrubal had given him, and Melvin's barely reliable recollections. They spotted and searched a couple of islands, but found nothing to indicate the presence of Gordon or the Luxembourgers, past or present.

"How is it, of all the times we could have gone to, we had to end up in one where we have to spend so much of it on cramped, stinky ships?" Jylling pondered irritably as he stood on deck.

"Most of the world is made up of water, no matter where you go. Odds are there's gonna be water," Dhlara's voice answered from above him. She had climbed partway up the rigging, hooked her arm around the rope to keep her secure, and was currently inspecting the horizon with a spyglass. Her hair was tied back in a ponytail, but the wind whipped loose strands of her hair across her face. She had ditched the dresses and skirts she'd worn in Charles Town to present a relatively normal appearance in favour of a loose white shirt and brown pants.

"And that's where I would expect to end up when a cramped and stinky ship shows up to abduct us," Hasdrubal added as he leaned on the sloop's railing. He, on the other hand, had continued to wear the clothes he'd worn in Charles Town, and kept the cane, but his old fez had returned to its place on top of his black, curly hair, instead of the tricorne hat.

"Well it's a crappy time to get stuck in," Jylling responded.

"There's worse," Hasdrubal countered. "Back at home, we have ships not much bigger than this, but they have hundreds of men rowing oars. This isn't that bad."

"Maybe it's not so bad for you, but I'm not from super long time ago B.C.. Even if we find Gordon, what then? We're still left to rot in this stupid place."

"We got here somehow, which means there's some way to get back out," Dhlara calmly reminded him.

"I don't want to remain in this time any more than you do," said Hasdrubal. "But we must bear the burdens and move forward."

"It'd be nice if those burdens didn't include tolerating a wooden tub full of drunk pirates," said Jylling.

"Hey, these are our men; they aren't pirates," Hasdrubal corrected him.

"I don't really see a lot of difference. They're just drunk under a different flag."

"Sometimes that alone makes all the difference."

"Hey, I think I see something," said Dhlara.

"Another island?" Hasdrubal asked.

"Sure looks like it. Hey, Captain!" she shouted.

"What is it, lass?" Kilik called from the quarterdeck.

"There's a bit of land over that way," she pointed at a spot on the horizon.

The captain leaned over and shouted something to the helmsman on the main deck, and the ship soon turned in the direction she had indicated. When they had sailed closer, Kilik summoned them to the bow and asked if any of them recognized that particular piece of land.

"That's the place," said Hasdrubal as he looked over the island's white sand beach and jungle interior through Dhlara's spyglass. He lowered it and handed it back to her.

"Are you sure?" Kilik asked.

"Without any doubt. A man has a way of remembering a place where he is shot."

"Whereabouts was your friend being kept?"

"On a beach on the opposite side."

"Did the frigate anchor there?"

"It was at the time."

"I don't see any masts above the trees," Kilik observed, having brought his own spyglass up to his eye. "She may have went off. Could be they took your prisoner with them and there's no one left."

"We ought to check, of course."

"Aye, that we'll do." He turned and shouted to the crew while pointing at the island with his spyglass, "We're bringing her in, lads! Take her in close!"

This was done, and when the *Royal James* had sailed close to the shallower water that surrounded the island the anchor was lowered and preparations were made for most of the crew to go ashore. Musketoons, pistols, and cutlasses were handed out and jolly boats readied.

"I'd like two, in fact," Hasdrubal said as one of the crew handed him a pistol. "Oh, and bring me a couple of those swords." His request was granted.

"Why do both you and Bonnet— I mean, Melvin always need two pistols?" Dhlara asked him.

"Have you ever fired one of them?"

"No."

"They take a long time to reload, and sometimes they won't fire at all. If I've got two, I can fire two shots immediately. But as for Melvin, he probably just finds it exciting to make more things go 'bang'."

"What about your...?" Dhlara looked down at his cane.

"I'll manage without it. It won't aid me as much in the sand and dirt, anyway. Here, take this." He handed her one of the cutlasses.

"What? I don't know how to use this."

"Yes, I know. But as I said, these sort of guns take a long time to reload and you'd probably not hit anything if you shot one. You've got a better chance of doing damage with a sword."

"I'd prefer not to do 'damage' at all."

"I'm not saying you would. Just take it; you'll like to have it if you come across someone who wants to damage you." He gave the other cutlass to Jylling, and then the three of them made their way into one of the jolly boats.

The boats ferried them and many of the crewmen to shore until about forty people stood on the beach, including Captain Kilik, who waved the trio over to him. A circle of men stood around the captain, most of whom stood taller than him, and the time travelers heard him giving instructions as they neared.

"Hobbes, Garrett, you'll keep your lot on either side of us. If you see anyone, stay out of sight and don't make violence until I give the command. There sure isn't the sign of a soul on this desert, but if there is, they may be awfully dangerous. You there, Curly, you seem to remember the most of this place. We'll follow your lead through this jungle."

"I am Hasdrubal Barca, Captain," the Carthaginian rejoined, staring Kilik down.

"Yes, well, we'll follow you through the jungle all the same."

"Come on, then!" Hasdrubal declared, waving his arm toward the lines of trees. Limping over the sand, he led his friends and his hired band of sailors into the dense wilderness. The ancillary groups of armed men to his right and left broke off, putting a small amount of distance between them and the center group, and then fanned out. As the line of about forty people cautiously advanced, passing between the trees, around pools of muck, and over collections of rocks, their voices were silent and they tried to make as little noise as possible as they walked.

Dhlara recognized the boulder from which they had glimpsed their chance to escape several months ago, and she pointed it out to Jylling. He glanced at it and nodded, but continued to look around at the jungle around them. He was half-crouched as he held his cutlass out in front of him, his body tense in anticipation of a fight. Dhlara had put her sword into her belt, but she kept a hand on it to prevent it from knocking into her leg. Instead of Jylling's apprehensive pose, she walked upright, but still carefully picked her path and studied her surroundings.

After a few minutes, a faint rustling sound came from behind them, and slowly grew louder. Looking back, Dhlara saw a large white sack running towards them. Most of it was flopped over and dragging on the ground, but something inside propelled it across the ground in a zigzag. One of the sailors aimed his pistol at the animated bag, but Dhlara held out her hand.

"No, we know what that is. You don't need to worry."

"Do we?" said Jylling.

The sack, in the middle of one of its zags, drove itself into a puddle of mud. At this, a familiar voice went, "Ack! Pllllbbttt! Pfffftt!"

"Oh. Man, he was supposed to stay on the ship!"

Dhlara scooped the sack up, taking care to dump Melvin back into the empty bottom rather than show him to everyone. She put her face in the opening and saw Melvin's muddy face smiling up at her.

"What are you doing?!" she hissed.

"There's all sorts of fun places to hide in!" Melvin happily told her.

"Sshhh!"

"Okay! Sometimes, if you hide in the right things, people will give you a ride, too," he whispered.

"We told you to stay in the cabin!"

"Because I'm super creepy!"

"Yes, because you're super creepy."

"Okay!"

"Can you at least go back to the boats and wait for us there?"

"Okay!"

She put him back onto the ground and adjusted the sack so that it covered his face, but not his legs. He took off running back the way he came. Looking around, Dhlara noticed the mariners staring at her with strange looks.

"Just a pet we brought on board," she explained hastily.

"Sounded like it was talkin' to you," said one of them.

"Nope... nope. Just me."

"Let's go; we're falling behind the wings," said Hasdrubal.

A bird call came from up ahead.

Kilik's head jerked toward the noise. "They've seen something," he warned.

The group silently moved forward until they saw the sand of a beach through the jungle. Garrett's wing on the left had drawn up to the last line of trees and each man concealed himself behind a trunk. Hasdrubal's center group crept up to the treeline and also hid themselves. Garrett, a wide, hulking giant of a man, caught the attention of the captain and the Carthaginian general by holding his arm up, then flattened his hand and pointed it at the beach.

About thirty yards away, nine barrels were standing upright in the sand. In front of the barrels was a rickety wooden table, which a pair of men were sitting at and playing cards. A short distance to the right of the barrels was what looked like a small camp. They could hear the men talking and laughing.

"Only two of them," Kilik noted. "Do any of you recognize them?"

"No, but those are probably Olinger's men," Hasdrubal answered. "Their prisoner was under those barrels, when we last were here."

"Probably a guard by the looks of it. Just two isn't much of one, of course, especially for the sort of man you've said is under there."

"It is strange. He may not be there, after all."

"We can easily overwhelm them, and then we can see what's there."

"Hold steady; it may not be that simple. Do you have your spyglass with you?"

As Kilik drew it from his coat and handed it to Hasdrubal, they heard frantic whispers behind them, accompanied by a rustling sound. Looking over, Dhlara saw, again, a mostly empty sack dragging itself across the ground. In its almost drunken movements, it avoided several sailors who tried to grab it, and ran off into the sand.

"Oh, crap," Jylling muttered.

"Well, your own crew has botched this," Kilik told them. "Do we fight them now?"

"Not yet. If there's more, maybe this will tell us," said Hasdrubal, watching Melvin.

The pair of guards watched the sack approach. Halfway across, Melvin tripped over the fabric and rolled out of the bag. The men at the table jumped up in shock, knocking their chairs over. Melvin waved at them, saying, "Hi! I'm Melvin, the—"

The instant he said his name, however, the barrels exploded into a geyser of sand. Splinters of wood mixed with the huge spray of sand as it all was flung up towards the sky. Before anyone had time to react or any of it even started to fall back down, Gordon emerged from the wall of sand. He sprinted towards his guards and shoulder charged one in the back, sending him flying forward. Before that one plowed face first into the sand, Gordon grabbed the second by his shirt collar and belt buckle and threw him onto the ground. He then bent over each of them and took something off their wrists.

"Hi!" Melvin said again.

"That fellow's on our side, yeah?" Kilik asked with a degree of concern.

"That's Gordon," said Hasdrubal, handing the spyglass back to the captain.

XV

Return Fire

Dhlara, Jylling, Hasdrubal, and Kilik came out from under the leafy canopy of jungle and strode across the soft sand of the beach to greet Gordon. As they approached, the spindly blonde bent over one of the men he'd tossed to the ground.

"Are you hurt?" they heard Gordon ask him.

"Uhhhnnn," he groaned. "Yeah, I'd say that hurt pretty bad, you freak." He started to reach for something under his shirt, but Gordon's hand snapped forward and held his arm back. With his other hand, Gordon pulled a twentieth century handgun out of the man's belt. Gordon tossed it aside and it landed with a puff of sand next to another handgun he'd already taken from the other guard.

"I'm sorry, I would have preferred not to hurt you, but I couldn't let you leave with these," said Gordon as he held up a pair of watches. "And I cannot let you hurt anyone else, either."

"Hey, Gordon! Are you okay?!" Dhlara called to him.

"Hello, Dhlara," he said, smiling at her. "I'm fine; it is good to be out in the sun again. Hello, Jylling, Hasdrubal. And hello, Melvin. I am glad to see you all again, though I am sorry to see you are not unharmed. I am flattered you came to free me. And hello, sir," he nodded at Kilik, "I'm afraid I don't know you, but if you are with them, then you are a friend to me."

"Humphery Kilik. Ain't nobody's friend, just business."

"Have you been down there this whole time?!" Jylling asked Gordon.

"Yes, I was."

"Why, if you could free yourself as you have?" asked Kilik.

"What was the point of having all these men come all this way just to watch you knock everything about on your own? I mean, I'm quite satisfied with getting paid for nothing, as I'm sure these lads are, but I don't see the sense in it."

"I did not know where they were," he answered, motioning to Dhlara, Jylling, and Hasdrubal, "if they were still in Muller's captivity, I did not want to provoke any harm coming to them."

"How's that?"

"I overheard the conversations of these men here, and I learned they were left here to observe my confinement, and if anything out of the ordinary happened, they had orders to use these devices to return to the Eruewerer immediately, which could be anywhere in the world. If Muller still held them, he could kill them the instant I tried to escape."

"So you just stayed quiet and sat here on this island?"

"Yes."

"Where is Muller now?" Dhlara asked. "Are these two the only people he left here?"

"I don't know where he's gone. The Eruewerer left several months ago, not long after we got here. As far as I know, these two are the only ones on this island."

"We've come with a ship; let's take you back and get you some food and find a place with a doctor so we can make sure you're alright."

"Alright?!" Kilik laughed. "This man is healthier than anyone else I've ever seen!"

"I'm fine, I assure you." Gordon straightened out his pinstripe waistcoat and smoothed back the few strands of hair that had gone astray. "More importantly, what has happened to you, Hasdrubal?"

"I got shot while we were getting away from Muller's men. The foot had to go."

"When did this happen?"

"Almost as soon as they put you in there."

"You all got away that long ago? I'm sorry I wasn't any help to you. If I had known… but I was trying to make sure you wouldn't get hurt."

"You are not at fault. We came here to help you."

"Are those our old watches?" Dhlara asked Gordon.

"Yes, they are. They are still altered so that they transport the wearer to the Eruewerer instead of the Ministry of Order, or at least I presume so, based on what I heard. I don't know how that works, or how to change it back, but it's more useful to have them than not, and I don't want Muller to receive any warning of my escape."

"Do you know of any way for us to get back to the Ministries?"

"No. The only way back I am aware of is by whatever method brought the Eruewerer to this time."

"When I tried to use my watch to go back to the Ministries," Jylling told them, "I got teleported into the cargo hold at the bottom of Olinger's ship, and there was this big machine glowing red down there. If the watch took me straight to that thing, that's probably what diverted my watch."

"But we have no idea where Muller's taken the ship," said Dhlara.

"Now that I have the watches," said Gordon, "we could find out in an instant where his ship is, assuming they still work as we've seen in the past. But anyone who went there would have no way of coming back to the rest of us unless they took control of the entire ship, which I don't think is very likely."

"You couldn't do that?" Kilik asked.

"I doubt I could. I would be willing to try it, if it is necessary, however."

"How do we know the Eruewerer's still in this time at all?" Dhlara wondered.

"We don't."

"Well, it sounds as if there's little point to standing around here right now," said Kilik. "Let's get these men back aboard the Revenge and talk over what we do from this point."

The group agreed, and they headed back into the jungle toward their ship. Kilik waved a group of his men over to pick up the Luxembourger guards and bring them along as prisoners.

"Who are you, then?" one of the crew called to Gordon as

they walked into the trees.

"I am Gordon."

"But who are you that you can do that?"

"Especially for being such a thin fellow," another chimed in.

"I just can," he answered.

"Where are you from? That's awfully fancy," said a third man who was looking at Gordon's clothes. A circle of curious sailors formed around the towering blonde figure.

"Leave him alone, you lot," Kilik ordered. "Back to the Revenge with you!"

"Are you hiring him on then, Captain?!"

"No, he's just a passenger. Now let's get moving."

The circle broke up and the men tramped off into the jungle, but their conversations with each other about what they had seen continued.

*

Once the whole crew was again aboard the sloop, the travelers in time and Kilik reconvened in the captain's cabin. A table had been brought in, as well as a few more chairs so that everyone could sit. Kilik sat down behind the desk and took a long stem pipe out from his coat.

"Where would we even start looking for a single ship, even it was here at all?" Jylling wondered.

"What kind of vessel is it, exactly?" Kilik asked.

"A frigate with forty guns, they said."

"Forty guns? And it weren't a navy ship?"

"No, not of any navy from this time."

"That's very unusual," the stout captain frowned as he packed tobacco into his pipe. "It's rare for anything other than a warship to have that many cannon."

"I've heard of one," came a voice from within his desk.

Kilik immediately stopped what he was doing and glared at the desk. He opened and closed a few drawers, then thumped his fist on the top. "Show yourself, you blasted devil," he ordered. One of the bottom drawers slid open and Melvin's face grinned up at him. "Get out of there and tell me what you mean," Kilik told him.

"Okay!" Melvin climbed out of the drawer and onto the desk top. "When I was with Captain Teach—"

"You were with Teach? The pirate?"

"Yep!"

"How did that happen? You said you were a captain; surely you weren't a captain with him."

"Yes I was!"

"I haven't heard of a head being a captain of any pirate crew."

"I wasn't a head, then! Wait, no, I was a head. And I still am a head. But! I had a body, *too*."

"What happened to it?"

"They hanged me, and I lost it."

"Lost what?"

"My body!"

"You became a pirate after Olinger kicked you off?" Gordon asked Melvin.

"I resorted to a life of crime!" Melvin answered gleefully.

"There's a lot that happened since then," said Dhlara. "We can tell you all about it in a bit."

"Hold on a moment… are you trying to tell me you're the living head of Stede Bonnet?" the captain asked, staring at Melvin skeptically.

"Yes!"

"You are an unholy abomination. But what about when you were with the pirate Teach?"

"We heard rumours last year that there was a ship of forty guns near Campeche."

"Hmmm… that's quite some time ago."

"I can't think of why they'd still be here, unless they've set up some sort of base in this time," said Gordon. "Maybe they've set up somewhere around Campeche."

"They did take us back to this time specifically, so maybe they already had a base here, and were just coming back to it," Dhlara pointed out.

"You all know more about this ship and the men who sail

it than I do," said Kilik. "If Campeche is where you'd like to go, we can go there."

"Hang on, where the heck is 'Campeche'?" asked Jylling.

"It is a coastal city hundreds of miles west of here, in the colony of New Spain."

"So, like, Mexico?"

"No, Mexico is many miles further west."

"How long will it take to get there from here?"

"About a week."

"Do we have any better ideas of where they could be?" Hasdrubal asked.

Kilik's brow furrowed in thought. "You saw it here, at this island, and that's the last place we know it's been. We could search the surrounding area here, ask around at ports and find out if anyone else has seen it. If I haven't heard about it already, though, and they're still around here, they may be trying to go unnoticed."

"So all we have to go on is one thing Melvin said he heard?" Jylling asked with a raised eyebrow.

"We're on his ship, you know," Dhlara reminded him. "He's done more in this time than any of the rest of us."

"Yeah! I'm helping!" Melvin clinked his metal hands together as he grinned.

"I would say we ought to inquire at the nearest ports first, talk to a few sailing men, and see if there is any more to be learned," Hasdrubal put forward. "If we are not pointed in a better direction, then let us go to Campeche."

"Do the rest of you wish to do any differently?" Kilik asked. Dhlara and Jylling shook their heads. "Then we'll put in at Saint Augustine." The meeting finished, Kilik took out a small stick, held it in the flame of a candle of his desk, then stuck the burning end into the bowl of his pipe.

Four chairs scraped against the wood flooring as everyone except Kilik and Melvin stood up and exited the cabin. They stepped out into the pale sunlight of a winter afternoon.

"How are you doing? Are you really okay?" Dhlara turned and asked Gordon.

He smiled warmly, "I am perfectly fine, and I am much

better now, thank you."

"Do you need food or anything? We've brought plenty on board with us."

"I am quite alright."

"Did they give you enough to eat while you were in there?"

"Not as much, but I am very much okay."

A group of the crew again formed around Gordon, and a young man who looked to be not much older than twenty approached him. "The boys and I have a disagreement; would you be willing to give us a demonstration of your strength again?"

"How would you like me to do that?" Gordon asked him.

"You don't need to do that," said Dhlara.

"It's alright, I don't mind."

"Well, Garrett over there is the strongest of us." The sailor pointed to the burly giant who had led the left wing of the landing party. He stood at the railing on the left, tying down a rope. "We've seen him carry a stone as big as a man."

Gordon walked over to Garrett. He only stood a few inches taller than the other, much wider, man. "Hello, Garrett." Gordon held out his hand and Garrett shook it.

"Good afternoon. I don't know what these fellows want us to prove, but we can try all the same."

"Oh, come now," the young man said. "We've got heavy things all over this ship, full barrels and the like, and each of you could lift them, or we could devise a test to match your powers against each other."

"How about we just toss you over the side instead?" Garrett grinned down at him. The group around them laughed.

"No, no, that doesn't mean much. I'm a very small fish, indeed. It'd be something if he could throw you." Smiling, the shorter man reached up and slapped Garrett's chest.

"Would that be an acceptable test?" Gordon asked.

The two sailors raised their eyebrows. "Can you do that?" the smaller one asked.

"Sure. Would you be okay with it?" he asked Garrett.

"Aye, you can try."

Gordon's arms snapped forward and gripped the bulky

mariner by his side and under his arm. Before Garrett had any time to react, Gordon had already flung him bodily into the air. He flailed awkwardly as he sailed over the heads of his comrades, fell past the side of the ship, and splashed into the ocean. In an uproar of amazement and laughter, the crowd of sailors rushed over to the port side to watch their soaked strongman climb back up the hull. Gordon leaned over the gunwale and offered his hand to Garrett, who took it, and was lifted back onto the deck.

"Are you alright?" Gordon asked him.

"That was a surprise," Garrett said as he took off his shirt and wrung the water out.

"Thank ya, sir," the now smiling young man said to Gordon. "I'm sure that I've won the wager!"

*

Over the next few days, the *Revenge* sailed into several ports. First was St. Augustine, a Spanish city on the coast of a river close to the ocean protected by a star fort. After asking around and learning nothing, the sloop continued on to an island off the east coast of Florida and its city of Nassau, which was even very recently an ideal pirate haven, but its new English governor Woodes Rogers had reasserted military control over the city and begun capturing and hanging pirates. Many people Melvin had known during his stint as the full-bodied Captain Bonnet were still on the island, as well as others who had been sympathetic to and known the dealings of pirates, but nobody had heard of the rogue frigate or its strange company of Luxembourgers.

So the *Revenge* set sail again, and went on to the Spanish city of Havana, a bustling trading hub inside a bay. It was larger than Charles Town, larger than any other settlement the time travelers had seen, and must have had similar troubles with pirates, because an imposing fortress stood guard at the mouth of the bay. At Nassau, Kilik had sent a couple groups of his men into the city to find anyone who had seen the *Eruewerer*, but Havana was Spanish, and none of his men spoke Spanish, so Dhlara, Jylling, and Hasdrubal alone went out to make inquiries.

Their day in Havana went much like the the ones in the other port cities; they repeated the same questions again and again to local business owners, dockworkers, and sailors, and none of them ever had anything to tell. Much like the others, that is, until they went into an inn called *La Posada Castor Canto*, and started to ask questions of the innkeeper. Overhearing, a barmaid came over to ask, "You're looking for someone?"

"We're looking for a ship, in particular," said Jylling.

"Well, there was a French man in here some months ago who said he was serving on a frigate, and it did look odd."

"Odd how?" Dhlara asked her.

"It was straighter, flatter than the ships I'm used to seeing. It must have been some strange French design. But the things he said were odder."

"Like what?"

"He drank quite a lot, and had many things to say to me that he imagined were pleasant, and he told me he was from a day many days from now, and that one day, we all would speak his language. He ended up getting thrown out."

"You said he was French?"

"His accent sounded French, and when he talked with his mates it sounded French to me. I don't know for sure, though."

"Did he say anything else?"

"Not that I recall. Who are you after?"

"We're hunting pirates, ma'am," said Hasdrubal.

"A woman aboard a pirate hunter?" she looked askance at Dhlara.

"Yes, that's right," Dhlara responded.

"Well, good luck," she smiled, but with a confused look in her eyes.

"Which way did his ship sail?" asked Hasdrubal.

"He said they were headed back west, I think, but I didn't see it leave."

"Thank you for your help," said Dhlara.

The barmaid nodded and returned to her work, and the

three of them hurried back to the *Revenge* to share what they had learned. Since this new information also pointed west, toward Campeche, the *Revenge* set off again soon after their return. They came out of the bay, passing the fortress, and sailed into the setting sun and its glittering reflection in the waters of the gulf, in search of the one ship that could bring them back to lands they once did know.

*

Dhlara held the butt of a musket against her shoulder and gazed down the barrel at a wood plank Hasdrubal had nailed to the opposite railing. The morning sunlight beat down on her, causing sweat to bead on her face. The weather had become increasingly warm as they had sailed south, surprisingly so, to the point where it was easy to forget it was still winter. Dhlara narrowed her eyes and, when she felt her weapon was in line with her target, she pulled the trigger; the hammer clicked down and the gun bucked as an explosion blasted out of the muzzle. The piece of wood splintered in half and the ball rocketed onward, destined to plunk down somewhere in the ocean.

"Very good," Hasdrubal nodded. "Your aim has gotten good enough. Next, you will need to learn to load and fire it quickly. Jylling, go ahead and take a shot."

"Yeah, yeah, alright." Dhlara handed him the musket. He dropped the stock onto the deck and held the end of the barrel so that the gun was vertical and poured powder into the muzzle from a horn. Closing the flask, he reached into a pouch hanging at his side and pulled out a ball of fiber, which he also put into the muzzle, before forcing it to the bottom of the barrel with a metal ramrod. A metal ball went in next, then another ball of fiber, and more jamming with the rod. He picked up the gun and placed the stock against his hip so that he could use one hand to pull the hammer back and pour some powder onto the metal plate below it. Finally finished, he cocked the hammer even further back, leveled the musket, and fired. Tiny pieces of the plank went flying; his shot had only grazed it.

"Good!" said Hasdrubal. "That's good! And you didn't forget the wadding this time."

"It's a bunch of work to end up shooting somebody," Jylling remarked.

"In my time, it takes significantly more effort to kill a man."

"But I don't want to kill anybody."

"Suppose we find the Eruewerer; what then? How will we be able to use it to get back? Olinger's men will not hesitate to shoot you."

"Yeah I get it, I gotta shoot the guy who wants to shoot me. I still don't want to have to kill anybody."

"We have to get out of here somehow," said Dhlara. "All of history is being changed, and we can't just be trapped and rendered useless like this by Olinger and people like him."

"I got it! Just saying I don't like it," Jylling reiterated. "How are we going to be fighting them, anyway? This thing seems seriously unwieldy for boarding a ship or something."

"Oh, of course you wouldn't use that to board them," said Hasdrubal. "You'd use pistols or a sword."

"Why aren't we learning to shoot those, then?!"

"You load them the same as a musket."

"I gotta imagine it's harder to aim with them, though."

"Oh, you don't aim. You'll be so close you just point it at his guts and boom, find out what he had for lunch."

Jylling winced and the colour left his face. "That's gross."

"Ah, well, we'll probably all die in the attempt anyway," Hasdrubal grinned at him.

"How is that helping us be ready?" asked Dhlara.

"I'll make you as ready as I can, but if they're here at all, they will number in the hundreds of men, and I would be surprised if they didn't have a stash of twentieth century guns with them. I ought to be realistic with you. You're not people who have known war or combat your whole lives."

Meanwhile, Gordon observed the target practice and its digression from further aft. Behind him were the helm and the helmsman, and beyond them stood Kilik. Far off to his left was the coast of the mainland.

"Why don't you go over there and practice handling arms?" the captain asked him. "That cripple, Barca knows something of it, it seems."

"I am already proficient in firing a gun," Gordon replied, his voice flat and calm. "Would you like me to show you?"

"No, I suppose not. I know better than to need to test your abilities; I take you for a man of your word. How have you come to that proficiency? Killed many men who've crossed you, have you?"

"No. I am a tracker, in a way."

"Oh, some sort of hunter? So you like to kill critters for sport, then? Ride around on your best horse with your best clothes and shoot everything that won't shoot back?" Kilik came beside Gordon and took the edge of his waistcoat between his fingers, feeling the fabric. "How fancy of you."

"No, not like that. Most of what I hunt is larger than the average human, and I have been shot at many times."

"A lot of puffed up pigs in expensive clothes are expansive about their own bravery."

Gordon shrugged. "I didn't say I am brave."

"You'd just have me believe you do brave deeds."

"I wouldn't have you believe anything."

Kilik let go of Gordon's waistcoat and clasped his hands behind his back. "What do you believe?"

Gordon turned his head and looked down at Kilik. "I don't understand what you mean."

"Are you a godly man, Mister Gordon?"

"No."

"Are you a drinking man?"

"No."

"Are you angry at these blackguards who held you prisoner?"

"No."

"Are you hunting them now, seeking to make violent revenge on them?"

"I'm sorry, I don't fully understand what is going on here."

"You're awfully calm, Mister Gordon."

"Is that a problem?"

"In my experience, when a man has been done a great injustice, he comes out with a great need. Sometimes it's to recite holy scripture, sometimes it's to drink 'til he can't stand for a week straight. But without those, it tends to be a murderous mood. And if you're a man who can shoot straight, strike like lightning, and who has the strength of a hundred beasts, it'd be a concern of mine what mood you're in."

"I feel perfectly fine, Captain. I won't hurt anyone. Is there something I could do to reassure you?"

"Not even my incessant queries incense you?"

"No."

"You are a very singular sort of man, Mister Gordon."

Gordon made no reply, instead returning his attention to the continuing musket blasts in front of him. Something caught his eye on the horizon, however, and he turned back to tell Kilik, "I believe there is a frigate ahead."

Startled, Kilik fished his spyglass out of his coat and put it to his eye. "By Jove, so there is. I am astonished; you have a remarkable eye." He continued to stare through his device as they drew closer to the distant ship. Eventually, he asked Gordon, "Are these people you're chasing expecting the five of you to be coming after them?"

"I wouldn't think so."

"That frigate does appear strange. It may be the one you're looking for. We're not far from Campeche now. If they're not on the lookout for us, we could sail past and survey their disposition as we make our way to Campeche, and put in there for supplies, and plan the next move. And perhaps hire a few more rough men if we mean to take her."

"I don't see any problem with that."

"Good. Now keep your eye on that ship; since your sight is as keen as your aim, I want you to tell me everything you see."

"Very well."

And so Kilik and Gordon studied the mystery vessel from afar as the *Revenge* passed by. It lay at anchor in the clear, blue shallow water not far from the shoreline. The shore itself was a thin line of a white sand beach at the foot of a hill made entirely green by thickly packed palm and logwood trees. On the beach near the anchored ship stood a group of buildings. Smoke wafted upward from a few of their chimneys as the small silhouettes of people passed back and forth between them. Further down the beach to the right, the hill jutted far out into the ocean. At the tip of this protrusion, numerous groups of boulders lay embedded in the sand. They watched, and watched, until the course of the *Revenge* caused the frigate and its camp to disappear behind the hill.

A few hours later, they arrived at Campeche, which had the appearance of a both a civilian settlement and a fortress. Standing a short distance inland from the docks were white and gray stone walls that surrounded the entire town. Only the tops of buildings were visible over the twenty-foot-tall fortifications. Beyond the town and the coast, there was nothing but rolling hills of lush wilderness under a blue sky in every direction. As soon as they docked, Kilik called the travelers in time into his cabin for another meeting.

"This morning, we sighted a frigate anchored at an encampment a few miles north," Kilik told them when they were all assembled. "It may be the ship you're looking for."

"Well, why didn't you tell us so we could take a look at it?" asked Jylling.

"We stayed some ways distant to avoid alarming them, so I don't think an untrained eye would recognize the peculiar vessel. Mister Gordon, however, is a man of exceptional parts, and I had him take a look, and he agrees with me."

"It did look like the Eruewerer, from what I could see," said Gordon.

"So what do we do now?" asked Dhlara.

"If it is a portion of their crew they have ashore, I would attack at night and board her, and attempt to sail her away. We can't take a broadside of forty guns on the open sea."

"We cannot match them man-for-man, either," said Hasdrubal. "That is a sound plan."

"Almost everyone will have to go over when we board her, but we will leave a few men behind to man the Revenge. I get the sense that you are a man who has been at sea, Hasdrubal

Barca."

"In much different ships than these, but yes, I am."

"I'll leave the Revenge under your command, then. You will only have a handful of men, but once we board the frigate, you'll take the Revenge back out to open water."

"I should like to be a part of the action, but I understand my position. Consider it done."

"We'll need to convince the men it's worth fighting against such a force."

"Then let's see what they have to say."

The group left the cabin and Kilik stepped up onto the quarterdeck. "Oi, lads, listen up!" The crew on deck gathered below of him. "As you are aware, we've been on the trail of a mighty warship. We now know her location: she lies at anchor up the coast, where those who crew her have made extensive encampments. Three nights from now, I will give orders for this vessel to approach her under cover of night, so that we may board and take her. They have many men ashore, and they do not anticipate our coming, so we may catch whoever is left aboard completely unawares. When she is under our direction, we will move off and not give battle to the men ashore. If all this is done, every man will receive a share of everything that we take. She is a rogue vessel from a distant country; none of you will be put on trial for taking her."

"How much does she carry?" one of the crew called. "For a sloop to fight such a man of war, she needs to be laden with coin!"

"I don't know precisely, but if they can settle and build as they have, they must have plenty of stores and the wealth to procure them. And I can tell you that if a man such as Mister Gordon here wants what is on her, she must hold rare cargo indeed."

"Is he going to fight?" another man called, pointing at Gordon. A murmur spread throughout the crew. "I'll fight if he will."

"I'll help capture the ship," Gordon answered, "but I won't kill anyone."

"Do any among you object to my plan?" Kilik asked. No

one spoke up. "Very well. We will sail in three days' time."

As Kilik stepped down from the quarterdeck, Dhlara asked him, "Why three days? What if they leave?"

"It's Christmas Day tomorrow. We've got a hold full of rum and I'm about to send out a party to find some boars. I'm not going to ask men to fight on Christmas, and we'll want to give them a day or two to sober up. We'll just have to hope the frigate is still there in a few days."

*

So the crew of the *Revenge* spent the next several days feasting and singing Christmas songs. Some of the men had gone out and come back with decorations such as tropical flowers and branches of pine, although one of them returned laughing about a part of a nativity scene he had spotted in the window of a local home and subsequently purchased from the owner, which turned out to be a porcelain figurine of a man in a red hat in a squatting position, his pants pulled halfway down, and a pile of excrement behind him.

Soon enough, however, the day of the attack came. The sun passed overhead and fell beyond the horizon, and a nearly full moon took its place in the sky. Under this pale white light, the *Revenge* took in its moorings and sailed out of Campeche's harbour. For several hours, it cut through the shimmering surface of the dark sea in its journey back north, until the familiar hill came up on the right. As they drew closer, the small bay behind the hill was revealed, as were the frigate that was still anchored near the shore and the wood buildings on the beach. Candlelight flickered in the windows of the houses. Kilik ordered everyone aboard to be quiet, and the *Revenge* silently glided toward the larger ship.

Dhlara jerked as an idea hit her. "Jylling!" she hissed, even though he was on deck right beside her. Each of them had a brace of pistols hung over their chest and a cutlass at their side.

"What?"

"Didn't you say that when you used your watch back when Olinger showed up outside the Ministries, it took you to a lower deck?"

"Yeah, the lowest one, as far as I know," he whispered. "Why?"

She spun around and rushed over to Gordon, who had climbed partway up the rigging to get a better view of the frigate. Trying to make as little noise as possible, she pulled heavily on the ropes and frantically waved at him. He craned his head downward to discover what the disturbance was and, upon spotting Dhlara, quickly came back down on deck.

"You've got our old watches, right?" she asked.

"Yes."

"Jylling said it took him to the Eruewerer's cargo hold when he tried to use it. What if, while the rest of us are taking the top deck, you use a watch to come in behind them? Or is that too dangerous?"

"That could work. Let's talk with Kilik about it so we can coordinate."

Together, they went to the captain, who was near the helm, and relayed Dhlara's idea to him. "That's brilliant!" he exclaimed in as hushed tones as he could. "How many people can you take over with you?"

"I only have two watches, so there could be at least one other person," said Gordon, "but I wouldn't like to put someone else in harm's way like that. If there's more people on that ship than we guess, or they're better prepared than we've assumed, we'll be trapped down there. I don't want to get anybody killed."

"What about that evil spirit you keep as a pet? Take him with you."

"Who?"

"I think he means Melvin," said Dhlara.

"Oh," said Gordon. "Yeah, I could give him the other watch. I don't want to get him hurt, either, though."

Kilik frowned and raised an eyebrow at Gordon as he stared up at him. "Son, he's a goddamned head. Ain't nobody born a head, so somebody hurt him enough to make him a head, and he doesn't seem to care. He'll be fine."

"I'll go ask him if he wants to do it," said Gordon.

"Hurry; we're almost upon her."

Gordon darted into the captain's cabin in search of Melvin while Dhlara returned to her spot next to Jylling. Now the *Revenge* was pulling up alongside the frigate, and they could see the word "Eruewerer" carved into its stern. The sounds of shouting and the clanging of a bell came down from the top deck of the *Eruewerer* above them. By the light of the moon, they saw a handful of the *Eruewerer's* sailors run up to the gunwale and fire their muskets down at them.

"RETURN FIRE!" Kilik bellowed. Shots erupted from the deck of the *Revenge* and the men at the railing above fell back. Grappling hooks were thrown across and lashed to the frigate. With a deafening yell, its crewmen leaped across the gap between the two ships. Dhlara and Jylling jumped over to grab onto the wooden hull of the *Eruewerer*. As they climbed, they could hear panicked and anguished cries coming from within the lower deck, along with a chaotic tramping of feet and random gunshots.

A gun port near Dhlara popped open; one of the *Eruewerer's* hands desperately tried to pull himself out of the ship, not noticing the boarding party on either side of him. A man of the *Revenge* grabbed him by his shirt collar and yanked him forward. He gave a yelp as he fell. Dhlara moved on, pulling herself up the hull as fast as she could. When she reached the top, she saw men scrambling up the stairways in the center onto the upper deck.

"Devils have come to take us in the night!" one shouted.

"Gordon's back!" another yelled as he ran for the gunwale. "He's pissed!" he added while he hurled himself over the side into the sea.

The crew of the *Revenge* on either side of her rushed past and vaulted over the railing. They charged the disorganized enemy with swords drawn and pistols blazing at close range. The melee did not last very long; the men of the *Eruewerer* quickly lost heart and followed the example of their comrades and leaped to the safety of the water below. Hoarse yells and gunshots still resounded from below; after clearing the upper deck of their enemies, most of the boarders rushed down the stairwells to the lower deck.

"You two!" Kilik called to Dhlara and Jylling, pointing his sword at them, before he descended the stairs himself. "Cut the lines so the *Revenge* may move off!"

Jylling looked around. "What the hell does that mean?"

"Come on, the ropes they threw over," Dhlara told him.

They split up and ran down the gunwale in either direction, stopping to hack the ropes holding the *Revenge* close to the *Eruewerer*. When the last one snapped and fell into the water, Dhlara cupped her hands around her mouth and shouted to Hasdrubal on the quarterdeck of the sloop, "GO!" He waved his fez in the air and took the helm. The *Revenge* pulled away from the frigate and turned to port, heading out to sea.

Meanwhile, the chaos below had quieted. Men poured back out onto the upper deck and rushed to make the *Eruewerer* ready to sail. As many of them scaled the rigging to unfurl the sails, musket fire rang out from beyond the starboard side. Bullets whizzed among them; a few found their mark and sent men falling back onto the deck.

"Go on, let out those sails!" Kilik shouted up to them. "Boatswain, we have to cut and run! The rest of you, to starboard! Unleash hell!"

The crew on deck sprinted to the starboard side of the ship. Standing in a row, they fired their pistols at the sea. Dhlara picked up a musket laying on the deck and ran up to the line. She scanned the water between the frigate and the shore, but couldn't see anything to shoot at. One spot lit up with flashes of fire and she heard bullets crash into the hull near her. Now she saw it: the men of the *Eruewerer* who had been ashore were now packed into longboats and rowing straight for their captured vessel. Those who weren't rowing were firing their muskets. She hurried to load her weapon as metal balls screamed through the air and the enemy drew closer every moment. When it was ready to fire, she pressed the butt against her shoulder, leveled the barrel at one of the jets of fire in the smoky darkness, and pulled the trigger. The gun kicked back. She dropped back to reload.

Near the stern, a pair of crewmen chopped the thick

anchor cable with axes. By the time they cut all the way through, the men on the yards had managed to unfurl the sails. As they were tied down, they caught the wind and bulged forward. The *Eruewerer* groaned as it was pulled along. The exchange of fire continued; the boats were very close now, forcing the defenders to fire nearly straight down. Men leaped from their little crafts onto the side of the frigate, only to be sent flailing into the water by bursts of musket balls. But soon the *Eruewerer* was leaving them behind in its wake, and a cheer went up from those on board when it veered to port and set a course to follow the *Revenge*.

Dhlara dropped her gun and ran up the stairs to the quarterdeck, then up the stairs to the poop deck, and watched the longboats desperately try to follow their stolen frigate. Her mouth opened in a broad smile; the ship that had held her and her friends as prisoners and had abandoned them on an uninhabited island was now under their command. They now had a way back. She pumped her fist in the air and cheered along with those she had just fought beside.

XVI

Rise and Fall

"AAAAHHHHHHHH!" Melvin tore up the stairwell and ran around the upper deck erratically with his mouth wide open in a constant scream.

"Melvin!" Jylling shouted at him. "Hey! Melvin! Enough! We've done it! It's over!"

"AAAAAAHHHH BUT THIS IS FUN AAAAAAHHHHH!" And then he skittered up over the gunwale and disappeared from sight as he climbed down the side of the ship, still screaming at the top of his non-existent lungs.

Gordon came up from the lower deck as Dhlara descended the stairs to the quarterdeck. "How did it go?" she asked him. "Are you hurt? Melvin seems... well, okay."

"I am fine. We caught them by surprise. He helped scare them."

"Has anyone seen Muller?" Jylling asked.

Gordon shook his head. "I haven't."

"He could have been ashore," said Dhlara.

"Good, let him rot in this miserable pirate-infested time," Jylling scoffed.

"All the pirates are what got us off that island and onto this ship, Jylling."

"Ah whatever."

"So the watches worked?"

"Yeah, they did," Gordon nodded. "Took us right to the device Jylling mentioned."

"It's down there? I'd like to see it."

"I'll show you."

Gordon picked up a lantern sitting on the deck near the

mizzen-mast and held it in front of him as he led them down into the gundeck. Inside the ship was even darker; the two rows of cannon, hanging hammocks, and scores of fallen human forms were only barely visible in the moonlight coming in from a few open gun ports. As she followed Gordon, Dhlara's foot kicked something; looking down, she saw a bent and twisted flintlock pistol. Near it were other damaged weapons, including a similarly contorted twentieth century handgun and several shattered swords.

By the light of Gordon's lantern, she saw more clearly the men slumped over cannon barrels and splayed out on the wood planking beneath them. Many were unconscious with broken bones or clutching at parts of their body and groaning. One man, upon seeing Gordon, curled up into a ball against the hull behind him and held his hands over his face saying, "No more! No more! I surrender!" Crewmen from the *Revenge* went from one fallen person to another collecting weapons from their prisoners.

Down a few more stairwells and the travelers in time were in the *Eruewerer*'s hold. Immediately, Dhlara noticed the glowing device in the center, bathing the barrels and chests around it in red light. It was as tall as her waist, about seven feet long, and had a rectangular shape. Walking over to inspect it more closely, she saw through glass panels on its sides a spiral of interlocked golden coloured gears whirling and rotating, churning the red water around them. An open bronze pipe sticking out of its side occasionally vented steam, while other pipes led out from the machine and up into the decking above their heads. They heard and felt a thumping, whirring hum resonating from it.

"So what is this thing?" asked Jylling.

"I'm not exactly sure," said Gordon, "but I think this is what enables this ship to travel through time. There is a tremendous amount of power being generated inside it, and I can see that it's made of materials that do not normally exist in this time."

"Can we use it?" asked Dhlara.

"I noticed some mechanisms near the helm that weren't

normal on a ship like this; they might interface with this…
generator. I will take a look at them, and this thing as well, to
see if I can put in a destination. We'll also have to find out if
we can activate it to bring us there, but the only way to do that
is push whatever looks like is responsible for doing that and
see what happens."

"And that destination would be back to the Ministries of
Time, right?"

"I should think so."

"If that wacko Olinger has access to all of those doors,
every year there's ever been or will be," said Jylling, "I don't
want to even imagine what kind of damage he could do to the
past. Everything we know could be gone already and we don't
know it yet."

"Not exactly. Time passes much more slowly at the edge,
where the Ministries are. If we could go back, we would get
there almost instantly after we left. We could still stop him."

Dhlara gasped. "We have his ship, all his men are captured
or back on that beach… it's just him and that small group he
attacked the Ministries with. Maybe that's all we have to deal
with to prevent him from turning the past into a colony of
Luxembourg!"

"If we can get this thing to work," Jylling pointed out.

"Well, we've got all the time in the world to figure it out."

Jylling glared at her. "That isn't funny."

"We should be prepared in case he has something more,
though. If he can just show up with a whole frigate, who
knows what else he can do. We ought to bring as many people
who are willing to fight as we can back with us."

"There is something odd about the people we've just
captured: some of them are Spaniards from this century. I
didn't see anyone like that the first time I was on this ship."

Jylling frowned and tousled his black hair with his hand.
"Why would that be?"

"They must have recruited men from the area around here.
Maybe Muller lost some of his men in a fight. I'm not sure. But
here they are."

"We can go back to Campeche and do our own recruiting,"

said Dhlara. "We should pay them beforehand, though. We can't promise a horde of rather mercenary sailors shares of the... command center of time, basically."

"Our own cash has run out. What do we pay them with?" Jylling wondered.

"There's treasure over there," a fourth voice said. Dhlara and Jylling jumped.

"Gah! Holy crap, Melvin!" Jylling shouted at the head hanging onto the deck above.

"There's treasure?" Dhlara asked him.

"Yup! Over there, in those chests!" He pointed behind them.

Gordon walked over, picked one up, placed it on the floor, and opened it. Gold coins spilled out onto the ground; it was entirely full of doubloons. "We'll have to count this up and split it with the crew," he said. "But if we pool our own shares we can definitely afford to recruit a couple hundred men."

"How did you know there were coins in there?" Dhlara asked Melvin.

"Gordon can see lots of stuff I can't," he answered, "but I can see *treasure* real good!" His eyes widened and he clacked his pincer hands together happily.

"Do you know anything about this, uh, thing here?" She motioned toward the glowing time travel machine.

Melvin immediately fell and cracked his head onto the planks below. He rolled over and ran over to the device. He pressed his ear to it and listened intently. He clinked a claw against the glass. He stuck out his tongue and licked it. He thought for a moment, tasting it fully, and answered, "Nope." With that, he made an engine noise with his mouth and scurried away.

"Well, at least he pointed out the crap ton of money," said Jylling.

"Hey! Is anyone down here?" someone called into the stairwell they had come down.

"Yes," Dhlara called back.

One of the crew walked down and saw the three of them. "The captain would like to see you."

"Alright, thank you. Come on, let's go up there," she said to the other two.

"Yeah, they're all about to be really happy to learn what's down here," said Jylling.

*

The news of the chests full of Spanish gold indeed delighted the men of the *Revenge*. They were quickly brought up to the upper deck and their contents tallied and divided. When the *Revenge* and the *Eruewerer* put in again at Campeche, the stories the crew told when they went ashore and the coin they spent at taverns while telling them prompted more men to volunteer for service on the sloop than the offered wage. The ships had been damaged by little more than small arms fire and were swiftly repaired, and the frigate's lost anchor and cable were replaced.

After a few days in port, their crew had grown to include over two hundred men. In preparation to return to the Ministries of Time, the *Revenge* was sold, since it could not be taken with them. Gordon said that he believed he had calibrated the machine correctly as well as identified the purpose of each unusual lever or dial near the helm, so, on New Year's Day, the *Eruewerer* sailed out into the open ocean to attempt time travel.

"Would you like to take the helm?" Kilik asked Gordon when they were beyond the sight of land. Dhlara, Jylling, and Melvin looked down at him from the poop deck. Hasdrubal stood near the cabin door.

"Yes, I think I should," he replied. Kilik stepped back and Gordon took his place, grasping one of the frigate's two wheels. "Your men will need to brace themselves; we're actually doing to dive straight into the water, if it works."

Kilik's brow furrowed, bewildered. "Into the sea? Are you mad?"

"Just trust us. We've done it before," Dhlara told him.

"Yeah! It was fun!" said Melvin.

Kilik stared at the grinning head for a moment, then

shrugged his shoulders. "I suppose you're right; I really have no notion of what is going on. BRACE YOURSELVES!" he shouted to the men on deck.

"BRACE!" The call was passed along. Dhlara wrapped her arms around the railing in front of her. Seeing Melvin uselessly trying to grip onto it himself with his much too small metal hands, she picked him up with one arm and tucked him against her body.

"Oh, hugs!" Melvin squealed.

"Well, here goes," said Gordon. He squeezed the handle of the lever to his right and pulled it down. They felt the planking beneath them lurch as the ship pitched forward. The prow dipped into the water and the water rushed up along the deck, swallowing up the frigate and everyone aboard until the stern disappeared beneath the swirling waves.

*

"It escaped, Mister President," one of Olinger's men reported to him.

"No matter; one less loony resident for us to evict from here," he replied. "I'm much more interested in why this particular wacky-doodle refuses to die."

"GDDDRGGGHRRHH!" the Minister of Order growled through the shirt in his mouth, struggling against the men holding him in place.

"You are going to die, you overstuffed English moron, because you have to. You have been quite enough of a nuisance, so you *will* cease to exist. Give me your pistol, Smitt." The officer handed Olinger his twentieth century style handgun. Olinger held it inches away from the Minister's stomach and fired eleven times. The Minister didn't even seem to notice.

"MRRRGRRR!"

"Huh. Apparently you're not finished with being impossibly irritating. Well, do you know what you have to look forward to, then?" Olinger grabbed the sides of the Minister's head and held their faces so close their noses nearly touched.

"I'm going to take you to the exact spot where the largest bomb in the history of the universe explodes, and I'm going to leave you there. And if somehow your charred skeletal ass still has some ridiculous English nonsense to say to me, I'll start tossing you into astronomical bodies. I will break you down into tiny, stupid, yelling atoms, and I'll feed them two by two into a particle accelerator."

"RRRRRDDDDRR!"

"Good. I'm glad your incredibly simple mind understands. Or doesn't. I don't care which. You're getting blown to bits anyway." Olinger threw himself down into the Minister's chair. He picked up the Minister's hat and put it on his head. "I'm the Minister of Order now, and the Minister of everything else, too. What other junk do you have?" He started opening the drawers of the desk.

"I saw a hammer down on that table," said Schmitt. "Could that be his?"

"It would have to be. Bring it to me."

"Yes, sir!" Schmitt walked down the stairs and down to the end of the table, picked up the hammer, and brought it back to Olinger.

"What do you use this for?" Olinger asked the Minister as he turned it over in his hands.

"GGRRRRNN!"

"Yes, well, I'll find out soon enough."

Meanwhile, a few miles distant, the frigate that had formerly belonged to him shot up out of the gently churning sea. Its prow pointed at the sky, it leaped clear of the ocean in an arc and splashed down again.

"We made it!" Dhlara shouted.

"I do think we've done it," Gordon remarked.

Kilik felt his coat with his hands. "I'm not wet at all."

"These waters aren't exactly water. We are at the edge of time itself."

"Son, don't bother explaining it to me. I'll never have the foggiest idea what you mean. All of this is utter madness. But there are riches and excitement to be had where you go, and that's all I need to understand."

Hasdrubal laughed. "The simpler life is the better one, isn't it?"

"Where are we, exactly?" said Jylling, looking around from atop the poop deck at the vast expanse of ocean around them.

"That's a good question," said Kilik. "Let me see here." He pulled out his spyglass, walked up to the poop deck, and scanned the horizon. "There... what looks like a fort out that way. And— oh, devil take us!" He exclaimed as he looked to port. "There's a damned fleet out there!"

"What?!" Dhlara exclaimed.

"Three frigates, at least! That's more than a fight; that's a death sentence. I don't suppose those are friendly?"

"No," said Gordon as he stepped up the stairs to join them.

"How is there suddenly three more ships out here?!" asked Jylling, practically spitting his words out in frustration.

"There aren't."

"Look!" Kilik held his spyglass up to the tall blonde and pointed a stubby finger at a spot on the horizon. "There they are!"

Gordon shook his head. "There's only one ship that I can see."

Kilik's brow furrowed. He stared up at Gordon, clearly doubting his intelligence. "That's why I'm giving you this here glass, so that you can see for yourself that there are in fact *three* frigates out there."

"Those are the Eruewerer. They're all the same ship; it's been back to the Ministries since we saw it last, apparently."

"...*What?!*" said Jylling, his face twisted in confusion.

"Okay, one of us has lost it. Somebody here is crazy," said Kilik.

"No, I think I get it," said Dhlara. "While we were with the pirates and in Charles Town, Muller used the Eruewerer to come back here three times, and... that's what you're seeing out there? Is that right?"

"Yes, that's it," said Gordon.

"Why would he do that, though?"

"It can't be for anything good," said Hasdrubal. "Actually,

this might explain the Spanish men among those we fought to take this ship. Muller might have been bringing men and equipment to the Ministries."

"So…" Kilik started, squinting his eyes, "what do you propose to do now? I don't know what you mean by any of this, but we can't give battle to three frigates, no matter what name they've got. There's definitely three of them out there, and if they're armed well at all, they would pound us into flinders."

"I don't know about that. We captured this frigate with far less than we have now. Under the right circumstances, we might be able to take them."

"No, we shouldn't fight them at all," Gordon countered. "We can't even let them know we're here; Muller's men clearly didn't have advance warning when we boarded. If any of those ships spot us, they can bring back that warning."

"Well, what do we now, then?" said Jylling.

"We should keep our distance until they all leave," said Gordon. "We know they'll go away at some point, because where the Eruewerer ends up is here, now, with us standing on it. As I said, there is only one ship, really."

"Very well then. DROP ANCHOR!" Kilik shouted down to the upper deck.

"No, don't—" Gordon started.

*

"I dare say they are terribly brave chaps!" Earl Ponceberry declared from his seat at the head of his dinner table, which was heavily laden with plates of turkey meat, dishes of gravy, bowls full of colorful fruit, piles of fresh bread, a wheel of cheese, and glasses full of different beverages. A pair of candelabras on the table and a few lamps by the wall lit the room, since it was evening, and curtains had been drawn over the nearby windows. A maid carrying dishes was exiting the room through the doorway behind him. Six other people, each as finely dressed as the Earl himself, sat at the sides of the table. One of them, a well-known Colonel, who the Earl had gone out of his way to invite only to watch his own wife eye the tall officer from across the table far more than he thought was proper, cleared his throat to voice his agreement.

"Quite! That is a most agreeable thing to say, and I would think any manly sort of gentleman would think so. But, alas, it seems there are many who are wanting in that regard."

"Oh yes, quite manly, quite manly indeed," the Earl's wife twittered, smiling at the Colonel.

"Well, a toast, then, I should say, to Mister Whymper," the Earl said as he raised his glass.

At that moment, the door across from Ponceberry burst apart, showering the room in wooden splinters, and a huge metal anchor flew into the room, shot through the air over the table, and jerked to a halt right in front of the Earl's face, as if to confront him over a forgotten dinner invitation. Holding onto the top arm of the anchor was a disembodied head with some sort of strange, metallic spider body. The hunk of metal and its passenger hung in the air for a split-second, then crashed into the table below. Much of the dinnerware fell over and smashed into pieces, which created a brief racket.

Its eyes wide, the head jerked back and forth, swiveling around to look at its new surroundings. "Whoah," it said, as amazed as anyone at its sudden entrance. "Hello! I'm Melvin, the previously embodied head!"

The dinner guests just stared at him in shock, silently sitting in their chairs; a few even had their hands in the air, still clutching silverware.

"Nice bowtie," the head complimented the Earl. "Bowties are cool. Ooooou, sweet rolls!" he exclaimed. He jumped down off the anchor and ran over to a broken plate and its scattered payload of baked goods. He sampled one with a huge bite. "Mmmmm... tashty!"

After a few seconds, however, the anchor scraped across the hardwood floor several inches back toward the now doorless doorway. The clatter of crashing dishes momentarily filled the room as the table was dragged with it.

"Oh, sorry, can't stay! That's my ride!" said the head. Clutching it with both of his tiny pincer claws, he held the roll out in front of him and scurried back onto the anchor. He sat down again on top of the arm and munched happily on his treat as the anchor slowly ground across the floor and out of the room.

*

"There isn't a bottom for it to hold on to," Gordon explained to Kilik while the crew hauled the anchor back up. "If it catches on something, it may be caught on a skyscraper in the twenty-third century for all we know."

"Do you want us to just drift about, then?" the captain asked him.

"I think that's all we can do, until this is the only Eruewerer left here."

"After that, let's go take back the Ministries from Olinger," said Dhlara.

"I agree," said Gordon.

"I'm sure this won't make any sense to me either, but what are these 'Ministries' you keep speaking of?" asked Kilik.

"The Ministries of Time," Dhlara explained. "They oversee the course of history, basically."

Melvin wandered over carrying a lump of what looked like a half-eaten sweet roll. "I'm the Minister of Maintenance!"

Kilik's eyes grew wide. "You mean to tell me *he's* actually in charge of history?"

"Not all of it," said Dhlara.

"That's obviously ridiculous. Nobody would put that thing in command of anything. Anyway, if we're going to be waiting these other ships out, I'll be in my quarters."

Gordon and Hasdrubal stayed on the poop deck to keep an eye on the center hub of the Ministries building and the three other instances of the *Eruewerer* that sailed up and docked with it while everyone else dispersed throughout the ship. The Carthaginian watched through a spyglass while Gordon simply stood and observed with his own eyes.

"Do you regret agreeing to help them?" Hasdrubal asked Gordon after a few minutes of silence.

"Who?"

"Those two, Dhlara and Jylling," the general said, putting down his telescope. "They brought you on this quest to fix time, and you almost got trapped in a distant time, or worse."

"No, I don't regret going with them. It wasn't their fault; they're trying to make things better. I'm just trying to help."

Hasdrubal scoffed. "Everybody's trying to make things better, but everybody's got a different idea what that means. In their case, they're trying to keep things the way they knew them, which I guess we all do. But why are you helping them? What are you trying to accomplish?"

Gordon shrugged. "I'm not trying to accomplish anything. There seems to be something wrong going on here and I'm trying to do the right thing. People assume I am so different because of how I am, but I don't know anything more about all of this than you do."

"Ah, the time they're from, they've forgotten about heroes. But I come from a place where we remember heroes and know their stories. You are not so strange to me."

"I am not a hero."

"You're not very much different from how one would describe a hero."

"Maybe not. What are you trying to accomplish, then?"

"I am a sworn enemy of Rome. Where Rome goes, there my family will be, with an army at our backs."

"What do the Romans have to do with all of this?"

"Napoleon is an Italian who styles himself a Roman. That's a Roman. If he wants his men to carry the eagles of Rome, then they will face the swords of Carthage."

"I see."

Hasdrubal went back to peering through the spyglass and they fell silent for a few moments. When he put it down again, he turned to look at Gordon with a penetrating expression. "I know the real reason you came along," he said.

"I... don't follow."

"I don't know why they cannot tell, but I've noticed the way you look at her. You have got an eye for Dhlara."

"I don't know what you mean."

Hasdrubal laughed. "No, of course you don't. You're too stiff to acknowledge it, aren't you? Well, we'll see, won't we?"

Gordon said nothing.

Hasdrubal slapped him on the back. "I'm going to go check on the ship's stores of rum. Want to join me? They aren't going any other place for the minute." He nodded at the docked frigates in the distance.

"No, thank you."

"You'll be standing watch, then?"

"Yes."

"Fair enough." Hasdrubal descended the stairs and went below, leaving Gordon alone to stare at the specks on the horizon. Several hours passed and he barely moved, standing rigidly still with his hands clasped behind his back. Eventually, the ships moved one by one away from the Ministries building and sunk back into the ocean, until the last one dropped its prow into the water and disappeared from sight.

"They've gone," Gordon called down from the poop deck.

"I'll let the captain know," Jylling replied from below and went into the cabin. After a moment, Kilik stepped out onto the quarterdeck.

"Let us bring her in, then, and see about this Olinger," he said. The sails were unfurled and the *Eruewerer* crossed the ocean between them and the Ministries building. "Bring her alongside," Kilik told the helmsman as the frigate neared the endless stretch of doorways. Dhlara noticed that the waterfalls that before had cascaded down from each door were no longer there; instead, the ocean calmly lapped at the building a few inches below the doorways.

"Ahoy there! You're late!" a voice called. One of the doors was open and a man in the doorway was holding a speaking horn to his mouth.

"Who are you, sir?!" Kilik shouted over the port side.

"Who are you?! That's our ship! What are you doing on it?!"

"Are you with Olinger?" Dhlara called.

"Why are you aboard the President's ship?!"

"We took it by force!" Hasdrubal declared.

"The President of the World Government of Luxembourg, Egmond Olinger retains the realms of space and time as the rightful property of his domain and will not suffer thieves nor trespassers. Surrender his ship and yourselves or die as traitorous dogs!"

"We'll do no such thing!" Hasdrubal yelled.

The man reached out to grab the handle of the door and slammed it shut. A moment later, every other door along the line flew open, and in every doorway was a cannon pointed at the *Eruewerer* and a group of men to fire it.

"BRACE YOUR—!" Kilik managed to bellow before the length of the narrow hallway opposite them roared fire and thunder, sending solid balls of iron blasting through the hull of the frigate, creating explosions of wood splinters all around them. Dhlara held her arm over her face and fell to the deck as the railing in front of her burst apart from the impact of a ball.

"MAN THE CANNONS! RETURN FIRE!"

Another volley from the Ministries pounded the ship. Ropes that had been cut through whipped around and bodies of men littered the deck. The planks Dhlara was kneeling on rumbled as the *Eruewerer* answered with a broadside of her own. Now it was the building's turn to take a beating. A ringing sound in her ears was all she could hear as she watched the cannons roaring beneath her punch holes in the building. Doors were cut in half and cannon crews in the doorways broken up by careening cannon balls. Thick smoke hung in the air as the frigate sailed alongside the hallway of doors and continued trading cannon shots along the way. Hasdrubal stepped up to the shattered gunwale near her and fired his pistol at the enemy gun crews. He looked down at her as he stood fully upright, even as the cannon shots whizzed through the air around him and sent the smoke around him whirling in their wake. He held out his second pistol to her. She took it and leaned to fire through the hole in the hull.

After several minutes of a deafening mixture of high pitched cries, the tremendous boom of cannonfire, and the cracking of small arms fire, Hasdrubal grabbed Dhlara's shoulder and pointed behind her. The foremast was slowly falling, stopped only by the ropes attached to it which were now snapping one by one and flying loose. Its base was deeply scarred by the battle and splintered as it broke in half. Sailors scattered as the huge piece of timber came crashing down onto the deck. The top of it and the sails attached there fell over into the water while the remaining ropes held the lower part on board.

The frigate began to turn to port, toward the building. Looking back at the quarterdeck, Dhlara saw Kilik at the helm whirling the damaged wheel to his left as fast as he could manage. His face turned a deeper shade of blotchy red as he shouted something. Gordon, who had been standing on the quarterdeck, suddenly bolted, racing down the length of the ship toward the front. Following him with her eyes, Dhlara watched him run up the prow, along the thin jibboom, and then leap into the air. By now, the *Eruewerer* was headed straight for the Ministries, and Gordon flew across the gap and slammed into the roof with his fist, sending up a shower of dust and shattered roofing tile. The hole he left was visible for only a moment, and then the *Eruewerer* followed his example, driving its bow into the hallway at full speed. The ship shuddered with the impact and slowly came to a halt as it ground through the building.

One of the crew jumped over the side onto the roof. Dhlara saw him place a ball with a fuse on the tiles, then run for cover further along the roof. It exploded, creating a hole that opened into the hallway of doors. The men of the *Eruewerer* rushed forward armed with cutlasses and pistols to jump down the hole.

When Dhlara, Jylling, and Hasdrubal made their way down through the hole, they found themselves in the middle of a desperate struggle. Their crew had captured several cannon and pointed them at Olinger's men. The guns bucked as they fired down the hallway. Both sides had established rough lines and exchanged musket and pistol fire. Behind them, only a few feet of hallway was not blocked by the bow of the *Eruewerer*.

"Come on, this way! The main part is this way!" Dhlara shouted to Hasdrubal and Jylling. They hurried through the narrow space to the other side of the hallway, which was a much different scene. None of their own men were there, but Olinger's men were all laid out on the ground, their weapons bent and several of their cannon overturned.

"Gordon's been through here," Hasdrubal remarked with a smirk.

They ran through the hallway past all of the disarray of Olinger's defeated men amid the unsettling relative silence, compared to what they had just emerged from. Finally, they came to the set of double doors Dhlara and Jylling had first passed through months ago. Opening them once again, they came into the library of the Ministry of Order, which was now scored with bullet holes. The Minister of Order's soldiers lay dead on the floor. A clapping noise came from the far end. Olinger sat at the Minister's desk, clapping his hands. The three of them approached cautiously.

"Well done! Really, very well done!" he called to them.

"Gordon?" Dhlara called, looking around.

"He's not here."

"Where is he?"

"While he was busy subduing my officers and guards, I used one of Wellington's old tricks to send him into that bronze globe thing." Olinger waved his hand at the Minister, who was tied up and gagged and being guarded on both sides by four of Olinger's men. "You remember how he likes to grab people and send them back here? That's how we all ended up here, isn't it? Turns out it's all in his hat." Olinger picked up the bicorne hat from the desk and spun it around on his finger. "So Gordon's in there, and apparently that machine is made of tougher stuff, because he hasn't come back out. Which is a splendid turn of events, because that means I am free to kill you all."

"Give it up, Olinger," said Jylling. "You've lost. You're not going to be dictator of the world."

Olinger laughed. "Just because you can hijack a ship doesn't mean you mean very much, insolent child. What have I lost? My men are still fighting, and they will defeat your pathetic group of whatever rabble you scraped together, and I will continue as if nothing happened. You've even brought my ship back for me. In fact, it looks like the three of you have lost more than I have. I have all of my feet. Schmitt!"

"Yes, President!" said one of the men near the Minister.

"Have you still got both of your feet?"

"I do, sir!"

"Two nobodies and an antiquated general who was only famous for being the *brother* of the guy who *lost* can't even run away from my men with success. You will be shot again, and again, and you will not leave here alive. You should have used your unimportance to hide, but now that you have delivered yourselves to me, I will gladly end you."

"You're not going to kill us," said Dhlara.

Olinger scoffed. "In a moment, we'll see how wrong you are."

"You haven't killed him," she pointed to the Minister. "And we know he's not exactly endearing. And you didn't kill us before."

Olinger laughed again. "You stupid girl. I've tried to kill him! And I'm still trying! Watch!" He picked up a handgun from the desk, inserted a magazine into it, and pointed it at the Minister.

"NO!" Dhlara shouted, but the Luxembourger was already firing. Eleven bangs resounded through the library. After the gun clicked empty, the Minister still struggled furiously against his captors.

"See?! It's absolutely ridiculous! And if you mean to tell me that if I do that to you, you won't die, then you will indeed vex me very seriously! But that's not going to happen."

Another gunshot cracked through the room, this time from behind them. The group ducked their heads in surprise. Olinger grabbed his chest and fell backwards, toppling his chair. Whipping her head around, Dhlara saw Kilik holding a musket amid a faint cloud of smoke.

"Did you just shoot him?"

"I can't fathom why you would be standing around talking to that blasted sheep's head. Any man who talks that much is a damn fool. Hey, the rest of you! Put down your weapons and come over here with your hands up!" Kilik ordered Olinger's four men holding the Minister. "Leave that man be and give up this fight like sensible people! There's plenty more of us, and a great number of you are dead by now!"

The man named Schmitt rushed over to the fallen body of his president. The other three disarmed themselves and walked down off the raised platform with their hands over their heads. The Minister ripped the shirt tied around his head out of his mouth and threw it to the ground. He swung his leg back and kicked Schmitt in the side.

"DAMNABLE SWINE!" He bellowed at the officer. He grabbed a fistful of the man's hair with one hand and threw him down the stairs. Turning back to the body near his desk, his face twisted up in disgust and he spat on it. "SOMEBODY CLEAN THIS FILTH UP!"

"Are you… alright?" Dhlara called to him.

"WHO THE BLOODY HELL ARE YOU?!"

"I, uh, you brought us here to stop Napoleon…"

"WELL THEN?!"

"…Well then what?"

"HAVE YOU DONE IT?!"

"No! We've been dealing with that guy next to you."

"WHAT ARE YOU WAITING FOR?! GET TO IT!"

"You're welcome!" Jylling shouted at him as Dhlara ran to the side room on the right that housed the time bathysphere. She yanked on a lever at its side and the bronze door swung open. Gordon ducked his head as he stepped out.

"Are you okay?" Dhlara asked him.

"I'm perfectly fine," Gordon answered. "What has happened? Is everyone okay? Olinger somehow stuck me in there."

"Kilik shot Olinger," she told him.

Gordon frowned. "That's unfortunate."

"He probably would have had all of us shot, if he had his way."

"Yes, and that would have been more unfortunate."

"Well, come on, let's go sort out the rest of this mess."

XVII

A Dangerous Meeting

Dhlara, Jylling, and Hasdrubal sat at the end of the long table in the Ministry of Order's library of records. Gordon stood nearby and, this time, Kilik sat on the bench with them, next to Jylling.

"Well, here we are again," said Hasdrubal as he leaned back in his chair and lifted his feet onto the table. They had moved the bodies of the Minister's soldiers and took them to an appropriate year to bury them, after getting the Minister to reactivate the time travel doors. Olinger's body was given to what was left of his men, who were made to return to Luxembourg in the year they had left it. The bullet holes in the records room remained, as did the battered ship they had crashed into the hallway. Barrels and crates unloaded from the *Eruewerer*'s earlier trips were piled up in the corners of the room.

"One world domination wacko down, one to go," said Jylling.

"I'm not one to say any fight is too daunting, but what can we actually do against him?" Hasdrubal asked. "We've done well raising this band of rogues, but they're very much less than an army."

"Against who? You're looking to fight somebody else already, are you?" asked Kilik.

"Napoleon," said Dhlara.

"Who the bloody hell is Napoleon?"

"He was the emperor of France about a hundred years after the year you came here from," Jylling explained.

"You're fighting all of France, now?"

"In a way."

"Why?"

"He has used time travel to change history," said Dhlara. "And a giant squid. He's used time travel and a giant squid to ensure the French empire one day rules the world."

"A giant squid? How giant?"

"We've seen it sink a whole ship," said Jylling.

"Blood and thunder!"

"And, I remind you, he has an entire army at Waterloo, too," said Hasdrubal. "And it's a fine army. We'd have to raise a large force indeed to turn the tide of that battle."

"Even if we could get an army of our own," said Jylling, "wouldn't we be screwing up history ourselves by using it to change the outcome of that fight?"

"It's already screwed up," said Dhlara.

"The future is meant to change," said Hasdrubal.

"It's not the future to us!" Jylling countered.

"Are you trying to stop Napoleon or make sure everything that happened in your past stays exactly the same?"

"Why can't I want to do both?"

"Because we have small resources and have to make the best of a bad situation. We have to stop Napoleon and that's it."

"What if we don't fight his army at all?" Dhlara pondered.

"He needs to lose the Battle of Waterloo, though," said Hasdrubal.

"Right, but he lost it anyway, with his army. What he changed was the squid. We just have to stop the squid."

"How do we do that?" said Jylling.

"When we saw him at Elba, that's the first time the squid shows up, right? He doesn't have it before Elba, and then he escapes from Elba on it. We've got a warship and a crew. Let's kill his squid."

"Whoah! Hold on, missy!" Kilik held his hands up. "Those men have fought two battles for you and they now have shiners enough for their wants. It ain't easy to ask any man to sign on to fight an emperor and his beasts of hell, even more so when he's got coin in his pockets. And that aside, we're shipwrecked!"

"It can be repaired," said Jylling. "And we can get a new crew."

Hasdrubal shook his head. "No, the men we have have seen and fought in this strange place, and they have learned that they can beat otherworldly foes. Greener men might abandon their guns once they see Napoleon's behemoth."

"You're all getting ahead of yourselves," said Kilik. "Let's repair our ship and let the men rest, and then let's see what can be done about your Napoleon."

"I think that's a good idea," said Dhlara.

*

Over the next few days, groups of sailors were sent back through door *1714* to bring back materials for repairs. The *Eruewerer*'s bow was fixed up and its foremast replaced before it was freed from the hole it had made in the hallway of doors. After that, work was started to rebuild that section of the building and patch up the damage to the frigate's hull that had been inflicted by cannonballs. Every night, so to speak, since the light over the edge of time never dimmed, singing and laughing filled the library of the Ministry of Order as the crew relaxed, much to the consternation of the Minister. Dhlara, Jylling, and the others continued to discuss how they could challenge Napoleon, but Dhlara's idea remained the best, and it became clear it was necessary to retain their current crew. So after the repairs were finished, Kilik summoned them to the deck of the *Eruewerer*, where the Minister wouldn't interrupt him.

"I'm here to ask you to fight one more battle," Kilik began, standing at the railing near one set of stairs leading down from the quarterdeck. The daylight that shone despite no sun in the sky shone down on him and the mass of men abovedeck. Dhlara, Jylling, Gordon, and Hasdrubal stood behind him. The throng of men below him on the upper deck booed and hissed. He held a hand up over his head. "I know we've been through many hardships thus far. But there is one more voyage, and then I will truly make you rich."

"Who do we have to fight?" one of the mariners shouted.

"There is a man who commands a gigantic tentacled creature of the deep. I ask you to help me kill the beast."

"How big is it?"

"As big as this ship, so I am told."

The crowd grumbled at this. "We've made enough money as it is." A man yelled. "These Olingers had plenty of money to take. We can't spend it if we're all dragged down to hell by a sea-monster!"

Dhlara stepped up beside Kilik. "We can give you more than money. I am from a time when machines as big as this ship, with as many people aboard, fly through the air like birds. A time when machines have carried people beyond the sky. It is a place beyond your imagination."

"So what?!"

"You can go live there. If you help us, you can live in a world greater than anything you've ever dreamed of."

"We've seen what these doors do! How about we go to your time and leave you to fight your monster on your own?!"

"You could do that. We can't stop you. But that place doesn't exist anymore. The man who controls the giant squid used it to rule the entire world. We've seen the future, and it is full of many more monsters, dragons, in fact, all under his command. You can live in the time I came from, but only after this man and his squid are defeated."

"We can't if we're dead!"

"Every fight we've asked you to take has not been more than you could handle. Everything we've asked of you has been something you could do, and we have always delivered on our promises. We promised to make you rich, and you are. I have seen the beast, and I'm telling you that we can kill it, and then you can go to a place where commonplace things hold more value than anything you can buy in your own time with the money you have now."

The crowd murmured as they talked amongst themselves.

After about a minute, Kilik asked them, "So are you with us?"

A few voiced their assent. "Aye."

"We'll do it."

The rest were reserved, but nodded agreement and didn't offer objections.

"Then we'll make ourselves ready and sail for battle tomorrow," said Kilik.

Jylling approached Dhlara as she stepped back from the railing. "You can't tell them they can come live in our time!" he protested.

"Why not?" she asked.

"We can't just dump a couple hundred pirates into the modern world!"

"They're not pirates."

"They're not much different, are they?"

"We need their help."

"You can't just screw with history like that!"

"That was a fine job, Dhlara," said Hasdrubal. "I agree with you. You did the right thing."

"We have to actually win, before I'll agree with that," said Kilik. "I haven't seen this squid. For all I know, it'll kill us all."

"Do you want to leave?" Dhlara asked him.

"No. I'm a foolish old sea-crab. I've had my fill of money and comforts; I'll go where there's adventure. Even if it does kill us all, isn't that a story?"

Hasdrubal laughed. "That is the way to live life, my friend."

"So, can you calibrate that contraption in the hold and take us wherever, or whenever it is we need to go?" Kilik asked Gordon.

"I have already done so. I believe it will put us extremely close."

"Then you may take the helm and await my command."

Gordon stepped forward and gripped the wheel.

"Prepare for action!" Kilik called.

The crowded upper deck came alive as men rushed to their stations. Once more, the sails unfurled, and, when they had gained enough speed, Gordon pulled the lever at his side, and the *Eruewerer* dived into the ocean.

*

When the frigate leaped back out of the water, Dhlara found herself immersed in total darkness, except for a mostly full moon. As she looked around, she folded her arms to warm herself against the much colder air. When her eyes adjusted, she saw the twinkling of stars in the night sky overhead, and the dim reflection of the moon's light on the surface of the sea, which seemed to entirely surround them.

"Where are we?" Kilik asked Gordon.

"We are near the island of Elba on February twenty-fifth, eighteen-fifteen." He walked over to the starboard gunwale and peered down into the water. The group watched him as he gazed intently at the shimmering waves.

"What is it?" asked Dhlara.

"I need a harpoon."

"Bring up a harpoon!" Kilik shouted.

The word went out, and a minute later a man came rushing up the stairs from the lower deck carrying a three-foot-long harpoon. Gordon took it from him, gripping the wooden handle, and held it in the air near his head. "It is coming," he said.

"Make ready! Prepare to fire!" Kilik yelled.

Gordon's arm shot forward, flinging the harpoon down. The sharp metal tip of the weapon sliced into the water and the entire length disappeared beneath. After a moment, a screeching, croaking noise resonated throughout the entire ship. A massive shape rose up out of the sea. It was difficult to see in the darkness, but it was nearly half as big as the ship itself. Everyone aboard stared in awe as the top of it rose above the deck of the frigate. And then it tilted backwards, away from the ship, and a mass of enormous tentacles stretched out in front of it, each blocking out narrow bands of stars as they waved and squirmed above the ship. The creature gave another screeching croak, this time much louder and shriller, and its entire length, from the tip of its tubular body down to the end of its tentacles, suddenly lit up in bright bioluminescent glows. Its main body gave off red coloured light with white blotches, while the tentacles gave off white and their suckers were coloured red. At the center of the splayed out tentacles was its beak, wide open and emitting a screech, and the area around it glowed orange.

"FIRE! FIRE! KILL IT!" Kilik bellowed as the tentacles reached for the *Eruewerer*.

The starboard length of the frigate roared back at the gigantic squid as cannon after cannon discharged. Billows of smoke shot out from the gun ports and wafted around the creature as cannonballs plunged into its flesh. It screamed in pain and charged forward. Its tentacles wrapped around the hull of the ship and thrashed across the deck, sending men and debris flying. Gordon grabbed a sword from one of the crew nearby and leaped onto the body of the squid. He buried the full length of the blade into the monster and jumped away, dodging a tentacle swatting at him.

One of the squid's arms slammed into the foremast and broke it, sending it into the ocean. Dhlara, Jylling, and Hasdrubal took up muskets and pistols and added to the crackling of gunshots. Firing, reloading, and firing again as men and beast screamed, wood splintered and cracked, and the cannon below continued to thunder. A luminescent arm swiped at the quarterdeck. The three of them hurled themselves onto the deck and it passed over their heads, but it struck Kilik, knocking him onto the upper deck, and ripped the helm away. After discarding the flinders of the wheel, the tentacle wrapped itself around the mizzenmast and snapped it in two.

"LOOK OUT!" Hasdrubal shouted as the huge timber fell towards them. Dhlara grabbed Jylling's arm to pull him out of its path. The mast toppled over, narrowly missing the two of them before it crashed into the quarterdeck. While they stared at the huge piece of wood that had nearly killed them, the squid moved aft. Its tentacles heaved its body up onto the ship and passed over the fallen mast. As they watched its beak pass overhead, they saw someone fall off the squid. The falling person tried to grab hold of the mizzenmast and managed to briefly slow his fall, but he lost his grip and dropped onto the quarterdeck near them. Dhlara thought for a moment it might be Gordon, but then she realized this person was much shorter and fatter. And then she saw the bicorne hat that had landed next to her.

"Napoleon?!" she exclaimed.

The man sat up and grimaced, holding his back. He had a head of somewhat short, soft hair with a receding hairline, thin lips, and a chubby face. His chin was slightly jutting and dimpled.

"WHAT?!" Jylling shouted. "GET HIM!"

Hasdrubal pointed his pistols at the man. "Don't move! You're our prisoner, now!"

"Am I?!" he asked, looking pointedly at the sea monster climbing over the stern of the ship.

"Tell it to stop!" Dhlara commanded him.

"How would you like me to do that?!" he asked.

"It's your giant squid thing! Get it to stop attacking us!"

"I have no idea how to do that!"

"What do you mean you don't know how?!"

"I don't have any power over that creature!"

"Hasdrubal, can you keep him here?!" Dhlara asked.

"He'll stay here, or I'll shoot him!"

"Come on!" Dhlara said to Jylling. "We have to help kill that thing!"

The squid had attached itself to the port side of the *Eruewerer* and was smashing anything it could lay its suckers on. One of its arms had gotten tangled up in the rigging and wrapped itself around the mainmast.

"TIE IT DOWN!" Dhlara shouted to those around her as she ran down to the upper deck. A dozen men grabbed the web of rigging and anchored it to other parts of the ship. Dhlara pulled out her sword and hacked at the tentacle. Jylling and a sailor with an axe joined her, each chopping at a section of the squid's limb. They hacked through several feet of slimy flesh until they had cut down to the wood of the mainmast. The men around her cheered as the tentacle relaxed and fell to the deck, but the severed appendage started to whip and whirl around. In its death throes, it struck Dhlara, knocking her down and slicing her leg with the serrated edges of its suction cups.

By now badly mauled, the squid wrapped its arms around the hull of the frigate. The *Eruewerer* creaked and shuddered around them as the enraged cephalopod squeezed with all of its might. Even the ship's strongest timbers cracked and splintered under such force. Taking Dhlara and Jylling's example, everyone left on deck rushed forward and attacked the tentacles. Gordon had climbed back onto the body of the squid and retrieved his harpoon from its flank and was now repeatedly thrusting the lance into its flesh. One by one, the crew sliced through the squid's tentacles and arms, until it couldn't even hold on to the frigate any longer. It gave out a hoarse groan as its body and the few appendages still attached slid off the ship and splashed back into the water. It groaned again, but weaker this time, and what was left of its form feebly thrashed around in the sea as it died. This time, everyone on deck cheered loudly.

Dhlara saw Kilik sitting against the gunwale. She went over to him and asked, "Are you alright?"

"My leg's broken," he told her with a choked voice. "But it's done."

"Yes, it's done," she echoed, looking over the side of the ship at the giant corpse. The brilliant coloured light its flesh gave off was slowly dimming.

The gun crews down below now came running up the stairwells onto the upper deck.

"We're taking on water, captain!" one of them reported to Kilik.

"How bad is it?"

"We're going down. We'll have to abandon ship."

"Gordon!" Dhlara shouted.

"Here!" a voice called, and he came climbing up over the gunwale with his clothes soaking wet.

"We're sinking! Can we make it back?!"

"I'm not sure. I'll have to go below and calibrate the time machine, and then we'll find out." He pointed at the man who had reported to Kilik. "Get everyone abovedeck!" Then he ran down the stairs with Dhlara following behind him.

"There are men overboard! We can't leave them behind!" Kilik called after them.

"We won't, captain!" Gordon replied.

They hurried down to the hold, which already had filled with several feet of seawater. Dhlara stopped at the stairs and watched Gordon wade through the rushing water to the red glow of the time machine. He turned some dials and flipped some switches on the top of the device.

"Got it! Now let's see if we can make it!" he said.

They ran back up to the quarterdeck. Gordon paused only for a split second as he passed Napoleon. He stopped at the spot where the helm used to be, but no longer was.

"Everyone hold on!" he shouted before he cranked the lever forward. The prow barely tipped forward, but they sank much more rapidly, until water poured in over the gunwales and overtook them.

*

Instead of leaping out of the water, the *Eruewerer* simply came bobbing up next to the Ministries of Time building. Only one of its masts stood tall; the others, like much of the rest of the ship, were broken and askew. Men climbed down onto the small dock near the Ministry of Maintenance. They caught ropes thrown to them and moored the ship.

"Quickly, everyone off! But don't go into the water!" Gordon ordered.

Many of the able-bodied crew rushed over the side to climb to safety, while others stopped to assist their wounded comrades. Dhlara and Gordon helped Kilik climb down the side of the ship, both descending alongside him and supporting him. This was repeated many times, by several groups of people while the frigate slowly sank beneath them, until everyone aboard had disembarked and safely stood on the dock. Napoleon remained under guard by several of the crew after he descended. When the last man stepped off, the gun ports were about even with the pier. Water poured in through each of them, and the ship quickly sank into the ocean of time.

The mooring ropes snapped as the *Eruewerer* disappeared beneath the waves one last time.

"Follow me; there are some we can still rescue!" said Gordon.

He led the group of about a hundred people through the closet that was the Ministry of Maintenance, through the lobby, past the shouting Minister of Order and his shelves of books, and into the hallway of doors.

Before exiting the lobby, however, Dhlara turned to Napoleon and said, "Not you. You… stay here."

"Oh, yeah, good idea," said Jylling.

"I'll stay and watch him," said Hasdrubal.

Dhlara and Jylling followed after Gordon. In the hallway, he had opened the 1815 door, where they saw the same night they had just left, and the same glowing, floating body of the squid. The door across from it had been opened, and groups of men carrying longboats filed out of one door and dropped their boats into the other. They rowed out into the night to pull their comrades who had fallen off the ship during the battle out of the cold water and bring them back to the Ministries. Gordon came out of the 1816 door helping to carry a boat.

"Do you need our help?" Dhlara asked him.

"We have enough people already to rescue everyone who can be rescued."

"Okay. We're going to go deal with Napoleon."

They headed back to the lobby, where the portly Frenchman was glaring at the Carthaginian who had two pistols pointed at him.

"Okay, who are you, exactly?" Dhlara asked him.

"I am Napoleon, Emperor of France. Who are you? Why do you hold me as a prisoner in such a manner?"

"I'm Dhlara, that's Jylling, and that's Hasdrubal."

"Hasdrubal?" said Napoleon. "You are named after the brother of Hannibal?"

"I am not named after him. I am Hasdrubal."

"*You* are one of the great Barca family?!"

"Yes."

"That is incredible! I am so glad to meet you!" Napoleon

252

stepped forward and held out his hand. Taken aback, Hasdrubal slowly holstered one of his pistols and shook the man's hand. "What gifts your family possessed! I learned a great deal from your family's battles, as did every general who lived after him."

"Well, thank you."

"What is this place? Where have you taken me? How is it that a person such as yourself still lives, when your birth was so many years ago?"

"You really don't know anything about where we are?" Dhlara asked him.

"I do not, but I should like to learn about it."

"I don't think it'd be a good idea to tell him," said Jylling.

"Why were you on that squid, then?"

"A spectre, a vision of myself as a very old man appeared to me, and gave the creature to me, saying that I could escape my captivity by riding on its back, and win back my throne with its might and terror."

"We saw that. You were on the beach with— with yourself," said Dhlara.

"How did you see that? Were you there? How could you have seen me, when your ship was so far from the shore?"

"Why were you alone on that beach at the exact moment your older self showed up?" asked Jylling. "Where were the rest of your men? You knew about the squid and you're lying to us."

"I did not know about the creature. This has been an extraordinary series of events, but the first of them occurred several years ago, while I was in Egypt. I went into the largest of the pyramids, and I alone entered the chamber of the great king, Cheops. There, the same vision of myself as an old man appeared to me, and told me that the greatest of destinies lay before me. First, I would make France an empire, and I would rule over her. Then my reign would end, and I would be banished to a small island. But, he said, I said, if I came alone to the shore of that island on February the twenty-fifth, I would once again be emperor, but not of France. Instead, I would rule the entire world."

"And that's all you know about any of this?" Dhlara asked him.

"That's all I know. Why have you stopped me? What do you mean to do?"

"We couldn't let you use the squid. That disrupts history," said Dhlara.

"What does that have to do with history?"

"That's not how history happened."

"Ah, do you mean to say that the events of my life have already played out, and they have been changed by the insertion of such an incredible creature?"

"Yes, that's what we mean."

"How remarkable! Do you intend to keep me captive at Elba, then?"

"Well, we hadn't really thought that far."

"Why don't we keep him here?" said Hasdrubal. "He can't create any more problems for us if we have his younger self hostage."

"That would change history, too," said Jylling. "He's supposed to escape Elba."

"I am?" the French general asked, his eyes lighting up.

"What would we do with him, anyway?" asked Dhlara. "And we can always go back and get him, if we need to. I think Jylling is right, we have to try to restore history as best we can."

Hasdrubal shrugged. "I don't see the point of it, but the monster is dead, so perhaps he no longer poses a threat. At least not this Napoleon."

"Alright, well, I guess we're taking you back to Elba," Dhlara told Napoleon.

"How are you going to accomplish this? Are you going to raise your ship from the depths, again? That is a most intriguing sort of vessel."

"You'll see. Follow me." She opened the door to the Ministry of Order and led the group into the library.

Upon spotting the Corsican, the Minister pointed at him and shouted, "BONAPARTE! SEIZE HIM FOR HIS CRIMES AGAINST TIME!"

"He's not the one you want," Dhlara told him as she

walked past him and down the stairs.

"WHAT?!"

"He's Napoleon from the past. If we don't return him to his own time, Waterloo will never happen. Is that what we're supposed to do, Minister?"

"No. Carry on. THEN STOP NAPOLEON!"

"We've already killed the squid," she called back.

"Very well then," the Minister muttered.

She abruptly stopped, then walked back up the stairs. "We lost those watches you gave us while we were battling it. We need new ones."

The Minister pulled three watches out of his desk and shoved them into her hand. "Here. But don't be so careless next time!"

After she handed a watch each to Hasdrubal and Jylling, the group walked over to the 1815 door, where the last survivors of the battle were being unloaded from the boats. Once they all were safe in the hallway, Dhlara closed the door, then opened it again. It opened into the same night, but back on the beach where they had seen both Napoleons for the first time. They stepped out into the sand. Napoleon's jaw dropped as he gazed around.

"We are back on the same beach I left! How did you do that? There was never a door here before," he said, looking back at the doorway standing in the sand. "How have you made it to appear here?"

"We aren't going to explain everything to you," she said. "Now you need to go back to your own time and live out the rest of your life as you normally did."

"Will I be seeing you again?" Napoleon asked. "If I try to return to France again, will you come back here again to stop me?"

"No, we won't," said Dhlara.

"You just couldn't do it with a great big squid," said Jylling.

"You are mysterious beings, Dhlara, Jylling, and Hasdrubal. But, on the whole, you have been honourable people. I will now return to running this little island. Farewell."

"Goodbye," said Dhlara.

The emperor turned away and walked up the sandy hill he had come down several hours ago. They stood on the beach watching him leave as the surf crashed behind them.

"So you killed my warsquid."

The three of them jumped from surprise. Dhlara whipped her head to the right, where the strange voice had come from. Standing there was an older Napoleon, with white, wispy tufts of hair poking out from under his bicorne hat and a more deeply wrinkled face. He still had a round, protruding gut. His lower lip stuck out over his upper one as he glared at them in the moonlight.

"Where did you come from?!" Jylling blurted out.

"I am always here," the old Minister of Chaos replied. "I am throughout time. Who are you, that you sought to kill my creation? It took a long time to craft such a unique animal."

"We just told you who we are!" said Jylling.

"You did no such thing. That man you just met is not me, nor was I ever him."

"Are you not Napoleon?" Dhlara asked.

"There are now two men that share that name. There is the man you have met, and then there is me, and his path is different than mine. But who are you?"

"I am Dhlara, and this is Jylling and Hasdrubal."

Napoleon grunted. "And why did you spy on me on this beach, and then hunt down my hand-crafted species of sea creature?"

"You can't change history like this," said Jylling.

"Yes, that's what I thought; you're working for the Minister of Order. But that is surprising, since you're the first in his employ to actually do something worth noticing. Why are you taking orders from him?"

"We're not taking orders," said Dhlara. "We're just trying to protect history."

"And stop you from ruling the world," said Hasdrubal.

"I am not trying to rule the world. The Minister of Order is mad, which anyone who possesses half a set of wits can clearly determine for themselves. At one time, he was a man of modest abilities, but the strain of his latest occupation have proved too much, and his mind has collapsed."

"We've seen the future. You ruined it," said Dhlara.

"And how did I do that?" the ex-Minister inquired.

"Everything was on fire and the sky was full of smoke, and you were riding a dragon and laughing."

Napoleon gave a long, croaking, wheezing laugh. "What year was this supposed to be?"

"Three thousand, I think."

"I've never had anything to do with any dragon, I've never been to the year three thousand, and I am not an arsonist. I am not here to set 'everything' on fire. That story is ridiculous."

"We saw it," said Jylling.

"You saw something. But as I said, the Minister of Order is mad. No one can say what you really saw. But it was not me. Let me tell you this: do not meddle in these affairs any longer. The events you are changing are beyond you. I oppose the Minister of Order, as should anyone who cares about the course of history. No one as stricken with madness as he is should have such power over the world. Go back to your homes and do not ally yourselves with him."

"Or what?" said Hasdrubal. "You'll make us regret it?"

"No. I was curious who killed my warsquid. I am not ill-disposed toward any of you, despite that. I am only giving you warning that you may find that the Minister of Order will make you regret your decision to help him."

With that, the older Napoleon abruptly vanished.

XVIII

Heading for Tomorrow

"Come on, let's go see if we've restored the course of history!" Dhlara called to Jylling and Hasdrubal as she ran into the hallway in the Ministry of Order.

The three of them sprinted to the 1815 door and opened it. Once again, it opened onto a scene of battle taking place in the streets of a little Belgian village. Gun smoke filled the air as musket fire furiously crackled all around them. The bodies of men in uniform lay everywhere on the ground, and more were added by charges and volleys of gunshots. But this time, no squid came tearing around the corner to beakily shriek its displeasure.

Dhlara closed the door and crossed the hallway to open the opposite door, marked '1816'. Beyond was the village square where Dhlara and Jylling had seen the statue of the squid, and had been shot at. But now there was no statue, and no one shot at them.

"Did we do it? Is everything alright?" said Jylling.

Dhlara walked out into the village. She went over to a man riding a cart that was being pulled by a mule. "Excuse me, sir, but could you tell me who rules over France?"

"King Louis, of course!"

"Of course!" Dhlara echoed, smiling as she turned back toward the door.

"Ha-hah! WE DID IT!" Jylling raised his fists in the air and gave a little hop. "We saved the world from Napoleon!"

"I've never heard of you," the Frenchman said. "I don't know that you had anything do with the fall of Napoleon."

"That's the point!" Jylling replied. "See, see?! That's not a squid pulling that cart! We fixed the world! SUCCESS!"

"By what magic is that madman standing in that doorway? Who are you people?"

"Oh. Whoops," Jylling blurted out. He lowered his hands and covered his mouth. Leaning his head out, he looked up and down at the door and doorway standing alone out in the middle of the street.

"Don't mind us!" Dhlara said hurriedly. "We're leaving and you won't be seeing us again!" She rejoined Hasdrubal and Jylling in the hallway and slammed the door shut behind her.

"We are some badass time travelers," said Jylling.

"We haven't fixed everything, you know," Dhlara reminded him.

"Right. Of course. We still have to go stop him from burning down, well, the whole world."

"He seemed pretty confident he wasn't there," said Dhlara.

"He's lying!" said Jylling.

Hasdrubal frowned. "I don't know. We should look into it. I wasn't there, so I didn't see what you saw in that year."

"Well, let's go to the three thousand door, and see what's there," said Dhlara.

The group walked down the hall until they came to the door labeled *3000* in gold numbers. Dhlara opened the door, and once again they saw an orange sun struggling to shine through a thick haze of black smoke. The sky was red, and far beneath them a vast inferno of fire raged. Something, some animal, roared in the distance.

"So far I'm seeing exactly what you described," Hasdrubal remarked. "But we don't know that this was a dragon, or Napoleon."

But as he spoke those words, a gigantic winged lizard came flying out of the smoke. A person wearing a bicorne hat rode on its back. The beast reared back in the air a few hundred feet from the door and beat its wings to hold it steady in the air. It drew back its head to take in a large breath, then vomited fire straight at the floating doorway. Dhlara slammed the door shut before it, or they, were incinerated.

"Yep. Definitely a dragon," said Jylling.

"I think it's time to consult our dragon wrestler," said Hasdrubal.

"Okay, let's go find Gordon."

They passed through the double doors leading into the records room and found Gordon near the wounded men laid out on the floor. Several doctors who were clearly from a time hundreds of years beyond that of the men around them moved among the wounded, treating their wounds and giving them medication.

"Your idea?" Dhlara asked him, pointing to the doctors. Gordon nodded. "That's really smart. This can wait, but we seem to have kind of a dragon problem."

"Dragon?" Gordon's eyebrow raised.

"When we open the door to the year three thousand, everything's on fire and there's a guy riding a dragon. Wellington said it was Napoleon who did that, but Napoleon showed up — the old one — and told us it wasn't him."

"Now that that squid's dead," Jylling said, "Napoleon loses Waterloo again. We checked. So shouldn't that have fixed anything that resulted from it in the future?"

Gordon shook his head. "It hasn't been long enough to take effect. Check the year three thousand again in a few hours. If it hasn't changed, then it isn't related to Waterloo. It is very strange that there is a dragon."

"Alright, we'll do that. Is there something we can do to help here?"

"Yes." Gordon had them help move medical equipment for the doctors and transcribe notes for them.

After several hours, most of the crew had been attended to, and Dhlara, Jylling, and Hasdrubal opened the door to 3000 again. The view before them was unchanged; fire raged and a dragon flew through the smoke. They went back to Gordon.

"The dragon's still there," Dhlara told him.

"That is troubling. Follow me."

He led them through the lobby and into the Ministry of Planning. The scores of people in labcoats inside the large white room scrambled to hide their work. He pushed through the crowd to the opposite wall.

"What are you doing bringing them in here again?" the Minister of Planning demanded as Gordon put his hand against the wall. A neon blue grid appeared on the wall and white light shone around his fingers.

"I have one dragon left to catch."

"But why are *they* here?! They aren't authorized!"

"They're helping me," Gordon replied, and the entire wall lifted up, revealing a beautiful land of rolling green hills under a blue summer sky. Mountains capped with snow rose up in the distance. On the top of one of the hills was a towering castle of stone. "Come on!" Gordon told them, and ran out into the grass. They ran out after him, but he was soon far ahead of them.

"We can't follow him! What is he thinking?" Jylling panted as Gordon sprinted over a hill and disappeared.

"I don't care what he says," said the Minister of Planning, "you can't be here!"

"We'll leave in a minute," said Dhlara. "But we have to wait for him."

"No, you need to leave *now*."

Then Gordon reappeared. The dragon they had seen Gordon capture when they had first met him came flying up over the hill straight at them, and Gordon sat astride its neck. Dhlara felt the ground shake when the mammoth lizard landed next to them.

"Get on!" Gordon called to them.

The three of them climbed onto the dragon's neck and it took off again, leaving the Minister of Planning far below its beating wings. Dhlara held onto the scaly neck beneath her as they flew over hill after hill.

"What is this place?" Dhlara asked Gordon when a white unicorn with wings flew alongside them.

"It's a stable. Or a storage facility. A mix of both. This is where the Ministry of Planning keeps their prototypes and unreleased content."

"What's with that castle? Is that where the Minister lives?"

"No, nobody lives there. Dragons like to destroy castles."

"Wait, what?!" Jylling shouted from behind them. "Are you

telling me that's a dragon *chew toy*?"

"You could say that," Gordon replied.

After flying for a few minutes, Dhlara saw a small white building far below. Gordon guided the dragon downward and it glided to a landing in front of the building. Gordon dismounted and put his hand against the wall. The front wall lifted up. Inside was what looked like the plain interior of a warehouse. Gordon patted the side of the dragon, coaxing it to walk forward into the room. Once it was inside, he closed the wall behind them, pulled something off the wall, and got back onto the dragon.

"...So, what are we doing in here?" Jylling asked.

Then the floor started to glow. It appeared to turn to liquid and began to swirl around faster and faster, forming a rainbow coloured vortex. The dragon, along with everyone on its back, slowly sank into the whirlpool floor.

*

Suddenly, they were falling through the air and smoke of what they recognized as the year 3000. The giant lizard hastily splayed out its wings, slowing its descent and turning the fall into a glide. They flew through the smoke for a few minutes, until they heard a roar.

"There it is!" said Dhlara as a dragon passed through the smoke in front of them.

Then they heard another roar from another direction. And another. The sky was full of dragons.

"Did we just make a terrible mistake?!" Jylling shouted.

"Scared?!" Hasdrubal shouted from behind him.

"Yes! Yes, I am very scared of a flock, a fleet, a *murder* of dragons!"

Hasdrubal laughed.

Gordon guided the dragon forward into a dive. Everyone behind him grabbed the neck even tighter. Their flying beast shot through the air, rocketing downward, straight toward another dragon. Their mount extended its clawed feet in preparation for impact. The two winged creatures collided, the one digging its talons into the back of the other. The lower one thrashed its tail and craned its head backward, gnashing its huge and plentiful teeth at its attacker. As they grasped at each other and fought mid-air, Gordon jumped off his dragon.

"What?!" she shouted.

"Hey! HEY!" Jylling yelled. "GET BACK UP HERE AND FLY THIS DRAGON SO WE DON'T DIE!"

After a moment, Gordon came climbing back up the dragon Dhlara and Jylling were riding. With one hand, he carried along with him a man in a bicorne hat and a blue and white general's uniform that was exactly the same as Napoleon's. As Gordon lifted him up onto the neck of the dragon in front of Dhlara, the man's hat flew away in the wind, and it became extremely clear to Dhlara by looking at his face that he was not Napoleon. Gordon sat back down, and the dragon released its claws from the back of the other one, which promptly flew away.

"You can't do this, Gordon! Let me go!" the man shouted.

Gordon made no reply. He guided the dragon down to a soft landing on a patch of grass. A city was nearby, and every building inside it was on fire. He pulled the other rider off the dragon's neck and planted him on the ground. The man had shoulder length brown hair and a flat nose.

"Who are you?" Gordon asked.

"I don't have to tell you!" the man declared.

"You don't seem very French to me."

"I don't have to tell you anything!"

"Uh, Gordon?" said Dhlara.

"Yes?"

"This isn't the year three thousand. My watch says this is nineteen twenty."

Gordon walked over and looked at the watch on her wrist and she held it out to him. The display indeed read, '1920'.

"How is this not three thousand?" Jylling asked. "This is the exact same time that the Minister of Order showed us behind the door for three thousand."

"Could he have changed the numbers on the door?" Dhlara asked Gordon.

"I suppose he could have. We'll have to find out more. *You're* coming with us," Gordon said to the pretend French general. "We're going to find out what's going on here." Gordon put him back on the dragon, climbed on himself, then slapped a metal disc onto the side of the animal's neck.

*

In a flash, they were back on the fields of the Ministry of Planning, in front of the Minister of Planning.

"Do you recognize this man?" Gordon asked the Minister, grabbing his captive by the collar and holding him up.

"No, I— well, actually, he looks like one of the Minister of Order's men."

"Were his men here?"

"Well of course they were."

"What do you mean 'of course they were'?"

"The Minister of Order requisitioned most of our dragons. Those men came here and took them away under his orders."

"Did they say what they were doing?"

"No. Why?"

"This man was riding a dragon in the year nineteen twenty, and there are many more out there. They've already burned down at least one city."

"*Are there*," the Minister hissed. "That's not an approved use of our equipment! I will revoke their authorization immediately!"

"I'll have to go see the Minister of Order about this."

"But you have to help us retrieve all of our dragons!"

"I will do that, later. After I find out why this has happened. I'll be back."

The group dismounted and left the Ministry of Planning. Gordon led the way back into the Ministry of Order. The Minister of Order sat at his desk opening and closing the same drawer over and over.

"Excuse me, Minister," said Gordon.

Shoomp, shoomp, shoomp, shoomp. The drawer opened, closed, opened, closed.

"Excuse me, sir."

Jylling pushed past Gordon and slammed his fist on the desk. "Hey! Way are you burning down cities?! What happened to not ruining history?!"

The Minister looked up at him. "What the devil are you talking about?!"

"When you showed us the year three thousand and how everything was a hellscape, you told us it was that way because Napoleon won Waterloo! But we were just there, and it's full of dragons being ridden by *your* men, who are dressed up like Napoleon for some reason, and there's a burning city, and it's not even the year three thousand! It's nineteen twenty!"

"Drastic measures had to be taken! Nobody understood the gravity of the situation but I! Napoleon has to be stopped!"

"So, so you ruined history to convince people to save it?!"

"Precisely, sir!"

"*What?!*"

The Minister stood up and pointed a finger at Jylling. "You may question my methods, sir, but I get results! Napoleon's squid is dead and Waterloo is won once again, and why is that?! Because of me!"

"*WHAT?!*" Jylling shouted.

"I took the necessary action! I gathered the requisite forces! The proper course of history can be recovered only by my force of will alone!"

"Burning down cities that have nothing to do with Napoleon isn't the proper course of history!"

"It's a place nobody cares about! It's worth the cost!"

"It isn't just a place! People lived there! It had a name!"

"Not one you've heard of!"

"Try me!"

"Meridian! Heard of it?!"

"No!"

"Exactly! Because it isn't important!"

"The people who lived there heard of it! They thought it was important!"

"They don't matter!"

"You're insane! And you're a liar!"

"DO NOT SLANDER ME, SIR! YOU ARE A SERVANT OF YOUR BETTERS!" Spittle flew from the Minister's mouth as he yelled. He walked around the desk and pushed his finger into Jylling's chest.

"Guys, guys!" shouted Dhlara. "Calm down! We can talk this over!"

"YOU! ARE! A! LIAR!" Jylling repeated.

Gordon quickly grabbed the Minister. With his free arm, however, the Minister punched Jylling in the face.

"UNHAND ME!" the Minister bellowed as Jylling reeled. "I SHALL STRIKE HIM AGAIN, SIR! TAKE YOUR HANDS OFF ME!"

Jylling put one hand down on the desk to catch his fall. As he felt his face with his other hand, he saw the hammer they had stolen from Napoleon lying on the desk. His fingers wrapped around the handle and his eyes grew wide with anger.

"NO!" Dhlara shouted.

Jylling returned the Minister's blow, slamming the hammer into his arm. At the moment of impact, the Minister of Order's entire body exploded into a shower of glitter. Gordon, Jylling, and Dhlara were instantly covered in a spray of shimmering sparkles. For a few seconds, everything was quiet. No one moved. The crowd of crewmen that had gathered below the raised part of the room the desk was on stared up in equally stunned silence.

"I believe you've killed him," said Hasdrubal.

Jylling spat out a mouthful of glitter. "Crap. How... how was I supposed to know that would happen? We saw him get shot a bunch and it didn't do anything."

"That's one of several reasons why people shouldn't just hit each other with hammers," said Dhlara.

"Hey, he hit me in the face!" Jylling protested.

"I know, I saw. But he's gone now. Or at least it seems like he is. You can never be quite sure with this place," she said, looking around at the walls of the Ministry.

"I think he's really gone," said Gordon. "That hammer is something very powerful."

"The Minister is responsible for what happened," said

Hasdrubal. "You don't hit somebody and expect them to not hit you back."

Jylling stared down at the pile of glitter. "Well... crap."

Melvin came running over with a dustpan and brush and started sweeping up the sparkling remains of the Minister of Order.

*

After Gordon and Jylling had scraped as much of the deceased Minister off of their skin as they could, Gordon returned to the Ministry of Planning and spent a day repeatedly going back to the skies over the city of Meridian in the year 1920 and using his metallic discs to tag the dragons one by one before they could participate in the destruction and send them back to the Ministry of Planning. By the time he was done, all of the dragons had been accounted for, and the city no longer turned into a raging inferno of dragonfire at any point in its past or future. After Gordon was done, all that happened over the city that day was a sudden flurry of dozens of dragons among the clouds, and then one by one they all disappeared again within a minute. To people on the ground, it just looked like a particularly odd flight of birds.

A few days later, Dhlara and Jylling sat at the end of the table in the library.

"Well, I guess somebody has to be Minister of Order or something now, right?" said Jylling.

"Does there?" Dhlara asked.

"Napoleon named that old lady Minister of Chaos when he left."

"But did he have to?"

"Yeah, I don't know."

"Maybe Gordon would know more about this sort of thing."

As they talked, Melvin scurried past them.

"He looks like he's up to something," said Dhlara.

Jylling laughed. "Ah, he's always up to something! He's a cool guy."

"Sure, I agree. But still, let's see what he's doing."

They got up and went into the lobby. The door to the Ministry of Maintenance was open. They entered the closet and made their way through Melvin's piles of junk. The door at the back was wide open, too, giving a view of the waves of the ocean of time gently lapping up against the pier. They stepped through the doorway and into the sun.

"Hello!" Melvin's voice came up from beneath them. He sat at a little desk proportionate to his size; his claw hands gripped a stack of similarly small papers in front of him. He was now wearing a set of spectacles, and his eyes darted back and forth behind them as he read whatever was written on the topmost sheet of paper. On the desk, facing outward, was a nameplate that read:

Melvin
Most Chief Emperor Supreme
Bureau of Tomorrow

"What's all this?" Jylling asked.

"There seem to be some shakeups around here," Melvin peered over his glasses at him, "so it's time for me to seize power!"

"I didn't know there was a Bureau of Tomorrow," said Dhlara.

"There wasn't!"

"Ah. You just created it, didn't you?" said Jylling, smiling.

"Yup!"

"So what's going to happen tomorrow?" Dhlara inquired.

"Who knows, man!" Melvin shouted gleefully, throwing his stack of papers into the air. He climbed up on top of the desk. "That's the great thing!" he continued, the sheets fluttering down around him. Dhlara caught glimpses of the pages as they fell; some of them had nothing but large question marks written on them, while others had stick figure drawings, and still others appeared to be entirely blank. "Anything can happen!" Melvin cried happily. "Nothing but new things, tomorrow! Doesn't that sound like an adventure?"

www.ingramcontent.com/pod-product-compliance
Lightning Source LLC
Chambersburg PA
CBHW020247180626
46810CB00006B/2408